A PERFECT GRAVE

Other books by Rick Mofina

EVERY FEAR

THE DYING HOUR

BE MINE

NO WAY BACK

BLOOD OF OTHERS

COLD FEAR

IF ANGELS FALL

Published by Pinnacle Books and
Kensington Publishing Corporation

A PERFECT GRAVE

RICK MOFINA

P

PINNACLE BOOKS
Kensington Publishing Corp.
www.kensingtonbooks.com

PINNACLE BOOKS are published by

Kensington Publishing Corp.
850 Third Avenue
New York, NY 10022

All Kensington titles, imprints, and distributed lines are available at special quantity discounts for bulk purchases for sales promotions, premiums, fund-raising, educational, or institutional use. Special book excerpts or customized printings can also be created to fit specific needs. For details, write or phone the office of the Kensington special sales manager: Kensington Publishing Corp., 850 Third Avenue, New York, NY 10022, attn: Specials Sales Deparment; phone 1-800-221-2647.

ISBN-13: 978-0-7860-1848-2
ISBN-10: 0-7860-1848-8

First printing: September 2007

10 9 8 7 6 5 4 3 2 1

Printed in the United States of America

*This book is for
my favorite sister-in-law.
You know who you are.*

Her sins, which are many, are forgiven, for she has loved much.

—Luke 7:47

1

For Sister Anne, death was always near.

But tonight, it *felt closer* and she didn't know why.

Tonight was like any other in the Compassionate Heart of Mercy Shelter at the fringe of Seattle's Pioneer Square District, where she was offering tomato soup to those who had lost hope. Their pasts haunted their faces. The pain of their lives stained their bodies with lesions, needle tracks, and prison tattoos.

Moving along the rows of plastic-covered bingo tables, Sister Anne saw how her "guests" occasionally looked up from their meals to the finger paintings on the basement walls, pictures taped there by the children of the shelter's day care program. Portraits of happy families holding hands under sunny skies and rainbows.

No dark clouds. No frowns. No tears.

Glimpses of heaven.

She was moved by the juxtaposition of the dreamy images and the cold realities of these unfortunate souls, handcuffed to mistakes, tragedies, and addictions, searching the artwork of inner-city children for answers.

Silent cries for help.

Offering help was Sister Anne's job. Her mission was to rescue broken people. To give them hot food, hope, and the courage to mend themselves.

"Would you like more soup, Willie?"

A gravelly whisper emerged from the crumb-specked beard of the former aircraft mechanic, who'd lost his job, his house, and finally, his family, to gambling.

"I don't want to trouble nobody, Sister."

"It's no trouble, dear. Sister Violet tells me you're doing well in recovery."

"Haven't missed a session in two months."

"Keep the faith, dear heart. You're my hero."

Sister Anne gripped his shoulder and pulled him close, indifferent to the smells of alcohol, cigarettes, body odor, and despair that were common here. The nuns of the order met the challenge of their mission, but Sister Anne embraced it.

For whether she was handing out wrapped sandwiches to homeless men, or comforting runaway teens and abused women, or whether she was entering prisons to counsel inmates, Sister Anne was a tireless warrior for charity.

She never lectured or preached; she served with humility, for she, too, had made mistakes. Yet none of the other sisters knew her story, or how she came to have her "God moment," which had inspired her devotion.

Sister Anne was private about her previous life.

In fact, upon first meeting her, few people figured Anne Braxton to be a nun. An easy thing to do since the Vatican's push in the 1960s to modernize the church. For the sisters of this small order, it meant they did not live a cloistered life behind the stone walls of a convent or maintain the tradition of wearing habits, wimples, and veils.

Tonight, Sister Anne wore faded jeans and a Seattle Seahawks sweatshirt, dotted with gravy and smelling of tuna casserole. With her scrubbed face and cropped hair feathered with gray, it was easy to peg her as a forty-something volunteer from a middle-class suburb. The small silver cross hanging from the black cord around her neck and her simple silver ring betrayed none of the inner fire that had fused her to her community.

For she had shouldered the anguish of those she'd worked so hard to help. Next to Willie was Beatrice, who'd been a schoolteacher in Ravenna when she accidentally backed her minivan over a six-year-old girl on a school trip. The girl died. Beatrice fell into a depression and was slipping away until the night police were called to the Aurora Avenue Bridge and talked her out of jumping into Lake Union. Since then, Sister Anne had been helping Beatrice forgive herself.

Sister Anne did the same with Cooper, a haunted soldier, whose tank took a direct hit in the rear. Everyone in the crew died. "Cooked alive."

Only Cooper got out.

Sister Anne prayed every day for Cooper, Beatrice, and Willie, refusing to let them believe they were worthless, unloved, and at fault for what had happened. No one is to blame, she would tell them, and the new people who arrived with similar tragedies every day at the shelter. Each one of them mattered and she wanted them to know that, especially at the end of the evening before they vanished into the night.

"Thank you for coming. God bless you and good luck." She hugged each of them as they departed.

Later, while collecting plates, her thoughts turned inward as she reexamined her past, her guilt clawing at her until she pushed it away.

But it kept returning.

Tonight, Sister Anne was the last to leave, staying behind to study the next day's menu. Again, the odd feeling drew her back through the years to the time when everything changed. It had been happening more and more over the past weeks, as if something was closing in on her.

Was God telling her something?

As she locked up, she stopped at the door and considered the line of prayer from St. Francis posted there: "It is in dying that we are born into eternal life."

She thought about it for a moment, then headed for the street. On the bus, she looked at the banner ads for unwanted pregnancies, condoms, distress centers, police tip lines urging people to report suspicious behavior. We live in a world of pain and we all have our crosses to bear.

She closed her eyes.

Her bus ascended the hills between First Hill and Yesler Terrace, toward a small enclave of clean, modest buildings straddling the eastern edges of the two neighborhoods. Mercifully, it was a short ride.

Echoes of distant sirens and a far-off car alarm greeted her at her stop, reminding her of a recent rash of car prowlings and a few break-ins at the fringes of her neighborhood.

Walking along the rain-slicked sidewalk, she saw the high-rise luxury condos of First Hill towering over the public housing properties of Yesler Terrace. Beyond them, across I-5, Seattle's glittering skyline rose into the night. To the north she saw the Space Needle, to the south, the stadiums where the Mariners and her beloved Seahawks played.

Sister Anne's home was a few short blocks away in the cluster of well-kept town houses. A generous parishioner had donated one to the archdiocese. Hers was the middle building. She reached for the door and stopped cold.

It was slightly ajar.

Goodness.

Her concern melted to annoyance. It had a temperamental mechanism. Upon entering, she'd detected the aroma of baked onions, pepperoni, peppers, and cheese and sighed. Her new neighbors, the young nuns from Canada, were partial to pizza every now and then but had yet to master the trick of completely locking the front door. Well, the silver lining here was that it spared her from fiddling with her front-door keys. Inside, the building was quiet as Sister Anne climbed the stairs to her second-floor apartment, where she lived alone.

Evening prayer, a cup of tea, and a bit of rest for her weary bones. She flicked on the lights of her small apartment and felt a ping of unease. Something wasn't right. She couldn't put her finger on it but something felt *wrong*.

Oh, it's nothing.

She was being silly because she was exhausted. But hanging up her jacket, she still couldn't shake a niggling feeling of *a presence*. Something in the air. The smell of cigarettes? But no one in this building smoked.

She stepped into the hallway leading to her bedroom and froze.

Her clothes cascaded from her dresser drawers. Her closet had been ransacked.

Someone's been here.

She looked toward her phone. A floorboard creaked and before she could react, a strong, gloved hand reached from behind and covered her mouth. A large, rock-hard arm hooked her neck in a viselike grip, crushing her windpipe, lifting her body. Her toes brushed against her hardwood floor as she was carried to the bathroom and her face thrust before the mirror.

The eyes of her attacker stared into hers.

He held her there long enough for her to recognize him and exhume long-buried pain. Then a knife blade glinted at her throat.

"Scream and you'll die," he said. "Understand?"

She nodded and he loosened his hold over her mouth.

"You know why I'm here."

She knew.

"It's gone," she swallowed. "I told you, it's gone."

"You're lying! Where is it?"

His grip tightened until she whimpered. The blade scraped over her skin, breaking it. Blood webbed down her neck, tears filled her eyes, and she said, "We can never erase the sins of our past."

His anger burned.

"No," he said, "but we can pay for them."

Her eyes widened suddenly as the blade sliced deep across her throat. Her hands tried to stem the blood.

"I forgive you," she whispered.

He let her collapse gently to the floor as if she were his dance partner. He watched her struggle for something in her pocket. A rosary. Her blood-stained fingers squeezed it. He watched for several moments until Sister Anne's face emptied of life. Then he returned to her bedroom and resumed shuffling through her personal papers and photographs.

Stopping at a recent snapshot of a boy. Searching the kid's eyes and face, the man studied it long and hard until he almost smiled. He now had the link to the thing that belonged to him.

All he had to do was claim it before time ran out.

2

Something was going on around Yesler Terrace.

Jason Wade, the lone reporter working the night cop desk at *The Seattle Mirror*, concentrated on the bank of radios scanning the major emergency frequencies for the city. Amid the traffic of nonstop chatter, he caught a telltale hint of emotion in a dispatcher's voice.

But the call was drowned out by police-coded cross-talk from unrelated transmissions. Jason cursed under his breath and locked on to the channel. Maybe he could pick it up again. He tried, but it was futile.

Sounded like some sort of activity in the Central District. East Precinct. But what?

One minute passed, then another. He heard nothing more. His call to the duty desk at the precinct went to voice mail. Instinct told him to keep the channel locked because he couldn't risk missing a single story these days.

Not on this shift.

On this shift, getting beat on a story would get him fired. He wrapped up a seventy-five-word metro brief on a stabbing near the university—a petty drug deal gone bad. The victim would live.

He finished his cold clubhouse sandwich from the cafeteria and surveyed the deserted newsroom. Most of the night copy crew had left after putting the first edition to bed. The editorial assistant was upstairs delivering papers to the executive offices. The last deskers on duty to handle any more late edition replates were in a far corner, marking time, discussing sports scores and a crossword puzzle.

Several floors below, the *Mirror*'s German-made presses were rolling off tomorrow's first edition, making the building hum. Sitting there, alone with the police radios, Jason took stock of his desk and his life. Here it was, amid the empty take-out containers, the stale junk food, the old news releases, old story files, used-up notebooks, and the front-page exclusives he'd broken for the *Mirror*.

He was a crime reporter at a major metropolitan daily.

It was all he'd ever wanted to be.

And now, it was all hanging by a thread.

In the two years since he'd won his staff job through the *Mirror*'s internship competition, he'd led the paper's coverage on many of its biggest crime stories, "with Pulitzer-caliber reporting," his former editors had written in his file. Sure, his way of nailing a story wasn't always smooth because he took things to the edge. And he faced some "difficult personal circumstances." But his passion eclipsed that of most staff veterans. And while he was still considered a rookie, there was talk of accelerating his junior reporter status to intermediate.

So how did it come to this?

How did he come to be an outcast on the most hated shift at the paper—the overnight cop beat? The answer

was buried in the crap on his desk, in the letters from
the lawyers with words that still burned him.

"*. . . possible proof of malice . . . erroneous reports implying
guilt . . . statements were untrue . . . defamatory action. . . .*"

Anguish and anger twisted in his gut.

*Stop this and forget about it. It's over, man, just leave it
alone.*

He cranked up the scanners and left his desk, thinking about other things. The *Mirror* was a few blocks
north of downtown, at Harrison and 4th. The newsroom was on the seventh floor; its far wall was made of
floor-to-ceiling glass that looked to the west. Watching
the running lights of the boats cutting across Elliott
Bay, he told himself for the millionth time that the
thing with Brian Pillar never should've happened.

It was two months ago.

Pillar had been lost and had stopped his van to ask
for directions from the two women standing on a corner. At that time, the Seattle police were conducting an
undercover prostitution sting. Jason had helped arrange
ride-along access for Cassie Appleton, a new general assignment reporter, and Joe Freel, a photographer for
the *Mirror*. Cassie was doing a profile of the neighborhood's outrage over a chronic hooker problem and increased crime.

It was Cassie's story, Eldon Reep, the metro editor,
told Jason. Other than getting her a ride-along, Cassie
did not need Jason's help.

Fine, but things took a twist when Brian Pillar was arrested for solicitation, along with ten other johns in the
sweep. The *Mirror* had exclusive news photos of "hookers" leaning into their vehicles, and pictures of the ac-
cused men being handcuffed, arrested, and taken to
jail.

Brian Pillar was a school principal.

"They just took him away! His wife's a paraplegic, or something. They've got three daughters," Cassie was breathless over the phone. "He should know better. I'm going to nail him by making him the lead in my feature."

Jason cautioned her. Jumping to conclusions at the outset of a sting could be risky.

"Cassie, you've got to be careful with these stories; sometimes guys are arrested but are never charged, for whatever reason. You should wait until you have it confirmed," he said.

"He's *so guilty*—you should've seen his face. I don't know this police stuff, Jason. Besides, the cops trust you. Can you help me confirm the charges? I called Eldon and he wants to run the story tomorrow on page one as hard news instead of a feature next week! I need help, now!"

"I'm not touching it. It's all yours. Good luck."

"Jason, listen," she dropped her voice. "I need your help. Eldon's afraid that the *Times* and *P-I* might get wind of the school principal's arrest and steal my story. He told me to tell you to help me. Please. I need this now."

Jason hated how this was being handled. First he was nudged from a crime story, then he was told to help— and by a reporter, not an editor. It spelled trouble. But after considering his situation, he made a snap decision, then made some calls. He confirmed that nine of the ten men were charged.

The one man not charged was Brian Pillar, the principal, he told Cassie.

"Turns out the guy was on his way to pick up some part for his wife's wheelchair and *really was lost*. The others were local street types, known to police, that sort of thing. Guess that takes your story down a peg," he said.

"Damn. Are you sure? Because the suburban school

principal is exactly what I need to make my story stronger." She was frantic. "I'll talk to Eldon."

Don't let the facts get in the way, Jason joked to no one. Seriously, with its drama diminished, Cassie's story would surely go deep inside the paper, he'd reasoned. But his jaw dropped the next morning as Brian Pillar's face stared back at him from a front-page story that featured him prominently as a "suspected john," along with the other men who were arrested.

Principal One of 10 "Johns" Arrested In Neighborhood Hooker Sting

Cassie's story quoted Pillar pleading with the *Mirror* not to publish his name or picture. "I had nothing to do with that sort of business. I'm begging you to please think of my wife, our daughters, my students. My school. Please."

But there was the news photo of Pillar in handcuffs along with the undeniable fact of his arrest, which was not the same as a charge. Even though he wasn't charged, he looked guilty in the *Mirror*'s photo and under that headline. The story also quoted an unsympathetic community activist. "I do not feel sorry for him. When these men are caught with their pants down, they will say anything, except the truth."

That morning Jason got a call from a detective he knew.

"Nice number today on the principal, Wade. We told you he'd been cleared. It was a case of being in the wrong place at the wrong time."

"It's not my story. I don't know why they played it like that. I guess Cassie will have to follow this up by talking to him and clarifying things."

"That might be a challenge, Ace."

"Why?"

"Brian Pillar hanged himself in his garage this morning with an extension cord. His oldest daughter found him, managed to cut him down with a hedge trimmer and call 9-1-1."

"Jesus, is he alive?"

"Barely."

Brian Pillar survived and recovered, and the *Mirror* paid him a "six-figure amount" in a quick out-of-court settlement that also involved a front-page retraction and a presentation on journalistic responsibility to be given by senior editors to Pillar's school board. Before all that happened, Cassie Appleton and Eldon Reep blamed Jason for the mess.

"How can you blame me? I was never part of Cassie's story."

"She called you for help," Reep said.

"And I told her he was not charged, that she'd better be careful."

"That's not Cassie's account. She's informed me that you clearly told her," Eldon picked up a legal pad with handwritten notes, "that all the men had been arrested and charged."

"She's dead wrong!"

"Are you calling her a liar?"

Jason met Reep's cold stare.

Be careful, he told himself.

Cassie Appleton was one of Reep's hires. Reep had replaced Fritz Spangler as metro editor a few months ago. Reep was a Seattle native who'd worked at the rival *Seattle Times* before leaving for Toronto to help launch the new daily, the *Canada News Observer*. After sixteen months, the new paper and Reep's marriage had folded. He wanted to return to Seattle, made some calls, and landed Spangler's old job.

Reep wanted to recharge the *Mirror*'s newsroom. One of his first new hires was Cassie Appleton. She'd worked at some small midwest triweekly but had won some obscure writing awards. She never smiled. She focused on her ambition to get the city hall beat, to use it as a stepping-stone to the state bureau in Olympia and then the *Mirror*'s national bureau in Washington, D.C.

According to the newsroom gossip, Cassie was a home wrecker who'd been cast out of her small town following a torrid affair with her managing editor.

Reep was rumored to have a thing for her.

So be very careful, Jason told himself.

"Answer me, Wade. Are you calling Cassie a liar?"

"Yes."

"And you can prove this, how?"

Jason couldn't prove it and immediately realized what was going to happen. He was going to be the scapegoat for this.

And he was right.

Eldon suspended him for a week, then put him on nights indefinitely while he decided his fate, informing Jason that one missed story, or one mistake, would end his employment with the *Mirror*.

"*—all units . . . we have a report of a . . .*"

The scanners yanked Jason's attention back to police matters and his desk. He adjusted the settings but was again frustrated by fragmented cross-talk coming out of the Central District area near First Hill—no wait—that's closer to Yesler Terrace. What the heck was happening out there?

"*. . . report of a second car prowling . . .*"

Car prowling? Is that all? No story there.

Jason was relieved, on the verge of releasing the channel and his concern when somewhere in the static storm of a broken transmission he heard, "*. . . nun's apartment . . . send it to you on your MDT . . .*"

Nun's apartment? What's going on? Jason knew there were several buildings owned by the Archdiocese. *And now they were using the Mobile Data Terminal.* Better try the precinct, he thought, reaching for his phone when it startled him by ringing with an incoming call.

"*Seattle Mirror.*"

"I'm calling for Jason Wade—is he at this number?"

"You got me."

The stranger's voice was coming from the din of a party crowd, the sounds of a cash register, and chinking glass.

"I'm calling about your father."

"*My father?* What about him? Is he all right?"

"He asked me to call, he says he needs you here right away."

"What, where is he and who are you? What's going on, is he hurt?"

"Look, I'm delivering the message. He's here at the Ice House Bar, he said you know where it is and that it's an emergency. I gotta go."

Bar.

Jason buried his face in his hands.

He's at a damn bar. I don't need this, Dad. Not now.

The scanner crackled with another fragment.

What was going on near Yesler Terrace?

3

Jesus Christ revealed his bleeding heart wrapped with thorns in the painting above Isabella Martell's couch as Detective Grace Garner listened to her lie about her grandson.

"No, Roberto, he no come here."

Grace threw a glance to Detective Dominic Perelli, her partner, tapped her pen in her notebook, then exhaled her disappointment.

"And you have no idea where he is?"

Isabella shook her head, blinking behind her thick glasses while staring into her hands, nearly arthritic now from years of scrubbing toilets in the Mutual Tower. Roberto beamed from his framed high school picture atop her Motorola TV. Nothing in his grin foretold that he would become a twenty-six-year-old drug-dealing pimp, who, at age twenty-three, would do nine months in prison for beating one of his girls.

According to an informant, Roberto was the last to see Sharla May Forrest alive before she was discovered behind an Aurora Avenue pawnshop.

She'd been strangled.

She was a teenage prostitute whose corpse had been found several weeks ago. And Grace still had next to nothing. No solid witnesses. Nothing but fragments and partials of trace evidence, nothing concrete. Nothing but a tip from a rival dealer happy to tell the SPD that "Sharla May owed Roberto and people saw him with her."

Whether the lead was valid or not, Grace needed to talk to Roberto Martell. Despite the fact that two days ago a neighbor had called police to complain about loud music coming from a Mustang with Roberto's plates idling in the street at this address, while a man matching Roberto's description had walked into this house, there was no way Isabella was going to give up the whereabouts of her flesh and blood.

"Hell, before she came to this country, she stared down the death squads who murdered her father," Perelli said later into a laminated menu at a Belltown diner where Grace brooded over coffee and everything else.

The Forrest case was growing as cold as the head-stone on Sharla May's grave. It seemed destined to remain unsolved like the last three murders Grace had caught. It was the same for the other detectives. Morale was flagging. In the last twenty months, eight veteran investigators had either retired or transferred out of Homicide. The toll was written in the unit's clearance rate, which had dropped from 80 percent to 55 percent.

"These sad stats say that killers stand a good chance of getting away with murder in this city," a *Seattle Mirror* columnist charged in a full-bore attack on the SPD.

This perception concerned the Commission, which concerned the chief, who pressured the deputy, who told the assistant chief, who summoned the captain, who instructed the lieutenants to issue an edict to the sergeants to pass to detectives.

"I've been ordered to tell you the obvious," Sergeant Stan Boulder, biting back on his anger, advised his team at the start of a recent shift. "We need a win and we need it fast." As his people grumbled, Boulder crumpled his memo, then pulled Grace into his office for a private moment.

"We're getting pissed on from every direction over this clearance crap."

"You paint a pretty picture."

"People are getting distracted, second-guessing, they need to stay focused, Grace."

"Yeah, we get that."

"You're one of my brightest, it's why we brought you on. We need to pull one out of the fire."

"Which one? I'll just run out and solve it, now."

"You know what I mean."

She did.

Grace always came at things with a fresh angle, a talent that had evolved during her teens, when her quick thinking had helped save lives during a shooting at her high school. In the aftermath, Grace knew she was going to become a cop.

She had graduated from college in the top 5 percent and considered applying to the FBI before deciding on the Seattle PD. As a patrol officer, she was decorated for tackling and disarming a fleeing robbery suspect. She soon made detective and worked in several units where she'd earned the praise of her commanders before becoming one of the youngest investigators to join Seattle's homicide squad.

She gave everything to the job, putting in sixty hours a week, allowing nothing else in her life. She was a loner. Had been ever since the school shooting. That's just the way it was. But over the last few years, as she grappled with death twenty-four hours a day, she didn't think she could stand being alone much longer.

Yet her attempts to do something about it hadn't really gone anywhere.

She went out with Jason Wade, the guy from the *Mirror*, a few times. There was chemistry, something electric between them, but work always seemed to get in the way. *Or maybe they let it get in the way.* Anyway, she broke it off before it got serious but he seemed hurt. She saw it in his face. Had she made a mistake?

She didn't know.

Then there was her disaster with Drew Wagner, the FBI agent. Upon transferring from Boston he pursued her with animal ferocity. God, he was so smooth, so good-looking. She never saw it coming. First, he says he's single because there's no ring, but she points to his tan line, so, all right, all right, he admits, he's divorced. She buys it, as he tells her about the heartache, and he does it so well. Later, she overhears him on a phone call to his wife and it's, all right, actually he's separated. The heartache stuff again and maybe Grace wants to believe him but she does a little checking and finally gets the truth. Turns out her all-star is only biding his time until his wife sells the house in Charlestown and *moves to Seattle with their kids.*

Some detective she was.

How could she have been so stupid? she asked her reflection in the diner's window, letting the question go into the night and back to Jason. Was she wrong not to work on something with him? There was just something about him that she liked. A brooding, brilliant honesty.

Stop it, Grace! Stop this "poor me" garbage!

Passing headlights stabbed at her for being selfish, hurling case images at her. Of Sharla May Forrest, a runaway not-yet-out-of-little-girlhood who was addicted to crack but kept a stuffed teddy bear on her bed and signed birthday cards to friends with happy faces. Of Sharla May's naked corpse in the urine, vomit, and dog shit alley, with a metal hanger garrotted around her neck, twisted at the back with a lead pipe so tight it nearly decapitated her.

And of Isabella Martell lying about Roberto while Jesus watched.

And of Special *Lying Bastard* Agent Drew Wagner at the mall with his wife and kids. And of Grace Garner alone with her unsolved murders, trying to get a handle on it all as someone was speaking her name.

"Grace. Grace," Perelli nudged her, holding out his cell phone, "It's Stan, he says your phone's dead."

"Garner."

"It's Boulder. We got a fresh one and you're the primary."

"Cripes, Stan, we got our hands full with the Forrest case. Can't Marty and Stallworth take it?"

"It's yours. Take down the address, it's near Yesler Terrace."

Grace pursed her lips as she jotted down the information.

"Who's the vic?"

"Anne Braxton. This will get profile. Big time."

"Why?"

"She's a nun, murdered in her residence."

4

Jason Wade grabbed a portable scanner and took the stairs to the parking lot, hating his situation.

He couldn't miss a story and he couldn't turn his back on his father. His old man was fresh at war with a ghost that had been stalking him for years, but he'd refused to talk about it.

Ever.

Even as it destroyed the things he loved, he would not open up to anyone. Even when it threatened to drag Jason down with him. Like tonight, man, he had to be careful. Whenever his father was seized by his demon, he reached out to Jason to rescue him.

Jason was all he had.

The cry of a gull and lonely horn of a distant boat echoed from the bay as he approached his 1969 Ford Falcon. He'd finally gotten around to getting it painted metallic red and it reflected the city lights as he wheeled through the streets. A few blocks east, the Space Needle ascended into the night, while south, the city's tallest buildings, Union Square, Washington Mutual, and the

Columbia Center dominated the skyline. Pike Place Market was near and a little farther, Pioneer Square.

Welcome to Seattle, baby.

Jet City. The Emerald City. Gatesville. Amazonia. Java Town.

The place where Jimi Hendrix learned to play guitar.

Rolling south near the stadiums he cast a glance in the direction of First Hill and Yesler Terrace and considered a detour. To where, though? He had no specific address to check out. He wasn't even certain anything was happening out there.

Cover yourself, man.

He called the East Precinct again. Voice mail again. He left a message. Then he alerted the editorial assistant at the paper to call him if he heard anything. He set his phone on vibrate, then slid *Layla* into his CD player. He was a disciple of classic rock and loved how Clapton's genius blended with the scanner's dispatches in an eerie mix against the night. He gathered speed as the song played and returned to his old man's situation.

Henry Wade was a private investigator, an ex-brewery worker, and an ex-Seattle cop. And for as long as Jason could remember, his father would not, or could not, ever bring himself to talk about the incident that had forced him off the Seattle PD and into a job at the brewery, where each day the thermos in his lunch bucket had been spiked with bourbon.

Whatever it was that he was trying to drown had ultimately cost him his marriage. Jason's mother had worked beside his father on the bottling line but eventually she walked out on both of them. She just couldn't take it any longer, she said in her note. The night before she left, she'd hugged Jason and her eyes looked as if she were dreading something on the horizon. In the days after,

Jason rode his bicycle all over the neighborhood searching for her until his old man told him she was gone.

"But don't you worry, Jay, she'll come back, you'll see."

The scanner crackled with a warehouse alarm.

Nothing to it. He adjusted the channels, then looked toward the bay as he guided his Falcon south until the brewery loomed. Man, he hated that place with its dark cluster of brick buildings, its stacks capped with red strobe lights spearing the night, the stench of hops permeating his car, reminding him of the worst days of his life.

His mother never returned and his old man's drinking never stopped.

Over time, it had pushed everything to the breaking point. It came just two years ago when his dad showed up drunk in the newsroom looking for him. The humiliation and shame of that night nearly cost Jason his job at the *Mirror*.

A job he'd shed blood to win.

But it also got his old man to admit that he had a problem.

He quit drinking and got counseling.

Nearly two years sober now and he was doing well, emerging from his self-imposed tomb a stronger man. Jason had reminded him that for a brief time in his life, he'd been a Seattle cop, a good one, and that he should do something about it.

He did.

First, he took early retirement from the brewery. Then enrolled in a few courses. He'd become a licensed private investigator with an agency run by an old cop buddy. He did well on his cases, even helped Jason out on a few news stories. His old man finally had it all under control. That's right, Jason thought, looking at the brewery fading in his rearview mirror, he was convinced they'd put all this crap behind them.

But here he was driving to another bar to rescue his father.

Risking everything he'd worked so hard to achieve.

It played out before him as he came upon the blue-collar neighborhood where he grew up, in the south, between Highway 509 and the west bank of the Duwamish River, not far from the shipyards and Boeing Field. It was here, ever since his mother had read him bedtime stories, that he'd dreamed of being a writer and had decided that being a reporter would give him a front-row seat to life's daily dramas. He studied them every morning on his first job in the business, delivering the *Seattle Mirror*.

Reading about other people's problems helped Jason forget his own.

He had tried to comprehend how his mother could just leave. As years passed, his grades plunged, his writing dream slipped away, and his father got him a job driving a forklift at the Pacific Peaks Brewery. They would rise at dawn, climb into his dad's pickup, and drive to the concentration of filthy brick buildings. For Jason it was a gate to hell and he vowed to pull himself out of it before he became a ghost, like his old man.

So, between loading trucks with beer, he read classic literature, saved his money, went to night school, improved his grades, enrolled in community college, and worked weekends at the brewery. He also got his own apartment, wrote for the campus paper, and freelanced news features to Seattle's big dailies.

One of his stories, a feature on Seattle beat cops, had caught the eye of a *Seattle Mirror* editor, who gave Jason the last spot in the intern program after another candidate had bailed.

It was Jason's shot at realizing his dream.

The *Mirror*'s internship program was notorious. Jason had to compete with five other young reporters, each of them from big journalism schools. And each of them had news experience as interns at places like *The New York Times, Chicago Tribune, Los Angeles Times,* and *Wall Street Journal.* They all went full tilt in a do-or-die competition for the one *Mirror* job that came at the end. After Jason had put everything on the line and broke a major exclusive, the *Mirror* awarded him a full-time staff reporter position.

It was all in jeopardy now because of the screwup over Brian Pillar and whatever awaited inside the bowels of the Ice House Bar.

Jason parked in the littered lot next to a burned-out Pacer, rotting there in the far corner where drug deals were closed and bladders relieved. He made another round of calls, left messages, and checked the scanner before switching it off. Nothing was popping on the air, yet he couldn't put aside his nagging feeling that something was going on up in Yesler Terrace.

The bar smelled of stale beer, cigarettes, sweat, and regret. A mournful honky-tonk song spilled from the jukebox; the wooden floor was littered with peanut shells and pull tabs. An assortment of losers populated the place. Two broken-down old-timers were at the bar. One was missing an arm, and in the glow of the neon beer signs above the bar, Jason noticed that the other had a patch over his eye.

Farther back, under the glow of lowered white lights, there was a pool table and a game in progress between a gap-toothed woman whose T-shirt strained the words DON'T TALK TO ME across her chest, and a tall slender man, whose arms were sleeved in tattoos. Beyond the game, six high-back booths lined the walls. All were empty except the one where Jason's father was sitting.

Alone, except for a glass filled with beer on the table before him.

It appeared untouched.

Henry Wade looked up from it to his son, who stood before him.

"You drink anything tonight, Dad?"

His old man shook his head.

Encouraged, Jason sat across from him in the booth, nodding to the white rag wrapped around his father's right hand.

"What happened?"

"Changing the blade in my utility knife to replace a bathroom tile."

"This is why you had the bar call me? Dad, I'm working now."

His father rubbed his temples as if to soothe something far more disturbing than a household mishap.

"Jay, you have to help me, son, I don't know what to do here."

Jason squirmed in his seat, then held up his finger.

"Hang on, it's my phone. I gotta take this." Jason fished through the front pocket of his jeans. "Dad, whatever you've got going on, I want you to go home just as soon as I—Wade—*Seattle Mirror*."

"Yeah, Wade—it's Grimshaw at the East Precinct. Got your damn messages."

"What's up near Yesler?"

"Report of a homicide."

"A homicide? Anything to it?"

"Something about a nun."

"A nun? Can you give me an address?"

"Let me see." Jason heard keyboard keys clicking, then the cop recited the location and Jason wrote it down in his notebook.

"Anybody else in the media calling you on this?"

"Not yet. We're just getting people out there."

"Thanks," Jason hung up. "Dad, I have to go, now. It was good that you called me and didn't drink. Now, I'm getting you home. We'll talk later. I have to go."

5

Jason got his old man into a cab and sent him home.

It was good that he'd called, good that he didn't drink and that he was trying to open up, but they'd have to talk later. Jason had his hands full with a story.

He laid rubber pulling his Falcon from the Ice House Bar and the neighborhood rushed by with his fears. Man, everything was at stake because after his dad and his job at the *Mirror*, what did he have in his life?

Seriously.

He had squat.

After things had ended with Valerie, he'd started up with Grace Garner and it was going great. Until she broke it off, saying that their jobs complicated things. That was a head-shaker. He thought they'd connected. He thought they had something real happening until— *wham*—she breaks it off.

He didn't get it.

Then he'd heard she was with some FBI guy. That was months ago. Jason hadn't seen her since and, if fate was kind, he wouldn't see her tonight. Picking through his CDs he played a live cut of Led Zeppelin's "Immigrant Song," from the *BBC Sessions*, letting its ferocity pound Grace out of his mind as he upshifted to the murder.

A nun.

Everyone would be all over this one. He had to get on top of it, had to concentrate on the story.

As he drove, he alerted the night news assistant to wake up the on-duty night photographer and get him to the scene. Then he tried in vain to reach the East Precinct sergeant for any new info, while gleaning whatever he could from his portable scanner. But he wasn't hearing much. Wheeling through the fringes of Yesler Terrace, he glanced up at the glittering condos of First Hill, soaring over the public housing projects.

This was not the crime scene.

He went farther, coming upon a tangle of marked cars, radios crackling, emergency lights washing a group of well-kept town houses in red.

Blood red.

Yellow crime-scene tape protected the yard of one of them. *The place of death.* People stood at the tape, craning their necks; others watched from their windows, balconies, and doorsteps as a uniformed officer waved Jason's Falcon away from the building.

"Can't stop here, pal."

Jason showed him his press ID.

"Take it on down the street."

After parking, he sifted among the newspapers and old take-out containers on his passenger seat for a fresh notebook and a pen that worked. He knew the anatomy of a homicide investigation, knew what to look for, and he took stock of the scene as he approached it. He couldn't believe it. No other news types in sight. Not even Chet Bonner, the Channel 93 night stalker, the camera guy who only came out at night.

Where was everybody? Had the press pack missed this one?

Judging from the array of official cars, this party had started long ago. There were unmarked Malibus, indicating the homicide detectives were here, the Crime Scene Investigation Unit vehicle was here, even the King County Medical Examiner's Office had its people on-site. He scanned the rubberneckers for a hint of someone who might have a bit of information. That's when a flash from above caught his attention.

Second story. Southwest window.

There it was again. A small explosion of brilliant light filling the room. Then another one as silhouetted figures moved, then stood dead still. Flash. Then the shadows repositioned themselves. Another flash. That would be the crime-scene people, or the homicide detectives, taking pictures.

Photographing the body of a dead nun.

Sadness rippled through him as he gnawed on the fact, holding it long enough for it to turn into quiet anger. What kind of sub-evolved life-form kills a nun? The camera flashes spilled into the night onto the building next door and the window directly opposite, illuminating a figure who was watching the scene. Looked like a woman, an older woman, cupping her face with her hands.

Here we go, he thought. That lady's got to know something.

The building was beyond the tape and not sealed. Patrol officers were coming and going. Some carried clipboards with documents that were likely preliminary witness statements, Jason judged from the glimpse he'd stolen.

"We're done in this building, Lyle," one officer said into his shoulder mike as he stopped Jason at the door with a question: "Do you live here, sir?"

"No, I'm a reporter with the *Mirror*, I've got business upstairs."

"Reporter?" The cop eyeballed him, checking out the silver stud earring in Jason's left lobe, then the few day's growth of whiskers that suggested a Vandyke.

"Got some ID for me?"

Jason held up his laminated photo ID. The officer reviewed it just as his radio crackled. *"Bobby, can you—"* Static garbled the call and the officer stepped away, speaking into his mike. "You're breaking up. Can you repeat that?"

"Bob, we need you out back, now."

Out back? Did they find something?

Jason had to make a judgment call. Go out back or get inside and attempt to get to a witness. At that moment, another officer approached, entered the building, and Jason caught the door before it closed. With the first officer distracted, Jason followed the second one into the building and, unopposed, made his way to the door of the second-story corner unit and knocked.

Several locks clicked before the door was opened by the woman he'd seen at the window. She looked to be in her late sixties, was wearing a long sweater and slippers. Worry creased her face.

"Yes?"

"Jason Wade, a reporter with the *Mirror*." He detected the thick smell of cats as he handed her his card. "Sorry to trouble you, but I was hoping you could help me with a moment of your time, please."

"The press? Goodness, no. I don't think I should say anything."

"Please, ma'am. I need to get a few things clear for my story."

"I'm sorry, dear."

"Ma'am, you know how people are always saying we get it wrong, or make it up. I need to get it right, please."

"I know, dear, but I just spoke to the officers and they told me not to talk to anybody until the detectives come by and talk to me." She looked back to her large window and the camera flashes that were ongoing next door. "I hope everything's all right," she turned back to Jason. "I gather it was some sort of robbery at Sister Anne's apartment. Probably those drug dealers. We've had some burglaries recently."

Some sort of robbery? She doesn't know what happened but she had a name.

"I'm sorry, you said, Sister Anne? And that's who lives in that unit with all the activity?"

"Yes, she's got a small apartment in the town house. Lives there with the other nuns. Saints, all of them. Devoted to the neighborhood. You know, they run the Compassionate Heart shelter downtown."

Over the woman's shoulder, through her window to the street, Jason saw the call letters of a TV news van. He didn't have time, he had to push this.

"Look, ma'am, that's the kind of information I need. Would it be okay for me to take some notes?"

"I shouldn't, I'm not sure. The police—"

"They'll probably tell us everything eventually but this will help."

"I guess it'd be all right. Everyone knows about our nuns, but I can't tell you everything I told the police."

Jason nodded as he wrote quickly.

"I understand, but did you see anything going on at Sister Anne's?"

As the woman pulled her hands to her face to consider his question, he glimpsed a car from the *Seattle Post-Intelligencer* roll to a stop outside, saw a photographer and reporter step from it while his source wrestled with a decision.

"Excuse me, ma'am, but did you notice anything out of the ordinary?"

"Yes, I saw something strange." The woman's face intensified as the curtain rose on an insight. "It's not a burglary, is it? Something's happened to Sister Anne."

6

Sister Anne stared at the ceiling.

Blood laced her face and the graying streaks of her dark hair. It drenched her Seattle Seahawks sweatshirt and jeans. Her bathroom floor was submerged under the torrent that had hemorrhaged from her gaping neck wound. The tiny silver cross she wore had slid down into it. Her rosary was entwined around her fingers in a blood-caked death grip.

The room flared with another burst of white light as the crime-scene photographer continued recording the scene.

Her eyes registered calm, peace, even acceptance. They were not frozen in the wide-eyed disbelief that was common among homicide victims, Grace Garner thought, sketching the scene, taking notes, and wondering if, in the dying moment of her life, Sister Anne saw God.

"Grace?" Perelli called from a few feet away. Like her, he was wearing shoe covers and white latex gloves while taking careful inventory of the small, cell-like bedroom. "Look at this. What do you think?"

The sheets of her narrow, single bed had been twisted.

Above it, the cross and painting of Mary had been pushed out of position. The wooden nightstand had been toppled; a King James Bible and a tattered paperback edition of *The Agony and the Ecstasy* were splayed on the floor, and pages torn from both books were scattered.

"I can't believe nobody in this building heard nothing," Perelli said.

Sister Anne's small closet and her four-drawer dresser had been rifled, her personal papers and photographs strewn about the room. The air held the scent of soap, laundered linen, and something familiar.

"I smell cigarettes and these nuns don't smoke," Grace said.

"Could be from our suspect?"

Grace nodded, frustrated that they had no witnesses and no weapon. No suspect description to put out. No path of inquiry to take. They had a canvass going but so far it had yielded nothing promising. She knew that the first hours of an investigation were critical and that the chances for a break melted with each minute.

She pushed a theory at Perelli.

"So he's in here looking for something and she comes upon him."

"What's the prick looking for?" Perelli pushed back. "She's a nun. She's got no money. There's no apparent sexual assault. She's got nothing. She's taken a vow of poverty, or something, right? Hell, her furniture's second-hand, donated stuff. So what's he want?"

"A crackhead from the shelter, maybe? And he's thinking, maybe there's a collection, a donation? He follows her from the shelter? I don't know, Dom. Maybe it's something else? We need a break here."

"There's no forced entry. No sign of it, anyway. They've got a problem with the lock at the front door downstairs. And this apartment door's got a simple warded lock. Hell, any child could use a toothbrush to beat it."

Grace flipped through her notes.

"Is it random, Grace, or you think she knew him?"

"I'm thinking it's time to talk to Sister Florence."

A handful of nuns lived in Sister Anne's building. The halls were adorned with pictures of saints. The main floor had a large common area with a kitchen and a dining room where the sisters ate meals together. Sister Florence was being comforted there by older women. All of them were wearing jogging pants, cotton night-gowns, or baggy pullover sweaters or T-shirts.

Their clothes were streaked brown with dried blood.

All were crying.

"I'm Detective Grace Garner and this is Detective Dominic Perelli," Grace said. "We're sorry for your loss. Please accept our sympathies."

"Why would anyone do this?" Monique, one of the older sisters, asked.

"We're going to do all we can to find out," Perelli said. "But we're going to need your help."

Grace consulted her notes. "We'd like to talk to Sister Florence, privately?"

Pressing a crumpled tissue to her mouth, Sister Florence nodded, then led Garner and Perelli along the creaking hardwood floor to the far end of the building and a room that served as a chapel. It had an organ, hard-back chairs, and a large stained-glass window, a gift made by inmates the nuns had counseled in prison.

A few sisters had left the chapel moments earlier after a prayer session for Sister Anne. Votive candles flickered in red, blue, green, orange, purple, and yellow glass cups. One had gone out. As Sister Florence relit it, Grace reviewed the short statement she'd given to the first responding officer. Sister Florence had moved to Seattle last summer from Quebec, where she was serving with the order in Montreal. At age twenty-nine, she was the youngest sister who lived here.

Sister Florence had discovered Sister Anne.

Grace met her green, tear-filled eyes. Her young well-scrubbed face was a portrait of heartbreak and un-shakeable faith as she recounted finding her friend.

"Tonight was our pizza and old movie night. We were watching *Norma Rae* and I decided to see if Sister Anne had returned and to invite her to join us."

"Was the downstairs front door locked?"

"We're not sure. It doesn't lock if you don't push it fully closed and we're all guilty of that at times, especially when you've got your hands full, like with a pizza."

"The pizza was delivered? Who received it?"

Sister Florence covered her face with her hands.

"I did."

"Did you lock the front door completely?"

"I don't know. I'm so sorry. I should've checked. Oh Lord, forgive me."

Grace gave her a moment.

"Tell us about your apartment doors and who has keys."

Sister Florence held out a key.

"We each have a key to our apartments and lock our doors when we're out, or need privacy. We know these old locks don't offer much security inside, but we're a family."

"Sister," Perelli had something on his chest, "with all due respect, you're living in the inner city, and with that front door practically open and your antique locks, don't you think you're taking a huge risk with your safety?"

"We never believed we had enemies."

"Until tonight," he said. "Get that front lock fixed

and the others changed. Grace, we'd need to get some uniforms posted here and have Central patrol this area."

"Okay, Dom." Sensing Perelli's growing anger over the nun's death, Grace steered matters back to the investigation. "Sister, can you think of anyone at all who might have wanted to hurt Sister Anne?"

"No."

"Someone from the shelter? An ex-criminal, or a husband or boyfriend looking for his abused wife, an addict, or someone violent or with psychological problems?"

"She was an angel of mercy. Everyone loved her."

"We understand the order was involved in spiritual counseling at prisons and for those released to the community."

"That's right."

"Did she ever mention a problem, or fear, concerning any of them?"

"No. Nothing like that."

"Maybe something in her background, or past?"

"She was so quiet about herself, entirely devoted to others. You might want to ask the sisters from Mother House."

"Mother House?"

"Headquarters of our order. Sister Vivian is on her way from Chicago."

"Sister, please think hard now. Did you notice, hear, or see anything different tonight?"

"No."

"No one heard anything strange going on? A struggle? A cry for help?"

Florence shut her eyes tight and shook her head.

"No, we didn't hear anything. Most of the nuns are older and their hearing isn't so good, so we usually play the sound of the movie quite loud. We even tell the pizza guy to knock hard."

"All right, so you went upstairs to see if Sister Anne had returned from the shelter and invite her for pizza and a movie. What happened?"

Sister Florence paused to swallow.

"Her door was open just a crack, usually our signal that you'll accept a visitor. Oh good, she's home, I thought and I knocked. But I didn't get a response, so I called in. And waited. She didn't answer. Again, I called her name and I entered—"

Sister Florence gasped and her voice broke with hushed anguish.

"I saw blood, then her foot, her leg, and she was so still. I saw her neck and didn't—couldn't—believe my eyes. But at the same time, I knew. It felt like slow motion. I knelt down and shouted her name. I took her into my arms. She was still warm. Then I heard this deafening roar as I tried yelling her name but she didn't answer and the others told me the deafening roar was me."

"You?" Perelli said.

"Screaming."

Perelli's lower jaw muscle was twitching as his anger seethed that someone would kill a nun.

"Then the others came," Florence said. "Someone called 9-1-1. Most all of the sisters have some sort of medical training. They checked for signs of life but we all knew that Sister Anne was dead. We were kneeling in her blood. So much blood. We took her hands and prayed over her. We didn't stop, even as we heard the sirens, even as the officers and paramedics thudded up the stairs with their radios going, we didn't stop praying." Sister Florence pressed her white-knuckled fists to her mouth. "We'll never stop praying for her."

As the tears flowed down her cheeks, her pain clawed at Grace and she was suddenly overwhelmed.

Sister Anne had lived a holy life, had devoted herself to helping those who were often beyond it. How could Grace Garner, a pathetically lonely self-doubting cop, on a losing streak, actually believe that she was skilled enough to find her killer? Grace's secret fear burned in her gut as she glanced to the votive candles, the flames quivering with the tiny light of hope.

"Sister, what prayers did you say when you found her?"

"The Twenty-third Psalm."

The Lord is my shepherd.

"That's a beautiful prayer," Grace said as a soft knock sounded at the door and a uniformed officer stuck his head into the chapel.

"My apologies for interrupting, Detective Garner, but they need you outside now. They've got something."

7

Steel glinted in the beam of the police officer's flashlight.

The officer was in the alley behind the town house with Kay Cataldo, a crime-scene investigator. They were crouched over a blackberry shrub next to a length of worn picket fence and the rusting frame of a bicycle. A second officer was taping off the area as Grace Garner approached.

"Where's the safe way in?" She didn't want to contaminate the scene.

"Close to the fence," Cataldo said.

"What do we have?"

"Officer Ryan Danko here's got the eyes of a hawk."

With great care, Cataldo spread the shrub's leaves, revealing a kitchen steak knife. It had a wooden handle and a six-inch serrated blade. Close inspection showed tiny reddish-brown flecks in some areas.

"This our weapon?"

"It's a candidate." Cataldo, aided by Danko, concentrated on taking photographs, measurements, and notes. "We'll type it against the victim. We'll process this knife, see if it matches anything the nuns use or if anything's missing from any drawers in there."

"What about foot impressions?"

"Got a partial inside and we'll use it when we cast around here."

"All right, and we better put the word out to watch for every tossed cigarette butt in the area."

"Our guy's a smoker?" Danko said.

"Just a hunch. Good work, Danko. Thanks, Kay."

Encouraged by the promise of evidence, Grace stepped aside and called Perelli.

"We may have a weapon. A blade. Serrated, about six inches. Wooden handle."

"Could be our break."

"Could be. You talk to the sisters about a volunteer list for the shelter and everyone she had contact with tonight. I'll follow up next door on the canvass."

"Sure. And Grace, this thing's already drawing heat. Reporters are calling in here trying to interview the nuns over the phone."

"Tell the sisters not to speak to the press, then get downtown to send someone up here to handle that. This is just the beginning."

Grace saw a news truck creeping down the alley toward the tape as she took stock of the surrounding buildings and windows, assessing lines of sight into the dimly lit area. She shone a penlight on her notes as she updated them and reviewed her sketches and the precanvass done by the responding officers, mining it for witnesses. There wasn't much to work with from the alley side.

But the front, now, the front was a different story.

In the front she had Bernice Burnett, age seventy-three, a widow and retired telephone operator. Lives in the adjacent building, alone with her cats. Bernice Burnett's big window looks into Sister Anne's second-floor apartment. Would she be reliable? Most witnesses weren't and Grace could feel time ticking away. She could not let this one get cold. She had to build on the positives. She had possible evidence, maybe a witness. Bit by bit, piece by piece, that's how you get it done, she told herself as she knocked on Bernice Burnett's door.

Locks clicked and it opened to a woman in a full-length sweater and fluffy slippers.

"Bernice Burnett?

"Yes."

Grace held out her identification.

"Detective Grace Garner. I'd like to talk to you about this evening, follow up on what you told the officer earlier. May I come in?"

"Oh. Yes, Detective, of course, but I've got—" Bernice glanced back to her visitor, Jason Wade.

"That's okay," Jason stood. "Thank you, Mrs. Burnett, you've been very helpful, I was just leaving."

Grace snapped her ID closed. She was annoyed. Annoyed as hell that a reporter was talking to her witness before her, the primary. And why, damn it, why did it have to be Jason Wade?

He didn't even glance at her until they were inches apart at the doorway, then he leveled a cold look at her. Or was it only a reflection of what he'd discovered in her eyes? Did he even know about her disaster with Agent Asshole? Well, to hell with it all, Grace. Do your job. Just do your damn job.

"Excuse me for a moment, Bernice, I'll be right back," Grace said.

She couldn't risk damage to her case by letting testimonial evidence become a headline. She followed Jason down the hall but he refused to stop.

"Will you hold on, please?"

He halted. But he refused to turn and face her, forcing her to walk around him until she stood before him.

"How did you get in this building?"

"Give me a break."

"All right, what did she tell you? What're you going to print? Are you going to hurt my investigation?"

"Ever heard of freedom of the press? I don't work for you, so back off."

Both of them were breathing hard; neither wanted to acknowledge what was raging beneath the surface, until finally Grace took the first step.

"Jason, look, maybe I made a mistake. I'm sorry if I hurt you."

"*If you hurt me?*" He shook his head. "I thought we had something good. That it was going somewhere. You just tossed me like yesterday's news without so much as a 'hey, we have to talk.'"

"So I suck at these things. I've always been alone. I—"

"You got a name on the victim, the nun?"

"What?"

Pages of his notebook snapped to a fresh one. His pen was poised.

"You're on the record. Can you confirm that it's Sister Anne Braxton?"

"No. We're not prepared to release—"

"Any indication on cause of death?"

"That will be confirmed by the Medical Ex—"

"I didn't ask you for confirmation, I asked for an indication?"

"Jason, come on."

"Was she shot, stabbed, beaten? Was it an act of God, Grace, tell me?"

"You're being rude."

"I'm doing my job. People around here are going to be outraged that someone would murder this nun. They call her an angel of the community. So you got a suspect yet?"

"This is how you want to play it?"

The jingle of keys interrupted them as a uniformed officer trotted up the stairs.

"Detective, we've got a bunch of media out front who're demanding to talk to you right now."

Without releasing Jason from her glare, she said, "Tell them to wait. We've got a press person coming to us from downtown."

The officer sized up Jason. "You got some trouble here, detective?"

"Mr. Wade here has breached the boundary of my scene. Escort him to the street and keep all press out of this building."

"No need for that," Jason said. "I'm finished here." He shot Grace a parting glare. "Believe me."

Bernice Burnett showed Grace a cherished photograph of her husband, the late Ambrose Burnett. He was a cabinetmaker who once did some of the custom work on the president's plane, Bernice recalled, while Lulu, her tabby, rubbed up against Grace Garner.

"You must be proud."

"Oh, I am. We have personal letters from the presidents who admired his work. Would you like to see them?"

"Another time, perhaps. Bernice, I'd like to come back to what you saw tonight. Your big window is beautiful."

"I like it."

"It rises from the floor to your ceiling. You've got a clear view of the building next door."

"Yes. I usually can see who comes and goes while I'm watching my usual TV shows. I like the old reruns of shows my husband enjoyed."

"Can you mark in your television guide at each point

in a show when you noticed something happening next door? It'll help me with a time line."

Bernice knitted her brow.

"Let's see, the pizza man came halfway through *Green Acres*. After him, the second man came."

"The second man? When was that?"

"When *Love Boat* started. I love that old show."

"Did you notice if the second man rang the bell?"

"No, it seemed like he just walked in like the door was open."

"Had you ever seen him before?"

"I couldn't be sure. He's hard to describe. Just a man, tall, I think."

"White, black, Asian?"

"Hard to say for certain. I think white."

"Any distinguishing clothing? Or in the way he walked?"

Bernice shook her head.

"I don't remember. It was dark; he was more like a silhouette. It was like he had business there. I thought maybe he was a priest. I thought nothing at all of it because the sisters get a lot of visitors."

"What came next?"

"Well, it was right near the end of *Love Boat* when I noticed strange lights in Sister Anne's apartment?"

"Strange, how?"

"Like someone was going around with a lamp, or flashlight. At first I thought Sister Anne may have lit a candle, for prayers, or maybe she'd lost power."

"Did you see Sister Anne arrive home?"

"No, I never did. I got up to get my cats some milk and I made myself a little snack, some cheese and crackers just before *Fantasy Island* started. Then I noticed it was all dark again."

"And after that?"

"Some time at the start of the show, the lights in her apartment came on and through her curtains, which were closed but are sheers, I saw shadows. The usual kind when Sister Anne is there, but then, I think I saw two figures inside."

Grace had been taking careful notes.

"And that's all you noticed tonight? A man at the door and unusual lights and movements in Sister Anne's apartment?"

"Well, that's what I told the officer, and that nice reporter, but come to think of it, I remember a bit more."

Grace looked up from her notebook.

"I saw a man leave the building. I think it was the same man who'd entered after the pizza man."

Has to be our guy, Grace thought as Bernice continued.

"He walked between the buildings to the back alley. No one ever goes that way. He was walking fast, not running, but walking fast. I thought, gosh, what's wrong? So I stood and watched him go that way."

"North?"

"If that way's north, that's right. I saw his arm move like he was tossing something small, then he stopped for a few seconds and I saw a red glow, like a flame at his head."

"Like he was lighting a cigarette?"

"Yes. And then he was gone."

"Anything after that?"

"I think I fell asleep. It was the sirens and all the commotion that woke me. Then a police officer came to my door."

Bernice took one of her cats, Lulu, into her arms and stood at her window watching the increased activity at the police tape below. More news crews and more police vehicles had arrived. Emergency lights strobed across her face.

Grace saw it reflected in the glass, saw Bernice's concern turn to fear, dawning with the realization that just out there, a few feet beyond her windowpane, an unseen horror had visited her neighbor. Lulu jumped from her arms.

"Is Sister Anne hurt?"

Grace went to her and gently touched her shoulder.

"It's something more serious than a burglary, isn't it?" Bernice asked.

"Much more serious."

Bernice could not breathe, her knees weakened. Grace steadied her, helping her into her chair, comforting her and gazing into the night, the same night that was hiding a killer.

8

The *Mirror*'s newsroom was empty when Jason Wade returned.

There was no way he would get the nun's murder into any late edition, as the last staffers on the night shift had left for home. The presses had long since completed their last run. The delivery trucks were gone and all over the metro area today's *Mirror* was already plopping on doorsteps.

The newsroom's silence was punctuated by the solitary clicking of his keyboard as he wrote about the murder for the *Mirror*'s online edition, to assure readers—*and his editor*—that he was on it. The *Seattle Times* and the *Post-Intelligencer* would be doing the same. TV and radio would be hammering on it all day today. And the Associated Press would surely move something soon.

He could not fall behind.

Jason made calls to Grace and the precinct to confirm the murdered nun's name. And ask her what was going on out back.

No luck at the precinct. And no luck with Grace. She probably wouldn't talk to him anyway. Well, he'd play it safe. He'd leave Sister Anne's name out of print until he was certain it's her, he advised himself while pounding out a tight item with bare-bones facts. And he held off using the exclusive stuff he'd gotten from Bernice Burnett. He didn't want to help his competition. He'd offer it all up later today when the *Mirror* put together a fuller story for tomorrow's paper. As he read it over, his cell phone rang.

The number was blocked.

"Wade."

"You the reporter who was asking about the murder by Yesler tonight?"

Jason didn't recognize the voice.

"Yes, who's calling?"

At the scene he'd floated his card to a group of young men gathered near the tape. Most were teens in hooded sweatshirts, watching and talking quietly. He'd figured they'd be good for knowing something and suspected that one of them was on the line now.

"You hearing if police got a suspect?" the caller asked.

"Nope, nothing. I didn't catch your name?"

"I got some information for you but first I want a deal, all right?"

"First, I want a name. Who are you?"

"Tango."

"Tango? That a real name?"

"As real as you need. You going to take this to the next level, or do I end it?"

"What do you want?"

"We trade. I tell you what I know, you tell me what you know, and we don't tell nobody where it's comin' from. Deal?"

Jason was interested, but guarded against giving up anything. "All right, but I've got nothing at this point."

"Come on, man, police always give you guys the inside track."

"All I know is what everyone knows: a woman was murdered."

"Yeah, but you got that she was a nun, right?"

"Really? What was her name?"

"Sister Anne."

"Sister Anne who?"

"Don't know, but word is she was stabbed and they found the knife out back. They were taking pictures and doing their CSI thing."

A knife. That was new. Jason made notes. "Anything else? What kind of knife? What kind of questions are the detectives asking neighbors?"

He was answered with silence.

"Got anything more for me, Tango? Anybody see anything? This connected to any other cases?"

"It might be something to do with a thing the Sister did a long time ago."

"Like what?"

"A gang thing. I can't say right now for sure, but this might be some kind of revenge thing."

"Revenge thing?"

"Payback."

"Payback against a nun?" Jason's grip tightened. "Payback for what? Tell me?"

"No. Can't do that yet. What've you got to trade with me?"

"Like I said, I've got squat. But you've got to give me your word you won't talk to other reporters."

"I'll try you out, that's the deal."

"Can I get a number?"

"No number, I'll call you, that's how it's got to work."

"What's your concern? Does this have something to do with you?"

"The sisters do all the good in the hood. Anyone thinks they can invade and hurt one, like what happened tonight, is going to pay. Vengeance is mine, understand?"

Jason understood.

On the crime beat you get strange calls. Whacked-out people claiming to have information. Or people claiming to be psychic. Disturbed people who confessed. Pathetic types who needed to feel important. And sometimes, people with the truth.

They all called.

Jason wasn't sure about this one. Tango offered possibilities on why Sister Anne was murdered. A gang thing? Maybe. Or maybe he was trying to play him for information.

Or maybe Tango was the killer?

There was no way for Jason to know.

It's why he had a habit of taping his calls. After the line went dead, he checked his microrecorder and replayed a bit. Good. He had it. He would follow up later. It might be useless. It might be gold. He returned to polishing his story. Once he finished, he e-mailed it to the *Mirror*'s web staff, who worked 24/7 in Redmond, a few miles east of Seattle.

It would be posted online within minutes.

Then he sent the morning assignment editor an e-mail with contacts and suggestions for the day side staff to follow when they got in, a few hours from now.

Leaning back in his chair, he finished the last of his potato chips, downed his Coke, and considered Tango's tip. *The nun's murder was payback for something she did.* What could that be? He ran a quick check of the *Mirror*'s databases but it didn't yield much.

His body ached for sleep and he contemplated things as he started his Falcon and headed home. Ever since the Brian Pillar fiasco, he'd embarked on a self-assigned special project. He'd been randomly mining old stories as candidates for anniversary features. Missing persons, unidentified corpses, unsolved murders and robberies.

Some went back for decades.

He'd learned the value of revisiting old files—most cops welcomed attention to their coldest cases. It often resulted in a fresh lead, a good read, and a new source. He'd also learned that it was critical to check all details of a fast-breaking crime story for links to previous cases.

But as for tonight—nothing had come up when he searched the scant details he had on the nun's murder. Other than a few urban-life features on the Sisters of the Compassionate Heart of Mercy and their work, there was nothing that would point to anything gang related. The shelter helped down-and-out types, people from the street, some with criminal records. Maybe the link was there, he thought, heading northbound on the Aurora Avenue Bridge.

He wasn't sure.

He found a soft-jazz station and glanced at the lights of Gas Works Park as he drove over Lake Union. He liked to come to the bridge to watch the sailboats, or the ships navigating the Ballard Locks and the Lake Washington Ship Canal on their way to the Pacific.

He looked in his rearview mirror at the twinkling lights and the skyline and his thoughts went beyond the city's beauty to a cold, hard truth he'd learned as a crime reporter. Death was his beat and for him metro Seattle was a burial ground. Cases like the Green River killer, Bundy, the mall shooter, the firefighter's arson, the unsolved hooker killings, the deadly heists, and the baby abduction marked its history like headstones.

And now we have a nun, slain near Yesler Terrace.

It would never stop.

It was Jason's job to understand it, write about it, to try to make sense of it while finding the nerve to ask a grieving mother, father, husband, wife, sister, brother, daughter, son, or friend for a picture of the victim.

"All of Seattle shares your loss."

Contrary to what most people thought of reporters, he hated that part of the job. It took a toll on him, too. Keeping his emotional distance from a story never, *ever* got easier, no matter how many tragedies he'd covered. It was always a struggle to keep from numbing himself with a few beers, because a few beers would lead to a few more.

Which would lead to . . .

Forget it.

He was exhausted and hungry as he came to the edge of Fremont and Wallingford, where he lived in a huge nineteenth-century house that had been carved into apartments. His one-bedroom unit was on the third floor.

He'd moved here when he was still in college and wanted to be on his own—for a lot of reasons. The big one being that he'd needed to put some distance between himself, his old man, the brewery, and the crap that had permeated their lives.

Since moving in, he hadn't changed the place at all. He had the same two secondhand leather sofas discarded by a dentist who was closing his office. They faced each other over the same low-standing coffee table, which was covered with newspapers. At the far end of his living room, a giant poster of Jimi Hendrix, his beloved god of rock, overlooked a thirty-gallon aquarium.

Jason was hungry and grabbed his last can of baked beans.

He loathed this, the loneliest time of his day. He put a spoonful of cold beans in his mouth to kill his self-pity and sat before his tank. It cast the room in a soft blue light. His tiny tropical fish gliding among the coral, the sunken ship, the diver, and bubbles soothed him as he chewed on his thoughts.

Had he been too hard on Grace? What was up with her, anyway? She seemed to want to call a truce. He wanted her to know that he was still pissed off at her. Still wounded.

And how long was he going to sulk?

She still drove him wild. He'd never met anyone like her and he couldn't believe she'd ended it with him. He couldn't get her out of his system. Maybe he should try to talk to her? God knows, he was going to need all the help he could get on this homicide.

After finishing his beans, he tossed the can, brushed his teeth, went to his bedroom, undressed, then fell into bed.

Tango.

And his line on payback for something Sister Anne did. What the hell was that? Could be something to it? He had to follow up on it, maybe even take it to Grace. Proceed with caution. Maybe that was the way to approach things with this story.

And with Grace.

He couldn't sleep. He was thirsty from the beans and went to his fridge. It was empty but for a half-eaten can of ravioli and an unopened beer. The bottle stood there as a personal test to prove that he was stronger than the temptation.

He settled for a glass of water from the tap.

See, he was not like his old man.

His father.

Cripes, he'd forgotten about his old man, getting the bar to call him when all he was doing was sitting there. Alone, staring into his glass. And that nasty cut on his hand. *"Jay, you have to help me, son, I don't know what to do here."* Something had been eating his father, something that was going to push him off the wagon, something that compelled him to call for help.

Guilt pricked at Jason's conscience and he glanced at the time. Why had he been called away just when his father needed him? He'd have to try him later. Man, he prayed it wasn't too late, that his old man had been able to hang on.

Jason rubbed his hands over his face, took in a long breath, then slowly let it out before picking up the printouts of the old stories he'd retrieved on the nuns with the Compassionate Heart of Mercy. He found Sister Anne's face in a group shot that accompanied one of the stories.

He stared at it.

She was smiling, but her eyes seemed to hold a measure of sadness.

9

Jason woke from a deep sleep and didn't know why.

Then his phone rang again. He cursed and grabbed it.

"You up, Wade?"

"No, what time is it?"

Eldon Reep's voice kick-started Jason's brain and he braced for trouble.

"Did we have the murdered nun's name last night, Wade?"

"It was never confirmed when I filed for our web edition—besides they usually wait to notify family."

"Her name is Sister Florence Roy, according to everybody but the *Mirror*."

"Florence Roy?"

"That's right, twenty-nine years old. Arrived at the order from Quebec. Our competition's got her damn picture online already. We've got squat. We look stupid. I don't like looking stupid, Wade."

"Listen, that name can't be right. Who confirmed it?"

"Did you even go to the scene?"

"Yes, I went to the scene. Who confirmed her name last night?"

"Neighbors, friends. Apparently, people all over this city."

"What about the Seattle PD or the ME? They complete an autopsy?"

"Get your ass in here, now."

"I'm on nights, I've hardly slept."

"Get in here now."

Tension knotted Jason's stomach as he showered. After shaving, he tried reaching Grace Garner for confirmation of the name. No luck. Dressing, he fired up his laptop, scanning Web sites of Seattle news outlets, where he met the face of Sister Florence Roy and a wave of self-doubt.

How could he have been so far off the mark?

While driving to the *Mirror,* Jason ate two apples for breakfast. As he listened to Led Zeppelin's "Fool in the Rain," he reflected on his competition's stories, finding some comfort in the fact nobody—*nobody so far*—had the angle that the homicide may be linked directly to something in the nun's past.

Whoever she was. Sister Florence. Sister Anne. Was his angle dead now?

Where would he take the story from here? He had to get a handle on it. But how? As he searched Seattle's skyline for answers, he remembered something important.

His old man.

Jason seized his cell phone, called his father but got his machine.

"It's me, I'm sorry, I'm jammed up with the story on the nun's murder. I want to talk about what's troubling you. Hang in there, okay?"

The metro editor's office was empty when Jason got to the newsroom, so he headed straight to his own desk and began working the phones, relieved when he connected with a trusted sergeant he knew.

"Man, I need help," Jason said, "Is Florence Roy the victim?"

"No. And this bull that's getting around about it is causing us grief. Good thing you held off, Wade, or you'd be off my Christmas card list."

"Great, I'm thrilled, can you tell me—wait, hold on, that's my cell. Got to take it."

Answering the call, Jason saw Eldon Reep far across the newsroom, emerging from a news meeting an unhappy man.

"Jason it's Grace returning your calls—all six of them."

"Thanks, I've got a lot of questions."

"You've got about thirty seconds."

"Who's Florence Roy?"

Grace took a moment to decide on the shape of the conversation, knowing that Jason often received information that could help, or hurt, an investigation. It was a delicate dance. "I'm off the record, got it," she said.

"Anything I use, I'll put to 'sources.' "

"Fine."

"Who's Florence?"

"She's the nun who found the victim. Some loudmouth TV reporter had called into the town house, got Florence's name from a distraught nun, got confused—got the story wrong—and now we have this mess. We're going to issue a statement clarifying things after the preliminary autopsy's done and ID's confirmed."

"When?"

"Should be later today."

"So is it Anne Braxton?"

"Don't publish Sister Braxton's name yet, Jason, until we put it out. But yes, you've got it right. The victim is Anne Louise Braxton."

"Have you notified her family yet? I'm going to start talking to people about her."

"We're sorting that out today with the sisters. Go ahead, but stay low-key."

"What was the last thing Sister Anne did before arriving at her apartment last night?"

"She'd worked at the shelter overseeing meals for street people. We're canvassing there and the driver of her bus route. You could put out that we're looking for people who took that bus. I'll text you the route and time."

Jason saw Reep standing at the doorway to his office.

"Wade! Get in my office, now!"

Jason held up his hand, indicating that he was nearly done on the phone.

"Grace, do you have any suspects?"

"I've got to go, Jason."

"Me, too, but you do have a weapon—a knife, right?"

"I can't talk about those things. I'm getting another call."

"What about a link to her past? I've heard this is tied to something in her past. Maybe even gang related, something about payback?"

"We're hearing a lot of rumors. It's too soon to rule anything in or out. Sorry, I have to go."

When the call ended, Jason buried his face in his hands, thinking that at least he had something to build on. Then his office line rang.

"You've got five seconds to haul your ass in here!" Reep said.

One wall in Eldon Reep's office was a theme park of "damn-I'm-good" displays of framed photographs and front pages. Jason stood before Reep's desk. Reep glared at him, then held a quarter-inch of air between his right thumb and forefinger before his eyes.

"I'm this close to suspending you, Wade."

"For what?"

"I understand you were in a bar last night when the nun murder broke."

"My father is a recovering alcoholic. He was struggling with a personal issue, and called for me from a bar, which was a family emergency. I was at the murder scene, on top of the Yesler story from the get-go."

"You can prove it?"

"It's all in my overnight note I'd sent to you. Did you read it?"

"If you were on the story, why did you miss the name?"

"I didn't. The victim is Sister Anne Braxton. Not Sister Florence Roy. Florence is the nun who found her. Why are you so quick to crap on the work of your own staff?"

"You listen to me, Wade. Our penetration in the metro market is eroding. If we keep losing circulation we'll have to cut staff. This is about our survival. It's crucial for us to be first."

"First to get it wrong? What kind of award do you win for that?"

Reep ignored Wade's last salvo, rolling up his sleeves, consulting his notes from the meeting.

"This is how we're hitting the story. Jenkins will do a metro column on good and evil in the city—innocence lost kinda crap. Anita Chavez is trying to pull information on the nun from the Mother House."

Jason took notes as Reep continued.

"Chad Osterman is on his way over to the Archdiocese. And Mirabella Talli will give us a feature on the history of nuns, the order, and its works. Wade, you will work on the investigation and profile the victim. And you damn well better give me exclusive breaking news that ensures that the *Mirror* owns this story. This is your chance to redeem yourself."

"Redeem myself for what?"

"The fiasco with Pillar."

"I resent this."

"Cassie Appleton has asked me to put her on the story. I'm assigning you to work with her."

"What! No thanks. I work alone."

"You work with her, or you don't work at the *Mirror*."

"Why are you doing this?"

"Cassie's had a rough time since Pillar. She needs to regain her confidence as a reporter in this city and build some street cred at this paper."

"You're making a big mistake."

Jason walked out of Reep's office, grabbed his jacket, and left the newsroom to pursue the story. As he stepped into the elevator, the red message light on his office phone began flashing.

10

Less than twenty-four hours after Sister Anne had offered hope to those who had lost it, her naked corpse lay under a sheet on a stainless tray.

Her spiritual journey had carried her to the white cinder-block walls of the autopsy room of the King County Medical Examiner's Office, in the Harborview Medical Center, downtown near the bay.

Her life had been reduced to this summary:

> *Anne Louise Braxton, Caucasian female, age 49 years, weight 131 pounds, height five feet six inches. Cause of death—hemorrhaging attributed to a fatal, deep force incise wound transecting the internal jugular and carotid arteries, consistent with a sharp, or serrated blade, of four to six inches in length. Decedent's identity confirmed through dental records and direct visual identification.*

In a small office beyond the autopsy room, Detective Garner watched Sister Vivian Lansing as she paused from reading the documents the medical examiner's staff had set before her and removed her glasses. Earlier that day she'd arrived from Chicago and was a bit jet-lagged. The sixty-year-old nun, who was a senior council member of the Compassionate Heart of Mercy, gently clasped the bridge of her nose.

"I need a moment," she said.

During the drive to the center, Sister Vivian had told Grace that she had known Anne Braxton since the younger nun had entered the order, some twenty-five years ago. That fact had stirred a whirlwind of emotions and memories of working alongside her in Ethiopia, Senegal, Haiti, the South Bronx, and Cabrini Green.

"You know what she told me, detective? She said that we face risks to deliver love, it's what God has in the cards for us."

While serving together, the two nuns had confronted more horror than most people would face in a thousand lifetimes.

Watching her now, Grace knew that nothing had prepared Sister Vivian for seeing her friend on that table, in that cold antiseptic room, *with her throat slashed*. Sister Vivian was struggling to reconcile her memories with the face she'd identified only moments ago.

Under the hum of florescent lights, Grace, Perelli, and Sister Ruth Hurley, a resident in the town house where Sister Ann was murdered, watched patiently as Sister Vivian composed herself before replacing her glasses and returning to the documents.

As she poised her fountain pen over the signature line, Grace noticed Sister Vivian's hand quiver before the pen scratched across the paper, followed by the snap of a page, then another signature before the ME staffer gathered the papers into a white legal-sized folder.

"Thank you, Sister," said the staffer wearing a lab coat. "Please accept our condolences. We'll contact you about releasing her to you through the funeral home. It should be later today."

"And her personal items?" Sister Ruth said. "Her clothes and her things?"

"Yes," Grace cleared her throat. "Those items have been collected by our forensic people. They'll work on them and hold them as evidence."

"I see."

"I think we're finished here, Sisters," Grace said. "There's another room, where we can talk, privately."

Grace guessed Sister Vivian at being close to six feet tall. Her neat white hair glowed against her dark skirt suit, a well-fitting simple design. She had the bearing of a ball-busting corporate CEO, Grace thought, catching the silver flash of the cross hanging from her neck when she sat at the large table in the empty conference room. Next to her, Sister Ruth, in her plain print jacket and black skirt, had the less imposing presence of a grade-school teacher quick to confiscate gum.

"We understand you brought Sister Anne's personal files from the town house and the Mother House in Chicago," Grace said. "Do they list her family?"

"No." Sister Vivian snapped open her valise. "We were her family." She slid two slim folders to Grace, who looked them over quickly, made a few notes in her case log, then passed them to Perelli.

"Do you have any suspects, Detective?" Sister Ruth asked.

"No," Grace said, "we've got other detectives canvassing the shelter, her route traveled from there to the town house and the neighborhood. And we're working on potential physical evidence."

The nuns nodded.

"Is there anyone Sister Anne may have had contact with who may have wanted to harm her?" Grace asked.

"I am not aware of anyone," Sister Vivian said "Are you, Ruth?"

"Everyone loved Anne."

"What about the people she helped at the shelter?" Grace asked. "We understand most of them have addictions, substance problems, many have criminal records. We're checking those we know, but does anything stand out? Altercations, threats, anything?"

"No, and this is what I cannot fathom," Sister Vivian said. "These are people she helped. She shouldered the burden of their trouble, so why would anyone want to harm her?"

"What about in the neighborhood?" Perelli said. "Anything out of the ordinary recently?"

Sister Ruth shook her head.

"She also helped women in abusive relationships," Perelli said. "Maybe a vengeful spouse or ex-partner thought Sister Anne turned his woman against him?"

"That's possible," Sister Ruth said. "We have encountered people with violent personalities or anger issues, but no one comes to mind."

"Sisters," Grace made a note, "we'd like you to volunteer all of the order's records on the people you've helped—names of abused women, ex-convicts, parolees, everyone you have on file for any reason. Staff lists, too. All of Sister Anne's case files, if she had any. Everything."

"But that is all confidential," Sister Ruth said.

"We can get a warrant," Grace said.

"We'll provide it to you," Sister Vivian said.

"But it's privileged," Sister Ruth said, "like the seal of the confession."

"Ruth, we're not ordained priests—none of it constitutes a confession. Police can exercise a warrant. And," Sister Vivian leveled her stare at Grace, "we can trust the detectives will honor the sensitivity of our files and the privacy of the people we are helping."

"Absolutely," Grace said.

"We'll not impede the investigation," Sister Vivian said to the other nun. "We'll arrange to provide the information."

"Thank you," Grace said. "Our crime-scene people will release Sister Anne's room later today. But for your security, you must replace the faulty lock on the town house and consider relocating for a time."

"Detective, thank you, but the sisters will not be moving," Sister Vivian said. "In fact, while I'm here, I'll stay in Sister Anne's room, once we clean it."

"But for your safety, until we make an arrest. Maybe the university," Grace said.

"That won't be necessary. We've already forgiven the person who took our dear Sister's life," Sister Vivian said. "Like the Holy Mother, we'll confront evil with love. We hold no hardness in our hearts for the person responsible. Nor do we hold any fear. We offer Mary's mercy because we accept whatever God has planned for us."

"We understand," Grace said. "Still, we'll talk to the precinct commander about having a couple of patrol cars sit on the town house."

The nuns nodded as Grace, again, flipped through Sister Anne's file from the order. It contained next to nothing in the way of personal information.

"Can you tell us anything about her background? This mentions nothing about a father, mother, sister, brother, or what she did before she became a nun."

Sister Vivian twisted her cross.

"She never wanted to talk about her life. As I recall, she was largely alone in this world until God called her to serve."

"This says something about Europe."

"Yes, the Order's Mother House, or headquarters, was in Paris. Anne Braxton was a young woman living alone in Europe when she entered the Order. Since then our Mother House relocated to Washington, D.C., then to Chicago. Anne had served all over the world before her work brought her here to Seattle."

"Can we get anything more about her personal history? It's like she just dropped out of the sky."

Sister Vivian nodded, promising to send out information requests to all the Order's missions around the world where Sister Anne had worked. She said that she believed that the nun who'd advised Anne when she was first accepted as a postulant may still be living.

"We're trying to locate her as well. But Detective Garner, isn't it more important to determine what happened here in the hours leading to her death than anything in her life from decades ago? Isn't that how you handle these things?"

Grace looked into the eyes of both nuns.

"Well, until we know the facts, everything is critical. And everyone's a suspect. That's how we handle these things, Sister."

11

Come on, come on, show us something.

Sister Anne's bloodstained Seattle Seahawks sweatshirt, jeans, bra, underwear, socks, and shoes were tacked to a large bulletin board in the Seattle Police Crime Scene Investigation Unit.

The clothes she had died in.

Her silver ring, cross, and rosary were up there, too.

And in one isolated corner: the knife used to kill her.

So far, the case refused to yield a break that would lead to a suspect.

But it would come.

It had to come, Kay Cataldo, a senior forensic scientist with the unit, assured herself, as she examined the board. She mentally crossed her fingers, willing her phone to ring with the call she was expecting.

Cataldo knew her stuff. She was an expert latent fingerprint examiner. She also had two degrees in forensic science and was about to get her PhD. She was qualified by the courts to give expert testimony on forensic matters. *So? What does the expert say now?* Cataldo challenged herself as she resumed studying her evidence inventory lists, test results, crime-scene photos, notes, and the autopsy report.

All puzzle pieces.

She was going to pull it together.

The scene had refused to give up anything useful. The guys at the Washington State Patrol crime lab offered to lend Kay's team a hand. They were taking a shot at the partial shoe impressions. The quality was terrible—practically a write-off; she bit her bottom lip, thinking she'd have to get back to them.

Maybe WSP would find something?

Cataldo's small, overworked crew had been going full bore without sleep since the call out to the homicide. They hadn't had much luck collecting trace, fiber, DNA, anything, for them to go on. They'd dusted and scoped the apartment, town house, everywhere and everything for latents. Nothing. The suspect must've worn gloves. Stabbings are intimate crimes where the killer is often cut in the struggle as the weapon becomes blood-slicked and difficult to control.

Not the case here.

Absolutely no indication of a struggle, no defense wounds. No indication of sexual assault, or other trauma. The only blood in evidence at the scene was Sister Anne's type: O positive. These facts alone would suggest either a come-from-behind lay-in-wait attack, or, a sudden full-frontal blitz attack, from someone she knew.

Go to the weapon.

The knife tossed among the shrubs in the alley. It had been washed, but while testing failed to yield any useable latents, washing failed to remove the traces of O-positive blood. Sister Anne's. And the fatal wound was consistent with the knife.

Cataldo scrutinized the knife then reread the report on the weapon.

It was a steak knife manufactured by a Swiss company. It had a six-inch blade made of forged stainless steel, containing 20 percent chromium. It was attached to a maple handle secured with three rivets. At the hilt, Cataldo noted a tiny insignia engraved into the blade.

A stylized maple leaf among the Alps.

The knife was not among the inventory of the cutlery in the nun's town house.

Cataldo's phone rang with the call she'd been waiting for.

"Kay, better get down here. I think we've got something."

"On my way, Gail."

Cataldo took a parting glance at the gruesome array of items on the board and dispatched a message to Sister Anne's killer.

"We're gaining on you."

Cataldo's van roared from the support facility at Airport Way South and she made good time before she arrived in the kitchen of the Compassionate Heart of Mercy Shelter. Her partner, Gail Genert, a senior Seattle police criminalist, was standing with two men.

"This is Sailor and Reggie Longbow. Gentlemen, this is Kay Cataldo, the investigator I told you about. Kay, Sailor and Reggie are in charge of the kitchen."

The two men nodded to the stainless-steel counter where the entire inventory of cutlery was spread. There were mismatches, different styles of flatware, plastic handled, wooden handled, all steel types. All sets had been neatly grouped. Genert and Cataldo each had crisp, full-scale photos of the murder weapon and placed them next to a group of steak knives matching the one in the pictures.

Sailor unfolded his large tattooed arms and placed

his hands on the counter. His voice sounded like it was churning in a cement mixer.

"All of our knives, forks, spoons, and whatnot have been donated over the years. From estates, people moving, hotels, schools, we get all kinds. That knife group is part of an eight-piece set." Cataldo had bent over to scrutinize the steak knives. The maple leaf/Alps insignia was identical to the one on the murder weapon.

"Go on," she told Sailor.

"Reggie's in charge of washing up and he noticed we came up short on one, about say what, two-three weeks ago, right, Reg?"

Longbow, who had a ponytail that nearly reached his waist, nodded.

Cataldo exchanged a poker glance with Genert, who saw the hint of a smile in her eyes.

"Do you have any idea how the knife in the set disappeared?"

Sailor shook his head.

"Could've been accidentally swept into the trash?" Cataldo nodded to the big Hobart dishwasher. "What about that?"

"Already checked it for strays. Found a spoon. No knives," Sailor said.

"Maybe someone took it?" Cataldo asked. "Any idea who?"

"We provide three meals a day to about two hundred people a sitting. Some are regulars. Some come once then you never see 'em again. You do the math."

"Gentleman," Cataldo said, "thank you for helping. We're not sure what we have here, but it's critical these details remain confidential. Circulation of this information would constitute obstruction of justice."

"Ma'am," Sailor said, "Reggie here's a mute and I generally don't talk to people. Outside of running the show back here, this is the longest conversation I've had in months. And I'm going to end it by saying I hope in my clean and sober heart you find Sister Anne's killer before we do. That woman was a saint."

Cataldo hurried outside, reached for her cell phone, and punched Grace Garner's number. When Grace answered, Cataldo said, "It appears the knife used to kill Sister Anne came from the shelter."

12

Was he closer to the murderer?

The line for dinner at the Compassionate Heart of Mercy Shelter began forming after 5:30 P.M. When the doors opened at six for the one-hour evening meal, it had grown to several dozen people.

Defeated old men in worn, stained clothes, teenagers with pierced faces, young mothers with small children, ex-cons, addicts, and drifters.

Was Sister Anne's killer here, among them?

Jason Wade adjusted his Mariners ball cap, pulled up the collar of his jacket, thrust his hands into his pockets, joined the line, and waited. The smell of hot food wafted from the window.

He'd missed getting down here for lunch, but was thankful that he was able to ditch Cassie at the paper. It gave him time to chase the story his way, alone, while dodging the messages Cassie had left on his cell, like the latest: *"Where are you, Jason? I want to meet up with you, call me."*

He'd spent the afternoon digging in Sister Anne's neighborhood. He'd door-knocked in the eastern fringes of Yesler Terrace and Jefferson Terrace and tried to bring Tango's tip about a possible link to gang payback into play.

But he got nothing.

He also burned up minutes on his cell phone working cop sources.

Again, nothing. And he couldn't reach Grace.

All Jason had was Sister Anne's name, a lead that a knife had been used, and about three hours to deadline for the first print edition. He didn't have a strong angle to advance the story and his stomach tensed when he spotted a TV news crew down the block going live. Jason envisioned Eldon Reep watching the report in the *Mirror* newsroom then demanding: *"What's Wade got? Have we heard from Wade?"*

The clock was ticking on him.

An emergency siren wailing in the distance pulled Jason's attention back to the line as it began filing into the shelter. It was evident from murmured conversations that most everyone now knew that a nun with the shelter had been murdered.

"Good to see you." A white-haired woman wearing a print top, with a silver cross around her neck, greeted each visitor by grasping their hand.

Jason held hers, leaned closer, then dropped his voice. "Sister, I'm a reporter with the *Seattle Mirror* and I am terribly sorry about the news."

"Thank you."

"I'd like to spend a moment here to get a sense of the mood. It's inspiring that you've kept the doors open, considering."

"God helps us persevere."

"Did you know the Sister?"

Sadness flitted across the woman's face, and her body language indicated that she'd prefer to see to the other visitors who were flowing around them. Jason moved on, coming next to a table with a jar for donations. He put a folded ten into the slot.

At the serving table he selected a tray, then a fork, spoon, and knife, letting his thoughts linger on the blade until he found himself looking over a food table at a large man wearing a full-length apron preparing a plate for him.

"Welcome friend. We have meatloaf, chicken, mashed potatoes, beans, some soup, and salad. How does a bit of everything sound?"

"A small bit of everything, please. I'll pass on the soup and salad, thank you."

After the chink of serving spoons against Jason's plate, he scanned the tables of the hall for a seat. Some people had collected into small groups and seemed to know each other, some were smiling, catching up. Others were far off, alone, hunched over their food and eating slowly in quiet desperation.

Jason took an empty spot between two large groups. To his far left there was a group of men. To his right were several young families with babies. As he ate, he listened to their conversations.

"I've been divorced for two years," a woman, who had a nose ring and appeared to be in her late teens, told the bald young man across from her. The man sitting next to the woman was holding a baby bundled in a yellow jumper. The man with the baby was wearing jeans and a vest and called to a man at the end of the table, "Yo, Dickie, heard what happened?"

"What?"

"One of the nuns here got murdered last night." The baby-holder took a mouthful of beans and bounced the baby on his knee.

Dickie had heard. "Cops were in here at breakfast and lunch asking questions."

"Which one was it who got killed?" the baby holder said.

"Dunno," Dickie said. "Hey Lex? You know which Sister got murdered?"

An obese man wearing glasses and sitting at the next table shook his head slowly.

At the far end of Jason's table, an unshaven man in his sixties with a mean scar down his cheek was sitting with six or seven quiet men. Scar man asked, "What did the cops want to know?"

The man with the baby shrugged. "Dickie, what did the cops ask you?"

"Where I was the night she got killed and if I had a record?"

A gentle rumble of laughter rose from the group of quiet men.

"Excuse me," Jason said, "but does anyone know if the police said anything about the homicide being gang related, or payback for something?"

Scar man eyed Jason coldly. "Who are you?"

"Jason Wade, a reporter with the *Seattle Mirror*."

"A reporter?"

The air tightened and Jason realized that he'd crossed a line. The way the men sat, arms defensively around their plates, their tattoos, their icy, hardened faces, he should've pegged them for ex-convicts, or parolees, before opening his mouth.

"I'm writing about the Sister's homicide."

"And how long were you going to sit there invading our privacy before you identified yourself, asshole?"

Jason felt everyone's eyes on him.

"Because you know what we do to assholes?"

Better back off, he thought, *back off and check out these guys later.*

"I haven't had much sleep. That was rude of me. Sorry, I wasn't thinking."

He picked up his tray and prepared to leave. The quiet men resumed eating with soft chuckling. As Jason moved off to find a new spot, someone touched his arm.

"What sort of story are you writing?" one of the young mothers asked.

"I need to get a sense of what kind of difference the Sister made down here and if anyone in particular was close to her, or knows what might've happened."

"You're talking about Sister Anne, right? Word is, it was her. She's been absent all day and she never misses, so we figured."

Jason nodded, noticing some of the young women had tears in their eyes.

"Sister Anne was an angel to us and our kids," the mother said, prompting nods from the others. "She was always getting doctors to look at them."

"And she was trying to help us finish school, or find a job," one mother said.

"Why would anyone want to hurt her?" one mother said. "Why?"

"I'd like to take your comments down, for my story. Please. It will let readers know what Seattle has lost. And it could help somebody to remember something that could lead to her killer."

The women agreed to let Jason quote them, except one who'd just come from Spokane, where she'd left her abusive husband. After talking for several minutes and passing his card around, Jason asked if they could direct him to any regulars at the shelter who were close to Sister Anne. The women considered a few people, but warned him that shelter people generally weren't much for talking.

"I got that." He glanced at the hard cases watching him.

After thanking the women, Jason left them to help

himself to a coffee in a ceramic mug donated by a local bank. Then he went to a far-off corner and reviewed his notes, flipping through pages, flagging the best quotes to go into his story. It wasn't great, but he had something. More important, he had just over two hours to deadline. Gulping the last of his coffee, he was set to return to the newsroom to start writing.

Someone stopped at his table.

"They say you're not a cop, is that true?" asked a man with black ball bearings for eyes.

"I'm a reporter with the *Mirror.*"

Jason displayed his photo ID and put a business card on the table for the stranger. The man was heavyset, in his forties, maybe. Hard to tell under his long hair and beard, flecked with crumbs. *A war vet?* He was wearing a dirty, tattered field jacket with desert camouflage pattern and military pants.

"I never talk to cops and they were here all day asking things about Sister Anne."

"You knew her?" Jason asked.

"She's the reason I'm still alive, know what I'm saying?"

No, Jason didn't know, but the man's intensity made him curious. The guy obviously had some problems.

"Can we talk about her?" Jason asked.

"No, I'm too upset, but there's something I want you to pass to police."

"What's your name?"

"Forget that, listen up and write this down."

Jason opened his notebook but wondered if the old soldier was going to be a nut job and a waste of time. Might as well humor him.

"A couple of weeks ago, this guy, a stranger, started showing up. He kept to himself and talked to no one but Sister Anne."

"What'd they talk about?"

"She never said. They always went off alone to a corner. It was weird. I watched them, see, because the thing
was, she always came away sorta sad, like whatever they
were talking about was her problem, not his. It was like
they were arguing."

"Did it get physical? Did he threaten her?"

"Couldn't say. It didn't look that way."

"You ever ask her about it?"

"I mind my own business. We all do in here."

"Has the guy been around today?"

"Haven't seen him for a few days. But somebody's got
to look into this guy."

"You know much about him, like his name, or what
he looked like?"

"Not really, the one thing I do remember is that I saw
him take a knife from here."

"A knife? Really?"

"A wooden-handled steak knife."

Jason made careful notes. As he struggled to absorb
the implication of the new information, his cell phone
rang. His caller ID displayed the number for Eldon
Reep.

"Sorry, I gotta take this." He answered, "Wade, *Mirror.*"

"You better haul your butt in here now, Jason,"
Cassie Appleton said.

*What the hell was this? Cassie calling from Reep's line, giv-
ing him orders.*

"Where's Eldon? I should be talking to him."

"Why did you ditch me? We're supposed to be working together."

"You don't need me to hold your hand."

"Eldon's in a meeting and since you're not answering my calls, he told me to call you on his line and give

you this message, which is to tell you you've got a dead-line and you'd better damn well get in here now with a story."

"I don't take orders from other reporters."

"You better listen to what I'm telling you, Jason, he's really ticked at you."

Jason ended the call and turned to resume his conversation with the old soldier.

But the man was gone.

13

Driving his Falcon from the shelter to the *Mirror*, Jason looked at his watch. Two hours before deadline, enough time to put a story together.

His cell phone rang. The number showed: *"Restricted."*

Most Seattle police phone numbers came up that way.

"Jason, it's Garner."

"Grace! Hang on!" He scanned his mirrors before pulling over. "What've you got that I can use?"

"The name's confirmed, Anne Louise Braxton. The press office is putting that out with a photo of her from the order, in about an hour."

"Any next of kin?"

"Apparently not. The order was her family, her life."

"Cause of death?"

"She was stabbed. That will be in the release and we won't go into details."

"Did you find the weapon? I've got sources saying you found a knife near the town house and I've got a

lead that the knife may have come from the shelter, so
I'm going with it."

"How did you get all that?"

"I'm a crime reporter, or did you forget already?"

"Jason, if you publish that now, it could damage our
case. We'll be chasing down every whack job who'll confess."

"I don't work for the Seattle PD. I'm going with what
I have, unless you tell me right now that it's dead
wrong?"

"I'm not confirming or denying it."

"So you do have a knife?"

"I'm not confirming that."

"You're not denying it. Grace, quit the BS. I think
you've got the knife. I won't say what kind of knife it is,
I'll qualify all my stuff as, 'police are investigating the
theory that . . .' you know the tune, okay?"

"I have to go."

"I think you owe me, Grace."

"What? I don't owe you squat. Grow up."

"Then tell me my stuff is wrong."

Silence hissed for several beats.

"Grace?"

"I don't work for the *Seattle Mirror.*"

"Give me a break."

"You can go with the knife, if you qualify it."

"I will. Any suspects?"

"I'm not getting into that."

"What about something from her past, something
gang related."

"Look, you know the procedure. We're tracing her
final movements, last twenty-four hours. Like I said, the
shelter, the bus ride, the hood. That's what we do. Now,
I have to go. And you keep my name out of the paper."

*   *   *

In the newsroom, Jason stepped from the elevator and glanced at the nearest clock, the one in sports above the blowup of a Seahawks touchdown. Most reporters had filed their stories and were gone. Others were putting on jackets, giving last-minute updates to copy editors, as the handoff from day side to night side had begun.

Jason had no time to talk to anyone.

At his desk, the red light on his phone was blinking with twelve messages. He logged on to the newsroom's system and had some two dozen unanswered e-mails. Ignoring everything, he transcribed his notes, putting up his best quotes, then crafted a rough lead and four or five paragraphs.

He'd taken a good bite out of the story.

Then he went to his phone messages, advancing them in rapid fire while simultaneously checking e-mails. Nothing critical. Then Jason winced when he heard his father's voice. "Still want to talk to you, son. Call when you can."

Jason mentally promised to call his dad after he filed.

"Wade! Get in here!"

Eldon Reep, the metro editor, hollered from the door to his office where Mack Pedge, the deputy managing editor, and Vic Beale, the *Mirror*'s night editor, were seated. Reep had loosened his tie and put his hands on his hips.

"Why in hell didn't you call in, Wade?" Reep said.

"My cell phone died and I was on to something at the shelter."

It was clear Pedge and Beale had no time for Reep's drama—their faces telling him to *discipline your staff on your time, not on our deadline.*

"What've you got for us that's strong enough for front?" Beale said.

"Homicide's got the murder weapon, a knife, and a

theory that it came from the shelter. She may have had some sort of incident with a visitor."

"And who backs that up?" Beale said.

"People I talked to down there. I also have a source inside the investigation."

"Can you shape your story," Pedge said, "so it leads by saying that detectives think the nun may have been murdered by one of the very people she tried to help?"

"Yes, as long as we qualify it as a theory."

"This is strong. Good work, Jason," Beale said. "We'll take twelve inches on front, then jump inside to the rest of the coverage. Go as long as you want, but we need it in under an hour."

After Beale and Pedge left, Reep closed the door.

"Wade, don't ever embarrass me like that again. When you're on a story, you call me every hour and tell me what you've got."

"I just got all of this now. Excuse me, but I've got to get writing."

"Hold up. Cassie's filing some material, I want you to put it into your story and give her credit. I told you to work with her, so put a double byline on top of the story."

"What'd she get?"

"Some color."

"I don't need it. Maybe somebody else can use it. I'm writing news." *Translation: I do not trust her stuff.*

Reep stepped close enough for Jason to know that he'd eaten something with garlic today. "You listen to me, smart-ass. You work for me and you'll do as you're told. Now shut up and get out of here."

Cursing under his breath, Jason got coffee, then sat down to finish his story. Halfway through, he detected a trace of perfume.

"There you are," Cassie Appleton stood next to his desk. "I've just sent you my half of our front-page story.

I told Eldon that we have to be careful we have our facts straight. See you tomorrow."

"Right. Bye."

When he'd finished his story, he opened Cassie's file. She had five hundred words copied directly from the Web site of the Sisters' order. Not a single live quote. Not a single news fact. The stuff was not even rewritten into news copy.

It was useless.

Jason didn't use a single word. He gritted his teeth and his stomach heaved as he typed her name next to his. It was ten minutes before deadline when he filed. Then he reviewed his e-mails and messages to be sure he hadn't forgotten anything.

His old man.

Fifteen minutes later, Jason was listening to Van Morrison and staring at Seattle's skyline and the bay as he headed south to the neighborhood where he grew up, at the fringe of South Park.

Driving through it gave him mixed feelings. He knew every building, every weather-worn tree, and every landmark that had been there since he was a kid.

His old man's truck, the Ford Ranger pickup, was in the driveway. Jason parked his Falcon behind it. There was no response when he knocked on the door but the lights were on inside.

Strange.

Jason found his key and went inside.

"Dad?"

Nothing.

At the kitchen table he found a family photo album. A few ancient snapshots were fanned out on the table, one of Jason, about seven years old with his new red bike. His mom had her arms around him. Their faces were radiant.

There was one of his old man smiling in the uniform

of the Seattle Police Department. That was a rare picture. Must've been before "the incident" that led him to quit the force after only a few years.

Would Jason ever really know why?

His dad never talked about it

Whatever happened back then had to be the reason his mother walked out on both of them. His old man worked hard to hold on to what was left of his life and in the last few years after he got on with Don Krofton's private investigation agency, he'd been doing well.

Until now.

He was battling something and he seemed to be losing.

What the hell was it?

Among the items on the table, Jason saw an empty envelope with Krofton's letterhead. It was recent, according to the postmark.

What was this all about?

Dad, I'm sorry I got tied up.

Jason started calling bars looking for his old man.

14

The next morning Henry Wade held the suspect in the sights of his handgun.

Finger on the trigger.

Life and death in a heartbeat. He couldn't do this. Not again

He had to do it.

All in a heartbeat.

Steady your grip. Focus. Look at the suspect. Is the threat real? The gun is death in your hand. You are going to kill someone.

Don't shoot or shoot? Is the threat real?

Decide now.

All in a heartbeat you are going to kill someone.

The air exploded.

Henry fired six rounds from his Glock, pressed the release button with his right thumb, ejected the magazine, inserted another one, securing it smoothly with the heel of his left hand before firing six more rounds.

Twelve rounds in under fifteen seconds. The threat was gone.

But his fear wasn't.

"Outstanding, Henry." Earl Webb, the firearms instructor, hit the button that retrieved the target. A B-27 silhouette. A man's upper torso. He assessed the scoring ring. "Nice clustering." Webb noted Henry's high score for the speed-loading segment of his firearm's qualification course.

"Let's go to the last one we talked about." Webb affixed the new target, hit the button for the clothesline chain to set it in position at the required distance, then instructed Henry to proceed.

Henry didn't move.

"Ready, Henry? Same steps. Go any time."

Henry stared at the target. It was a B-29 silhouette. A man's upper torso, reduced in size. Fifty feet away. *Confronting him at fifty feet.* Pulling him back in time, reminding him that *the suspect was approximately fifty feet away.*

The victim was . . .

Henry's scalp tingled.

"Go ahead." Webb's thumb was poised on the timer.

He was being tested.

Again.

God help me.

Henry fired six rounds, ejected the magazine, inserted another one, and fired six more, all in less than ten seconds. Webb retrieved the target. Henry's clustering was even tighter than with the B-27.

As if he was determined to kill something.

"Impressive." Webb noted the scoring. "That's it, you've completed everything and because of your background and the fact you're already a licensed PI, I expect you'll be getting your firearms ticket real soon. Nice work."

Webb extended his hand. Henry hesitated. *What the hell did he have to be happy about?* But Webb didn't know.

No one really did.

Wheeling his pickup from the Washington State Criminal Justice Training Commission, near SeaTac International, Henry could hear the whine of a jet on its landing approach. As it drew closer, its engines screamed overhead like the truth descending upon him. He would be licensed to carry a gun again.

Authorized to take another person's life.

Are you able to live with that the rest of your life?

In the seat next to him, the pages of his study guide lifted in the breeze.

His nightmare had been resurrected.

Bile surged up the back of his throat. He pulled to the shoulder, slammed on his brakes, got out, doubled over, and vomited. He stayed there until the jet passed and the sky was quiet again.

Back behind the wheel, heading to where he needed to go, Henry dragged his forearm across his mouth. He ached for a drink. He battled the craving. He had to face this head-on and he had to face it sober.

It was that simple.

He'd gone more than two years now without touching alcohol, ever since he almost lost Jason and took early retirement from the brewery. That's when Don Krofton, an old ex-cop pal, had hired him for his private investigative agency to work as an unarmed private detective.

Unarmed.

That suited Henry just fine.

Jason and Krofton had pulled him from the hell where he'd been trapped for some twenty-five years. Since he started working as a PI, Henry and Jason had grown closer. Sometimes Henry helped him on his stories, sometimes Jason helped him on his cases.

Partners.

Henry cherished what they had but now he feared he could lose it all.

Recently, a couple of the agency's files involved some unexpected violence, so Krofton ordered all of his investigators to become licensed by the state to carry and use firearms. "No exceptions, Henry," Krofton told him. "Unless you want to pack it in, and I don't think you want to do that."

It was true.

For as far back as he could remember, Henry had wanted to be a Seattle police officer and work his way up to detective. He'd never imagined that things would turn out the way they did. In the early days, he and Sally were happy. They had Jason and his job as a cop was great.

Then it all went wrong.

It had started as a routine day. Then they got the call. That call.

Twenty-five years ago.

God, he still couldn't stomach thinking about it. Or talking about it.

Ever.

After it happened, Henry quit the force then tried to become a private detective but failed. Things got bad financially. He and Sally ended up working in the brewery. He shut down, stopped living. For Sally, it was like being condemned to life in a mausoleum. She couldn't take it, so she left.

It broke Jason's heart.

The kid used to ride his bike all over the neighborhood looking for her while Henry crawled into a bottle and sat in the dark, mourning it all.

"She'll be back. I can fix it, Jay. Just wait. She'll be back. You'll see."

Jason soon learned it was a lie. Sally never came back. Henry didn't blame her. He became a lost cause who had fallen into an abyss and Jason realized that he had to get away, or be dragged down with him.

But Jay refused to give up searching for his mother.

Years later, he'd spend hours at the library, looking for her name and maiden name in old out-of-town phone books. He'd read obituaries and news stories about deaths. He'd keep records of those he checked, thinking the day would come when he would find her.

The boy just wanted to put his family back together.

Maybe that's how his journalistic dream truly started for him. Born out of his mother's desertion, Henry thought as he drove.

God, he was so proud of his son.

Only recently did Henry come to see how strong Jason was, how much he needed him, because it was his son who'd saved him. The night Henry turned up drunk in the newsroom was the rock bottom moment. He had humiliated Jason, had nearly cost him his job. That's when Jason kicked him into AA.

That's what saved him.

After Henry got sober, Krofton gave him a chance and took him on at the agency.

But now he had to carry a gun again and it pushed Henry to the brink.

For it had released his demons. He could feel them starting to circle round him, feel them closing in.

He needed a drink.

He needed Jason.

15

Rhonda Boland looked at Sister Anne's picture on the front page of the *Seattle Mirror.*

Sister Anne had beautiful eyes. A kind face. Rhonda would have liked to have known her. She needed a link to God these days.

Rhonda looked away from the paper and flipped through an old issue of *Woman's World.* But she was unable to concentrate. Her concern went down the hall of Dr. Hillier's office to the room where he was examining her twelve-year-old son, Brady.

Again.

Three months ago, Brady had complained of headaches and dizziness. Rhonda took him to their doctor. After a neurological exam, he referred them to Dr. Hillier, a specialist, who asked a lot of questions, ran tests, made notes, then arranged for Brady to go to the hospital for a brain scan.

It was scary seeing him swallowed by that big tomb-like device, but he was brave and it went okay.

That was last week.

Then Dr. Hillier's office called her this morning, asking her to bring Brady in.

"But his next appointment is not for three days. Did they find something?"

"Dr. Hillier would like to see Brady," the receptionist's voice was professionally and clinically neutral.

Please don't let this be bad news. Please.

Rhonda had to plead with the head cashier at the supermarket to let her leave work, again. Rhonda couldn't afford to keep missing shifts. And she had to pull Brady out of school, again. He couldn't afford missing more school. His grades were slipping.

A month or so back, his teacher had called to say, "For weeks now, Brady's been distracted in class and he's had a couple of outbursts, which is out of character for him. He's usually very quiet and polite. Is there stress at home, Mrs. Boland?"

Stress at home?

Only the kind that comes in the year after your husband dies suddenly.

Sitting in the doctor's waiting room, Rhonda grappled with worry. Maybe Brady's problem was a diet- or vitamin-related thing because she'd let him eat a little too much junk food. She'd let a few things slide since Jack died because he'd left her alone to face a world of trouble and some days it was so hard.

Please, let it be nothing.

"Mrs. Boland," the receptionist said, "Dr. Hillier will see you now."

She led Rhonda to the doctor's office, across the hall from the examining room from the room where Brady was. Hillier was behind his desk, a file with several colored pages open before him. He was on the phone and motioned for Rhonda to take the chair opposite him.

He kept clicking his pen.

She studied his face, his body language, for a clue of what to expect, as he wrapped up the call. The pen clicking did not stop. He studied the file.

"Mrs. Boland, I know we've already asked you, but please try hard to remember. Has Brady ever had a head injury? A mild or severe fall, or blow to the head? Brady doesn't recall any incident and there's nothing in his file."

"You mean, one where I took him to the doctor, or the hospital?"

"Any kind of head injury," the pen clicking stopped, "even unreported."

"Unreported?"

"Did you, or your husband ever discipline Brady? Physically?"

Hillier watched her face redden at what he was suggesting.

Was Brady abused?

"No. Nothing like that, I told you."

"I apologize, but as his doctor I have to ask."

Rhonda waved it off and Hillier considered other sources.

"Maybe a little playground mishap? Horseplay with Dad in the living room?"

"Well, one time, he had this little bump. Here." She touched her left temple. "But it was nothing."

"What happened?"

"He told me he was in the garage helping his dad clean up and he banged his head against the workbench. Just a tap. It was over a year before his father passed away."

Hillier absorbed it for a moment, nodded, noting it in the file.

"Brady seems to be exhibiting the symptoms of prolonged postconcussion syndrome, arising from some trauma to his head, which he could've experienced even a couple of years ago. However, that's only part of the problem, which may, or may not, be related to what we found."

Hillier stopped and thought for a moment. Then he showed Rhonda color computer images of Brady's brain scan, then elaborated about things with long, Greek-sounding names before reading the fear in her face. He tossed his pen on his desk, rubbed his eyes under his glasses, then softened his voice.

"The scan shows a growing mass of cells in his brain. A tumor."

"Oh God!"

"If it's not removed, this tumor will kill him within sixteen to twenty months. I'm very sorry."

Rhonda's hands flew to her mouth in time to stifle her scream.

Hillier helped her to the small sofa and comforted her.

"You can't let him die! Please, is there anything you can do?"

Hillier looked hard into her eyes.

"There is something we can attempt. I've consulted with my colleagues. It's extremely complex, but because of its behavior and location, we can't remove the tumor just yet. At this immediate point the procedure is too risky. Brady would not survive the surgery."

"I don't understand. You've got to help him."

"In two to three months it will advance to a stage where we'll have a better chance at surgically removing all of it safely."

"Then he'll be okay?"

"His chances of survival are good. We'd put them at seventy-five percent."

"And without the surgery, what are his chances?"

"Zero."

Hillier passed Rhonda a box of tissues. Her hands

shook as she grasped at the hope that Brady could be helped.

"He has to have the operation. You have to cut this thing out of him."

Hillier understood.

"But will he suffer?" Rhonda asked. "Will he be in pain as the tumor grows and he waits for the operation?"

"No. He'll be fine. Now that we know what we're dealing with, we can give him medication for his other symptoms. He'll be fine."

After a long moment passed, Rhonda noticed that Hillier's door was open a crack. She glimpsed through it. Across the hall, she saw Brady sitting on the examination table, reading his *Thrasher* magazine. His feet swinging in those new sneakers he'd begged her to buy for him.

Brady was her world.

Rhonda watched the nurse help him with his jacket, then take him down the hall to the front to wait for her. Still with Dr. Hillier, Rhonda asked, "Did you tell Brady?"

"No, but I will, if you prefer."

"No, I'll tell him."

"We'll give you a packet of information and numbers of support groups, people experienced in these things."

Rhonda went to the window. She watched the buses, cars, bike couriers, people going about their lives. "So," she looked at the tissue clenched in her fist. "Is this surgery expensive?"

Dr. Hillier inhaled thoughtfully and returned to his desk.

"Yes."

"You know my insurance is basic. How expensive are we talking?"

"Yes, I understand. I don't know the precise figures."

"Can you give me an estimate?"

"I really couldn't, there are many factors."

"Please, Dr. Hillier, I may be just a supermarket clerk, but I'm not stupid. I know you know."

"Maybe sixty to seventy thousand."

Rhonda turned.

"Seventy thousand dollars? That's more than double what I earn in a year."

"I know."

"I'm already facing several thousand in medical bills I can't pay."

"I know."

"My husband left us in debt."

"I know this is overwhelming, but these things can be negotiated between your insurance company and the hospital and there are financial arrangements."

"I don't know what I'm going to do. I just don't know."

"You're going to go home and help Brady. He needs you to get through this."

Rhonda nodded and pulled herself together. She went to the waiting room where Brady was looking at the *Seattle Mirror* and the picture of the murdered nun. Rhonda didn't want him reading that. They'd had enough bad news for today. Tenderly, she tugged him from the newspaper.

"Let's go, hon."

"Mom, I remember her," Brady pointed at Sister Anne. "She was with the nuns who come to my school for our charity fair every year."

"I know, honey, they do good work."

"They made food, set up games, sang, and juggled; they weren't like real nuns. They were cool, mom. The teachers took lots of pictures of us doing stuff with them. Why would somebody want to kill her?"

"I don't know, sweetie."

Why would God give a twelve-year-old boy a death sentence?

"Mom!"

Rhonda had pulled Brady to her, holding him tight, to keep them both from falling off the earth.

16

Sister Anne's blood churned and bubbled like liquid rust in the cleaning bucket. There was so much, Sister Denise thought, wringing her sponge.

It was as if the floor had been painted with it.

This room would never be the same. It no longer held the fragrance of fresh linen and soap. It smelled of the ammonia she'd mixed in the cold water, haunting her as she scrubbed over the mosaic of smeared, bloodied shoe prints.

Some of them belonged to the killer, the detectives had told her.

After the forensic analysts had finished processing Sister Anne's apartment, they'd released it to the nuns, urging the sisters to let a private company that specialized in cleaning crime scenes "restore" the apartment for them.

"It would be less traumatic," one concerned officer, a former altar boy, said as they were leaving.

"Thank you, officer," Sister Vivian turned to Sister Denise and said, "but Sister Denise will take care of it for us."

Surprise stung Denise's face and the young officer pretended not to notice.

How could Sister Vivian do something like that without first discussing it with me? Denise thought later. *Because Vivian had a reputation for being an arrogant tyrant, that's why.*

As she scrubbed, Denise grappled with anger and anguish. She abhorred the way Vivian was dominating people, especially given this horrible time. But Anne had been Denise's friend, and, in some way, by washing the blood from her room, she was honoring her memory.

Like Anne and the others, Denise lived in the town house. She was a nurse at the shelter and was regarded by the sisters to be the toughest in the group because she was raised in New York. Her mother had been an emergency nurse; her father had been a New York City cop.

Growing up in a rough Brooklyn neighborhood, Denise had seen some unforgettable things, but washing her friend's blood from the floor where she had been murdered was one of the hardest moments she'd ever faced in her life. She struggled with her tears each time she poured a bucket of reddish water down the sink.

She was alone with her grim work, contemplating life, death, and God's plan, when a shadow rose on the wall. Denise turned to see that Sister Paula, the most timid of the women who lived here, had ventured into the apartment.

Paula didn't speak as she cast a glance round, absorbing the eerie aura of death, gazing at the pasty, reddish streaks for a long moment. Then gently, she touched the walls, the counter, the light switch, the things Anne had touched, as if caressing a memory, or feeling the last of her presence.

This was a brave step for her, Denise thought. Paula was born in a small town near Omaha, Nebraska, the daughter of an insurance salesman. She was soft-spoken and meek.

"I'm sorry for interrupting, Den," she said. "But I had to see that it really happened." She twisted a tissue in her hands. "I mean, Vivian tells us to be strong. To go beyond being the humble bride-of-Christ thing, be progressive urban warriors of light. But how do we do that knowing that Anne was murdered right here in our home? And her killer's still out there. I really don't think I can handle this."

Denise washed her hands quickly, then put her arms around Paula to comfort her.

"I'm so sorry," Paula said, "I'll try to be strong like you and the others."

"You've got nothing to be sorry for, it's okay. It's perfectly fine to feel the way you feel. Be angry. Be afraid. Be confused. Be human. That's how God made us."

"Please forgive me."

"For what? You're like Thomas, you have to see and touch the wounds before you believe. So you can carry on in faith."

"I suppose I am. I just don't understand how she can be gone."

"She's not, Paula, her good work will live on."

"But her killer is still out there."

"The lock on the front door's been reinforced. The windows, too."

"I know, but he's still out there."

Downstairs, the doorbell of the town house was sounded by another visitor, part of the continuing stream of neighbors, local politicians, and Sister Anne's guests from the street. They arrived to offer their condolences, flowers, home-baked cakes, cash donations, casseroles, or colorful cards in crayon scrawl made by the children from the day care. People also phoned or e-mailed with heart-warming messages of sympathy and support.

After taking a call on the town house phone, Sister Ruth approached Sister Vivian, who was on her cell phone instructing the order's lawyer to help her volunteer the order's staff and client lists to Detectives Garner and Perelli.

"Excuse me, Vivian, the Archdiocese is calling. They're offering Saint James Cathedral for the funeral."

"The Cathedral? Thank them. Tell them we'll consider it and get back to them."

Nearby, in the cramped office of the townhouse, Sister Monique's eyes widened at the computer monitor when she saw an e-mail with the ".va" extension. The Vatican, she whispered to herself before reading the short message. It was from the cardinal who was secretary of state, who reported directly to the Holy Father on all actions of the Church outside of Rome.

Sister Monique printed the e-mail and hurried from the computer to read it to Sister Vivian: "The cardinal conveys personal condolences from the Supreme Pontiff, who has dispatched an Emissary from the Holy See in Washington, D.C., to represent the Holy Father at the funeral, or for any requirements of the order at this difficult time."

Sister Vivian did not share Sister Monique's awe. As she removed her glasses to weigh matters, she said, "It appears the boys, who've always been wary of progressive nuns, now want to ride in the slipstream of Sister Anne's good work."

The younger nun's face flushed.

"Monique, surely you're aware that most men in the upper ranks of the old guard want us to remain socially isolated in convents, making jams and candles."

Sister Monique didn't speak and Vivian suddenly cut herself off and waved her hand to silence the subject.

She was exhausted.

The night before, she'd slept on a couch in the living room. Well, she lay there, at least, grieving and looking at Anne's file and photos of her, remembering her friend's overwhelming capacity for forgiveness.

Through the years, they'd worked together in so many places around the world. But when it came to Anne Braxton's family background and her life before she became a nun, Vivian knew nothing. Unfortunately, it was exactly as Detective Garner had said, it was like Anne had "just dropped out of the sky."

It saddened Vivian.

No family to contact. No mother, father, brothers, or sisters. No one listed in her personal file. Nothing. Information on her biography was arriving in small pieces from the missions where she'd served, and the former mother houses in Paris and Washington, D.C. But nothing that preceded her call to a religious life.

Vivian was trying to locate the nun who'd first advised Anne when she was accepted as a postulant. And there was belief in some circles that the old nun was responsible for screening Anne in Paris, and had retired somewhere in Africa or Canada.

One thing Vivian knew for certain about Anne was that in life she was happiest in her sweatshirts and jeans, helping those who felt they were beyond it, offering grace to those who felt undeserving of it.

Anne Braxton would abhor any pomp imposed upon her in death.

"Excuse me, Sister Vivian?" Sister Ruth appeared and pulled her from her thoughts. "What should I tell the Archdiocese? They require an answer. It seems a number of weddings are also taking place in the next few days."

"Tell them no thank you. We'll have her funeral—a celebration of her life—in the shelter she helped found. In the very dining room where she gave so much of herself." Vivian slipped on her glasses "Let the Vatican's emissary pull up to it in his luxury sedan. Should be a nice juxtaposition for the news cameras."

Vivian tapped the printout of the Vatican e-mail to her chin, returning to her pondering about the old nun who had screened Anne, wondering if she was still alive and considering ways to locate her.

"Where's Denise? Is she done with the room yet? I'd like to lay down for a bit and I've got another job for her."

Upstairs, Sister Denise was alone again and almost finished cleaning Sister Anne's apartment.

Upon making a final inspection, she noticed that some blood had spilled into the hall closet next to the bathroom. A slender thread had meandered along the floor, like a tributary on a map, pointing to a secret destination. Denise freshened her bucket with cold water and ammonia, then used a soft-headed toothbrush to scrub dried blood from the seams between the floor boards.

That's strange.

The gap between two boards—as thin as the edge of a credit card—had widened ever so slightly. A loose board. It appeared that with the proper manipulation, the board could be completely lifted from the row covering the closet floor.

Curious, Denise found a pair of manicure scissors in the bathroom, opened them, and used a blade to pry the loose board out. Two adjacent boards were also loose. Denise pried them out as well.

Something was under the floor.

Something rectangular.

Denise opened the closet door wider to allow more light on the hole before she reached in to get the mysterious object hidden under the floor.

It was a cardboard box.

17

In the twilight hour before dawn, Grace Garner sat alone in the empty homicide squad room, feeling the crushing weight of the case on her shoulders.

It increased with every word of the morning's headlines.

The *Seattle Times* had NUN'S MURDER CONCERNS VATICAN—HOLY SEE ASKS CHIEF FOR UPDATE. While the *Post-Intelligencer* had SISTERS PLAN SHELTER SERVICE FOR SLAIN 'ANGEL OF MERCY,' and the *Seattle Mirror* had lined POLICE FOCUS ON WEAPON—A KNIFE FROM NUN'S SHELTER on page one above the fold.

Each of the headlines hit Grace like a blow to her stomach. After digesting every article, she set the papers aside to work. As she reached for a re-canvass report, her cell phone rang. It was her sergeant.

"It's Stan, you see today's papers yet?"

"Yes."

"The heat's on us to clear this one fast, Grace. My predawn wake-up call came from the chief. He said the commissioner, the mayor, even the governor, have 'expressed deep interest' in Sister Anne's case."

"I'm writing that down."

"Grace."

"And what's their interest in the murder of a seventeen-year-old hooker? Or, a homeless down-and-out loser—"

"Grace."

"This kind of political crap sickens me. We go flat out, Stan. We don't need to be told the obvious."

"It's in my job description to tell you the obvious. By the way, we're bringing in detectives from Robbery to help. Case status meeting's at 7:30 A.M."

After the call, Grace noticed a message that had come last night from Cynthia Fairchild, with the King County Prosecuting Attorney's Office, requesting an update. Came in about midnight. They were leaning on Cindy, too.

The pressure was coming from all fronts.

Grace had a stack of messages and shuffled them into priority. First things first. She brewed herself some fresh coffee, then began working on her candidates for suspects, so far.

The full autopsy report and observations by the King County Medical Examiner's Office on the angle and force of the wound suggested that Sister Anne's killer was strong, likely over six feet tall and weighing more than two hundred pounds. Reviews of the shelter's staff and client lists had, so far, yielded the following subjects who fell into that category:

Haines Stenten Smith, Caucasian male, age 37, weight 235 pounds, height six feet, six inches. Recently released from Washington Corrections Center after serving time for choking a woman in a Tacoma park. Witnesses said he held a knife to the face of a volunteer at the shelter five months ago but was intoxicated at the time. Smith could not account for his whereabouts the night Sister Anne was murdered.

Louis Justice Topper, African American male, age 33,

weight 220 pounds, height six feet, three inches. Recently released from Coyote Ridge. A crack dealer who'd stabbed female crack addicts for nonpayment. Three weeks ago he'd flown into a rage at the shelter and threatened a client with his fists. A friend said Topper had "gone off his medication."

Johnny Lee Frickson, Caucasian male, age 43, weight 280 pounds, height six feet, two inches. A Level 2 Sex Offender who'd attacked women aged 40–60, in their apartments in Seattle. After undergoing treatment, Frickson qualified for a work-release addiction recovery program. One night, last month, after dessert at the shelter, Frickson lost his temper and shouted threatening gibberish at several nuns. Detectives interviewed him in a downtown flophouse. A neighbor alibied Frickson, placing him in the flophouse that night of the murder. Detectives were seeking more sources on Frickson's alibi.

Ritchie Belmar Brown, Caucasian male, age 52, weight 240 pounds, height six feet, four inches. Brown was recently released from King County Jail. He'd served several months after trying to run down the organ player in the Seattle church parking lot where Brown was a Bible studies instructor. Legal action had bankrupted Brown's struggling taxidermy business. He frequented Sister Anne's shelter, where he began telling anyone who'd listen that the Catholic Church was the cause of his personal troubles. The detectives who'd interviewed Brown strongly recommended they go back on him because he kept changing his account of where he was the night Sister Anne was slain.

Each of them had a connection to Sister Anne. Before their release, she'd visited each of them in jail, as she had visited many prisoners, to offer spiritual guidance.

Each of these men had access to a shelter knife. Each of them was a smoker, which fit with Grace's single witness account.

Still, Grace did not like any of them for the murder. Nothing registered with her. They were all violent, dangerous men, but her instincts had not locked on to any of them.

And these four heroes were not her only potential suspects.

The shelter had people who were not regulars, those who drifted in and out. Sister Anne could have been stalked. And there were also "walk-ins." Strangers who appeared every day, like anonymous ghosts.

Sister Anne also counseled abused women who sought sanctuary. Through these situations, she often came in contact with their vengeful partners. Threats were common in these cases.

Grace faced many possibilities.

She needed solid evidence, a fingerprint that put someone at the crime scene. DNA. A credible witness. Something.

Grace went to her notes and reviewed Sister Anne's last moments. After leaving the shelter, she took the bus. No one indicated if she was alone, or was followed. Grace and Perelli interviewed the bus driver, who'd helped them find his few passengers. They were regulars and the driver pinpointed their stops and buildings, too. But it had yielded nothing. No one got off anywhere near Sister Anne's stop.

And the one witness account from Bernice Burnett, who lived next door to the nuns, suggested a stranger had been in Sister Anne's apartment when she arrived—and was a smoker. She recalled him lighting up in the alley when he left.

Grace flipped through other files. It would take time

to collect and analyze cigarette butts from the alley to compare with possible DNA from the suspects who could already be legitimately placed in the vicinity of the crime.

That made for a weak case against the four men she was considering so far. All of that evidence would be challenged in court.

Okay, back to square one.

So the guy's in her place like he's looking for something. But what? Nothing's missing. Nuns have nothing; they vow to live a nonmaterialistic life. Maybe that's it? He's a two-bit criminal. Has no idea she's a nun. He's getting pissed off that she's got squat to steal. Sister Anne discovers him and boom, he kills her.

There was the tip from a couple of confidential informants that someone had been talking on the street about a gang thing. It was the same line Jason Wade was working on. Some kind of revenge thing, because Sister Anne had helped some banger in trouble. The fact was she helped anyone who needed it. The "gang connection" to the murder was just talk coming from a gangster named Tango whose crew was devoted to the Sister. About five weeks back, she had comforted one of the members who got stabbed outside the shelter by a rival gangster. Sister Anne had called an ambulance and saved his life. Tango just wanted to put the word out that if it was an act by an enemy, his people would exact vengeance.

So far, nothing came of the gang angle.

It might've been a false lead, but it showed how much people loved Sister Anne.

Grace put her head in her hands and took stock of the empty squad room. Perelli and his family smiled at her from the framed photo on his desk. The other detectives had pictures of their kids on their desks, even the divorced dads who lost custody.

No one smiled from a photograph at Grace. Suddenly she felt utterly alone. Everybody had somebody. Everybody belonged to somebody.

It hit Grace that her life was similar to that of the nuns. They had taken a vow to give up any chance of ever getting married, of having children, of growing old with a husband and grandchildren.

But they belonged to the church, worked together doing God's work. In a sense, Grace worked for God, too. The God of Justice. But outside of being a homicide cop, Grace had no life. Even her attempt to find one with the FBI agent ended in disaster.

He was a married lying bastard.

Grace caught Jason Wade's byline and felt something stir.

She did have a thing for him. He was a few years younger but she was drawn to him. Something about him attracted her, his intensity, his razor-sharp intelligence. The guy exuded some kind of heat. It felt so right with him. Maybe that's what scared her. They were both loners, both intense. So why did she break it off with him?

Had she made the biggest mistake of her life?

A wailing siren pulled Grace from her reverie to underscore the urgency of her case. She needed a break, something to put her on the right investigative path.

Grace shook her head at her notes on Sister Vivian, who had yet to provide her with more files on Sister Anne's past. CALL HER THIS A.M.! Grace underlined in her notebook.

She stared at Sister Anne's photograph in the newspapers.

A kind, smiling face.

Grace covered Sister Anne's mouth with her fingers and looked into her eyes.

I need you to help me. Tell me what to do, where to look. Help me.

Grace's phone rang and she answered it without removing her eyes from Sister Anne.

"Good, Grace," Kay Cataldo said. "I figured you'd be in."

"What's up?"

"Got a break with the evidence that brings us a step closer to the killer."

18

After Jason looked at his grease-stained menu, with higher prices penned over lower ones, he counted four dead flies on the windowsill of his booth at Ivan's.

He didn't mind; it was his kind of place. A small, twenty-four-hour diner on a side street off Aurora. The smell of bacon, onions, and coffee mingled with the soft conversations of working people, weary night crews who'd just clocked out and sober-faced day crews about to punch in.

In one corner, a biker couple had fallen asleep. No one cared. No one needed their booth. Jason's old man said he'd meet him here at 7:30 A.M. It was 7:50 A.M. Give him a bit more time, he was likely tied up in traffic.

Jason looked through the window's grime to the street and thought, maybe this would be it? Maybe his dad would tell him whatever it was he was trying to tell him the other night at the Ice House Bar. Before the nun's murder had eclipsed everything.

"You have to help me, son, I don't know what to do here."

Jason shuddered at the memory of his dad poised over a beer. It triggered a torrent of searing images from his life: his mother walking out, his old man showing up drunk in the newsroom that night a few years back. *"Where's my boy? How come you don't call me, don't I matter anymore, Jay?"* The shame from the final humiliation had forced his old man to face his problem, to get help and to start turning his life around.

And was it all because of what had happened to him when he was a Seattle cop?

For years, Jason had secretly tried to learn more about his father's past. He'd dug up a few scraps of information here and there but never enough to get a full sense of the events that had forced him off the job. His dad had refused to discuss whatever had happened. With anyone.

Ever.

All that Jason knew, sitting here this morning, was that he would do all that he could to help his father confront his demon, kill it, and bury it forever. Because his old man had already paid too great a price, had already come too far, to surrender to it now.

While waiting, Jason took his empty coffee cup to the counter.

The gum-snapping waitress topped it off with a "thanks, sweetie," before Jason returned to his other problem: how to pursue the nun murder story today.

He studied this morning's front page.

Okay, so he'd already used the knife angle in print. But he held back on how the guy who stole it from the shelter supposedly had some kind of heated discussion with Sister Anne.

Was that guy her killer?

Jason needed to dig up more, then consider taking it to Grace to see if he could leverage it into a major exclusive, so the *Mirror* would own the story. He entertained pleasant thoughts about her until his father arrived.

Jason ordered a BLT, milk, and more coffee.

"Just coffee," Henry Wade told the waitress.

"I'm sorry that I kept blowing you off when you wanted to talk," Jason said.

His old man shrugged off his apologies.

"You've got the big story, I understand."

"All right, so let's talk. Are you ready to finally tell me what happened to you when you were a police officer? Why you left the force?"

As his father rubbed his chin, Jason saw that he'd nicked himself shaving.

"This is all about the thing you wanted me to help you with, Dad, right?"

Henry looked out the window searching for the place to start. "I don't expect the name Vernon Pearce to mean much to you."

"He was your partner when you were a cop."

"How did you know that?"

"Look, after all these years, all the crap our family, well, what's left of it, has been through, do you think I was going to let you keep your secret locked up?"

"You know everything, then?"

"No. But I tried to learn everything, without you finding out. I dug wherever I could. I dug carefully because I didn't want anything getting back to you because I thought you'd stop me."

"So what more did you find out?"

"Not much, just that something happened because you quit and Vern kind of disappeared, or something."

"Vern was a seasoned uniformed police officer. A Vietnam veteran. A diehard street cop who took me under his wing. He taught me everything about police work. How to handle myself when someone takes a swing at me, or if I was outnumbered. Taught me the basics of investigations, about police politics, how to make a judgment call, when to let somebody go with a warning, or when to be the meanest mother on the street."

"You got along, then?"

"We were like brothers."

"So what happened?"

"We'd been partnered for just over a year, in uniform and on patrol. In total command of our zone. Handling crap, the thin blue line. I loved my job and being Vern's partner. God, it was good. Then one day we get called to an armed robbery in progress and—"

Henry rubbed his face.

"I've never really talked about this."

"I know, Dad, take it easy."

"The call went all weird on us. It ended with a person getting shot. The suspect was arrested and pleaded guilty."

"Can you tell me who got shot, Dad?"

His father stared at him, his eyes clouded with fear.

"Can you tell me the date?" Jason pulled out his notebook.

"Put that away, son. Please and let me finish."

"Why?"

"Please."

Jason tucked his notebook away.

"More coffee?" the gum-chewing waitress asked.

They both accepted refills from her.

"Dad," Jason said, after she left, "I looked through the old clippings from the time you were on the job, armed robberies, shootings. Your name never came up."

"Not every cop who responds to a call gets named in the news reports," Henry said. "All I can say is it was tragic." He rubbed his lips. "It took a toll on me and it took a toll on Vern."

"What happened?"

Henry stared into his black coffee.

"We gave so much to the job, we became the job. We

put our lives on the line every time we went out. And in a split second, in a heartbeat, everything changes. Your life changes."

"Dad, what happened?"

"Vern took things very hard. But he never said a word to me. So I never realized how things were eating him up, until that day."

"What day?"

"The last day I saw him."

"When was that?"

"One day, a few months later. Vern was late for work. I told the sergeant that his car had broken down, then I called Vern at his home. He answered. He was home alone. I told him I was swinging by to pick him up for our shift."

"What did he say?"

"He said—" Henry stopped to blink several times. "He said sure, pal, come and get me. So I got to his place. Knocked. No answer, so I tried the door. It was unlocked. I got in and the first thing I heard was the loud static scratching of an old vinyl record that had played to the end. I called for Vern but heard nothing.

"The place was a mess. It smelled kind of bad, like nothing had been washed, or cleaned. Clothes were heaped, the TV was on but muted. Vern never had a hair out of place.

"I called for him again, heard a muffled sound from a bedroom. The door was half open. When I entered I saw Vern in his uniform and he had this strange look on his face. He was holding his off-duty gun, a Colt. I thought he was cleaning it or something. Vern looks at it, looks at me—says 'sorry, Henry'—sticks the gun in his mouth, and pulls the trigger. A portion of his skull and brain matter splashed over his wedding photo on the wall."

"Jesus."

"I don't recall what happened after that. They told me that when they found me, I was on the floor cradling his head in my lap."

"Dad, I'm so sorry."

"Maybe a piece of me died with Vern that day. I was finished as a cop."

"Did he leave a note? What was he sorry for?"

"No note. His wife walked out on him. That call had taken a toll on Vern and me."

"Well, what happened?"

"I don't want to get into that. This is hard for me."

"Sure. Sure."

"The thing is, after I packed it in, I got a small disability pension and started drinking. I swore I never ever wanted to touch a gun again."

"I understand."

"Now here I am, a private detective with Krofton and he's issued this order for all of his people to get themselves licensed to be armed. I'm having a very hard time with it all."

"Are you going to do it?"

"It's done."

"It's done? Wow. Well, think of it as a good thing, that you're strong enough to stare this business down and put it behind you and hope you'll never have to use the damned gun."

Henry embraced Jason's encouragement because it was what he needed to hear.

"That's what I'll do."

Jason patted his father's hand.

"Thank you for telling me this, Dad. I understand things now."

"Thank you," Henry said, "for not giving up on me, son."

"Are you kidding? We're partners." Jason spun the newspaper around with his story on the front page.

"Maybe you could help me with this story, Dad?"

Henry looked at the headline and Sister Anne Braxton's picture.

Jason ordered more coffee.

19

"No— I've— No! You've already connected me to that department—"

Rhonda Boland failed to get the receptionist at the insurance company to understand Brady's situation.

"Would you just listen to me? Please. He's just been diagnosed. Please, don't put me on hold again, just listen, please—"

The line clicked. Elevator music flowed into her ear. "Rhinestone Cowboy."

Rhonda squeezed the phone and stared at the mound of papers growing on her kitchen table. She'd circled the help-wanted ads in her search for a second job. They needed bartenders at the Pacific Eden Rose Hotel, which wasn't far.

Still holding, she considered her bank statements, employee benefit handbooks, forms, and insurance policies with fine print that only a lawyer could decipher. Even her late husband's papers were on the table. Even though there was no chance that *anything* regarding Jack Boland could ever help her at this stage, Rhonda had dug them out anyway.

Whatever it took to save Brady.

There was nothing in Jack's material. She pushed it all to the extreme end of the table and saw the booklet again. The one left by Gail, the volunteer from the support group, who'd visited earlier that morning.

"The information here will help you, Rhonda. It'll guide your decision on what and when to tell Brady," Gail said.

Still on hold, Rhonda took in the cover again. Beams of brilliant light parted the clouds over the title: *Will I Go to Heaven?*

The line clicked. The receptionist had returned.

"Yes I'm still holding," Rhonda said. "Please, let me explain, I've got special circumstances and need to know—"

More "Rhinestone Cowboy."

Rhonda shut her eyes and cursed, letting anger and fear roll through her. *Hope no one you love ever gets sick.* She reached for the booklet, then glanced at the clock over her sink. Brady would be home from school soon.

That's when she'd planned to tell him. Everything. She'd intended to tell him the moment they'd left the doctor's office but couldn't do it.

"So am I kinda sick, or something, Mom?" he'd asked as they walked to the car.

How do you tell your son that death is waiting for him? She couldn't do it. Not there, in the parking lot.

"The doctor's not sure. He needs to check some things. Want some ice cream?"

"Okay."

Rhonda had stalled for time. Gail at the support group said it was a normal reaction, part of "the parental need to process the information."

Oh God, Brady would be home this afternoon.

Rhonda stifled a sob, glanced at her fridge door. The story of their lives was there in a cluttered patchwork of odds and ends.

Brady's last report card. He had been doing so well before all this started. His gold certificate for his science project. He wanted to build passenger space jets. The birthday card he'd made for her. *"My Mom Is The Best Mom In The World."* The Mariners calendar, marked with home and away games, her shifts at the supermarket, Brady's appointments with Dr. Hillier. And the new specialist, Dr. Choy.

The calendar was also marked with "D-Days." Those were the days when payment was due for the debts Jack had left her. When he died suddenly, Rhonda was shocked to learn that his small business was on the verge of bankruptcy; she had no legal protection and next to no life insurance. It meant she had to close his business and slowly pay off his outstanding bills with her job as a supermarket cashier.

Some days she hated Jack.

Some days she missed him and mourned the time in her life when she had believed that Jack Boland was her salvation.

Rhonda had grown up in the middle of nowhere in Utah, where her stepfather would beat her and her mother. Her mother seemed to just accept it. Her stepfather was an unemployed food inspector and a self-pitying bastard who blamed his life on "the goddamn government." When he reached for a claw hammer to use on them, Rhonda packed her bags and bought a bus ticket to Las Vegas.

She got a job at a bar off the Strip serving drinks to rollers, saved her tips, and took dance lessons because she wanted to be a showgirl, then an actress. She'd been in Vegas, dreaming her dream for some six years, thinking of leaving, when she met Jack Boland after serving him rum and Coke at the blackjack table. He was a quiet player who'd given her sad, warm smiles and huge tips for about a week before asking her out.

Jack was a gentleman. A good-looking guy, in a dark mysterious way. Rhonda was not bothered by the fact he was about twenty years older than she was. He was a charmer, a professional gambler and pretty much a loner, who'd lived all over the country. He said that once he'd set his eyes on her, it was time to settle down.

She told him she'd had enough of Vegas and wanted to start a family. Take a shot at the white-picket-fence dream with a good-hearted man.

Jack smiled, said it was a good dream.

"What do you say you and me roll the dice on dreams, Rhonda?"

They got married and moved to Jack's old hometown, Seattle, where he started a small landscaping business. He took out a loan for a big new truck, a couple of riding mowers, tillers, and all sorts of new equipment. He even subcontracted jobs to other small companies, creating the impression his one-man operation was larger than it was.

They lived modestly.

Jack stopped gambling and remained a private man. They didn't go out much. After they were married, he told Rhonda he'd always been alone since he'd lost his family in a fire when he was a boy growing up in the midwest. It was something that haunted him and he never really talked about it. She soon found out that he was prone to brood, drink, lose his temper, punch a wall.

But he never laid a hand on her.

Still, it broke her heart because she'd thought she'd escaped Utah.

Rhonda was no quitter. In the years after Brady was born, things changed. Jack appeared to find some peace. As Brady got older, Jack would take him along on landscaping jobs. But money got tight and Rhonda got a job at the supermarket to help with the bills.

Every now and then, Jack would find a few bucks

when things were dire. He'd say a big job had paid off. In her heart, Rhonda suspected Jack was gambling again but she never questioned him because his payoffs had always saved them.

Still, Jack's temper seethed near the surface as he complained about his business and not having the freedom to live the way a man should. He seemed to be battling something.

Rhonda begged him to talk to her, but he refused and went off by himself, which made things worse because his rage seemed to be growing.

One ugly night, Jack, in drunken fury, raised his hand to Rhonda. She seized it.

"If you ever hit me, it'll be the last time you see me and Brady."

Jack stared right through her like she wasn't even there.

Then one day she came home from a bad shift at work. That's when she'd noticed Brady had a fresh bruise on his head. She asked about it at dinner.

"What happened, sweetie?"

Brady looked to Jack for the answer.

"He banged it on my workbench helping me."

"Banged it on the bench? How the heck did that happen?"

"That's how it happened. So drop it," Jack sucked air through his teeth while gnawing on a chicken wing.

That night after Brady got into bed, Rhonda softly pressed him for more details.

"Brady, what really happened?"

"Mom, I was clumsy."

"You're not clumsy. Tell me what happened."

"Dad said that I—Mom. I'm clumsy. I dropped a tool on Dad's foot. Okay?"

Her blood bubbled.

"Did he hit you?"

Brady turned to the wall.

Rhonda marched from Brady's room. Jack was on his sixth, or seventh, beer and still gnawing on chicken wings when she lit into him.

"Did you hit him?"

Jack glared at her while still chewing, his jaw muscles tightening.

"He dropped a drill on my foot. I hardly touched him."

"You bastard!"

"Don't make this a big deal, Rhonda," Jack gnawed on his chicken bone. "I'm warning you."

"You stupid coward."

Jack ground into the chicken, sprang to his feet, swung at her head, missed, shifted his weight to swing again, and suddenly his eyes widened and he clawed at his throat.

He was choking.

Rhonda thudded his back, wrapped her arms around him, put her hands together and tried to press into his upper chest. Jack fell to his knees, collapsing on their living room floor, gasped for several minutes, then stopped breathing.

Right there.

With Brady watching.

Rhonda tried mouth-to-mouth and CPR while Brady called 911.

There was nothing they could've done, the doctors said later.

A chicken bone had become wedged in his throat.

Rhonda was suddenly a young widowed mother, trapped in a maelstrom of horrible emotions that lasted for months. So when the doctor had asked if Brady had ever had a head injury, she couldn't tell him the whole truth because she believed it had been all her fault.

She feared that the doctor would call social services and—*they could take Brady.*

There had been a point in her life when she truly believed Jack was her salvation. But it was so long ago it seemed like a distant, dying star. Little by little as each day passed, Jack had become a hard man to love. In fact, all the love she'd ever had for him evaporated the day she buried him.

Brady was the only good thing to come out of her marriage.

The only good thing in her life.

And now, after all she'd been through, God has somehow seen fit to take Brady away from her. *And now,* as she tried to fight back tears, the line in her hand clicked and this woman at the insurance company was going to put her on hold—

"No! *Damn it!* Don't put me on hold again you, stupid, stupid—!"

Rhonda slammed the phone down, drove her face into her hands in time to muffle her scream.

Helpless. She was utterly helpless.

Rhonda sat in her kitchen letting her anger ebb until she heard a noise.

What was that?

She stopped breathing to listen.

20

It sounded as if something had fallen over in the garage.

Rhonda waited and listened.

Nothing.

Strange.

Was she so stressed that her mind was playing tricks on her? Maybe it was the echo of her own sob.

No. She definitely heard something.

It came from the garage. Maybe it was Brady and his friends? She glanced at the clock. It was a bit early for him to be home from school just yet. Besides, he didn't like going in the garage much.

Neither did she.

It was like a mausoleum. That's where Jack spent a lot of time. A lot of his stuff was still out there. Stuff she had trouble selling, or giving away. She'd better go check because, if she didn't, it would trouble her tonight.

She took the key from the peg.

It was a two-car garage connected to the house with a breezeway. Rhonda hardly used it. This is silly. She was probably hearing things, she told herself, sliding the key in the side door.

Dust motes swirled in the columns of late-afternoon sunlight shooting through the side window. Standing in the doorway, with her hand on the handle, Rhonda looked around.

Three broken lawn mowers that he used to cannibalize for parts lined one wall. Two ladders were suspended on hooks on the opposite wall. Extra sheets of drywall and scrap pieces of plywood stood in one corner. The tall refrigerator was in another corner. Brady's wading pool, his old tricycle, and baby things cluttered one area. Old baby toys and broken lawn furniture. The barbeque.

Reminders of happier days.

It was odd.

She could feel a presence.

Jack's workbench was still cluttered with old tools. Junk, really. And such a mess. She should just toss everything. Next to the bench stood the row of his old mismatched file cabinets where he kept God knows what. Landscaper stuff. Not the important papers. Those all went to the accountant and lawyers.

Nothing seemed out of place.

Maybe the neighbor's cat got in through a vent? Or a squirrel? Hopefully not a mouse.

No. It was nothing.

Rhonda tightened her hold on the door handle and prepared to leave. As she took a last look around, something caught her eye. The way the light reflected on the file cabinet. The middle drawer of the second cabinet was open.

Now that's strange.

They're all supposed to be locked. There's nothing important in there but she distinctly remembered locking them all. She looked at the stuff in the drawer. Just useless files on lawns and maintenance. But how could that drawer be open?

How could that be?

Maybe she'd forgotten?

Maybe she'd been out here looking through Jack's papers and had forgotten? She stood there thinking until she heard Brady's voice, faint, from the house.

"Hi, Mom, I'm home."

"I'm coming!" she called back.

This was silly.

She snapped the file drawer closed, then left, pulling the garage door closed behind her without seeing the stranger standing in the darkened corner next to the refrigerator.

He was holding a large knife.

And he was skilled at using it.

21

It was relentless.

Something familiar gnawed at Chuck DePew, something he felt could break this case wide open.

But what was it?

At the Washington State Patrol's Crime Lab in Seattle, DePew studied an enlarged photograph on his oversized computer monitor. He'd seen this before. But when? He thrust his hands into the pockets of his lab coat and ground his teeth; a lifelong habit signaling his Zen-like style of problem solving.

The image looked like a TV weather map, a confusion of isobaric contours, troughs, and radiating temperature patterns.

DePew then typed several commands. As the new data loaded, he took stock of his worktable with the evidence collected in and around the scene where Sister Anne Braxton was murdered.

The key item was a cast of a partial shoe impression taken from the alley behind her apartment, near the blackberry bush where the killer had tossed the knife. The cast was collected by Kay Cataldo's crew with the

Seattle Police CSI unit. They'd done a nice job, producing a little work of art in dental stone that offered a three-dimensional copy of the partial.

A right shoe impression was the first thing DePew thought when Kay first showed it to him earlier. "Any chance you could help us out here, Chuck?" Kay's SPD unit was smaller than the WSP team and constantly overwhelmed. But then again, so was DePew.

"There's not much to go on here," he said.

"I'll give you my Sonics tickets if you guys can do anything with this and the lift of the partials we took from her apartment."

"Are they good?"

"The impressions?"

"The tickets."

"Center court, fifteenth row."

"I'll see what I can do," DePew winked.

He was a senior forensic scientist and a certified court expert. After setting aside his own file, he set to work on Cataldo's case. The nun's murder had profile and everyone in the building knew the pressure that came with a high-profile case. DePew photographed the cast of the partial shoe impression, then he loaded clean, clear images into his computer.

Next, he analyzed the information from the alley, comparing it with the cast—the soil, the depth, weather condition, the pressure and stress points of the partial impression.

Now, where things got tricky was with the partial impressions Kay's people took from the hardwood floor of the apartment. They'd found impressions in the blood that had pooled around her, but they were smeared, the quality virtually unusable. The curious thing was they were not indicative of a set of exit tracks. The killer likely removed his shoes until he was out of the building.

Very smart.

But he never thought about his entrance because beyond the blood, they got lucky. Invisible to the naked eye in the microscopic layer of dust on the hardwood floor, he left something. Something they could work with. Using an electrostatic lifter they got a couple of partials on the clear floor a few feet from Sister Anne's body.

A right shoe impression.

DePew analyzed the sharpest one, along with the field notes, photographed it, loaded it into his computer. And here we are: DePew's computer screen split and he set to work configuring the two photographs to the identical scale and attitude.

Good, he thought.

Then he transposed one image over the other and began looking for points of comparison the same way he would examine fingerprints because DePew knew that shoe impressions can be as unique as fingerprints. The shape of the outsole, its size, its design, the material used to manufacture it, the wear patterns, the weight and gait of the wearer, all serve to create a unique impression.

And here, DePew thought as his computer beeped, we have a very consistent pattern of these right partials.

One taken from the murder scene. One taken from the alley where the murder weapon was found. He enlarged the transposed image dramatically, until it felt like the impressions had swallowed him.

The partials lacked any manufacturer's logo, lettering, or numbering, but that was no problem. DePew focused on the wear and cut characteristics. The edges had channeling, with an array of lugs and polygons; there was a waffle pattern, but here was the clincher: this mark on the fifth ridge, indicating a stone, or for-

A PERFECT GRAVE   141

eign object was wedged into it with this nice little "x" cut.

It is in both exhibits. DePew was getting ahead of himself but he would duly swear on the Holy Bible that this is the shoe of Sister Anne's killer.

Beautiful.

Now, why was that sense of familiarity gnawing at him even more?

By his calculations, DePew figured the shoe was a men's size 11, a North American sports shoe. DePew moved quickly to check the reference books of brands and manufacturers' designs and outsole producers, importers, and exporters who might know this impression.

But he stopped cold.

He had it.

DePew went to his file cabinet, flipped through case files until he found one in particular, pulled out a computer disk. Inserted it. He clicked through attachments and notes from the earlier case until he found images of shoe impressions.

He captured the outsole, configured it, then transposed it with the shoe impression from the nun's homicide. DePew assessed the characteristics. There was no way this was the same shoe. The earlier case was a male size 9, taken from a burglary at a gas station near Tacoma. They'd cleared that one and the offender was back in prison.

DePew was not concerned. In fact, he almost smiled.

The style and brand were definitely similar. In fact, DePew had a photograph of the type of shoe.

It was a sports shoe, a men's tennis shoe.

Standard state clothing that was issued only by the Washington Department of Corrections.

Whoever killed Sister Anne had done time.

22

Home from school, Brady came through the door the usual way.

A pack-drop to the hall floor and a beeline for the fridge.

"Hey, Mom."

"Have a good day?"

"Uhh-huh. No math homework. I thought we had chocolate milk."

"You finished it last night. How're you feeling?"

"Okay, I guess."

"Did you take your medicine at lunch?"

"Yup, did the doctor tell you what I got, or anything?"

Brady turned with the orange juice box he'd started at breakfast. "Today, I told Justin and Ryan about the MRI, how it was like going into a deep-sleep chamber in space. They thought it was cool."

Rhonda watched his attention go to the papers, then to the booklet as he read the title: *Will I Go to Heaven?* She watched him blink a few times, open it, and begin reading. Awareness rolled over him and Rhonda felt the light in their lives darken.

Brady didn't move.

She watched his chest rise and fall as he continued reading, understanding.

His eyes rose from the booklet to hers.

"Mom?"

"I know. We need to talk, sweetheart."

He set the booklet and the unfinished juice box on the counter.

"Let's go to your room."

Brady's room was all hard-core boy: walls papered with posters of Superman, King Kong, Spider-Man, and the Mariners; shelves lined with adventure books, model Blackhawk choppers and Humvees. In one corner, his skateboard rose like a rocket from his clothes heap. On his small desk, the secondhand computer Rhonda had picked up at a church donation sale. It was the best she could do. The N key stuck but Brady never complained.

Taking it all in, Rhonda succumbed to the reality that she might never see Brady's life go beyond his world right here and now. That she might never see him with his first girlfriend, his first car, never see him graduate from high school, go to college, start a career, get married, never hold her first grandchild.

"Don't cry, Mom."

Rhonda sat him on his bed next to her.

"Oh sweetheart. I'm sorry."

"I'm really sick with something and I could die, right?"

She searched his eyes.

"Brady."

"Mom, am I right?"

She nodded.

"How did you know?"

"By the way you hugged me at the doctor's office and stuff. I just knew it was serious."

She looked at him.

"And before, at the hospital, by the way everyone was acting and being so nice to me, the nurses, the doctors, like being all extra nice and everything."

Her eyes were shiny as she nodded.

"So is it cancer or leprosy or something?"

"You have a mass of cells, a tumor in your head and you're going to need an operation to remove it."

"Will it hurt?"

"No," she shook her head, "but you have to have it."

"And if I don't have it, I could die, right?"

Rhonda's chin crumpled, her tears flowed.

"Yes."

"And if I have the operation, I won't die, right?"

"Yes, the chances are tons better that you'll be fine with the operation."

"So when do I have it?"

"In a couple of months."

Brady thought for a long moment.

"How'd I get this tumor? Is it hered—hair—did, you know, was I born with it?"

"They're not sure."

"Could it be from the time Dad hit me for dropping the drill on his foot?"

"Why do you say that?"

"Because the doctor kept asking me if I ever played sports, or got hit hard in the head. I never told him about Dad. I didn't think it was right."

"I understand, honey."

"I don't hate him or anything. Sometimes I miss him."

"Me, too."

"So how did I get it?"

"No one knows for sure how people get them."

Brady looked at everything in his room, his second-hand computer, his old clothes, aware of how his mother struggled with money.

"This operation will probably cost us a lot, huh?"

Rhonda stared at the crumpled tissue in her hands.

"Don't worry about that. I'm going to get a second job. Nights likely, just to help us through a tight patch. So I'll talk to Alice about having someone watch you."

"Mom, I'm old enough to watch myself."

"I'm not old enough to let you watch yourself."

Suddenly Rhonda felt the breath squeeze out of her as Brady locked his arms around her, holding her tighter than ever.

"I don't want to die, Mom. I don't want to go away from you."

Rhonda fought to find her voice.

"I'm not going to let that happen. I'm going to be right here with you. You're going to be brave and have the operation and be as good as new and I'll be beside you every step of the way, okay?"

Brady didn't answer. He buried his face under her chin.

"Okay, sweetheart?"

She felt him nod.

"We're in this together," she said.

She heard him sniffle before he pulled away, wiped his tears, then took her hand and held it tight. They sat that way for a long time, saying nothing, just sitting there, like the time they sat near the edge of the Grand Canyon.

Eventually Brady pulled away from her.

"Mom, there's something I want to do and I want you to say it's okay."

"What is it?"

"I have to show you something. Wait here."

He ran down the hall to his bag and rummaged

through it before returning with a hastily folded page ripped from the newspaper. He unfolded it and passed it to her.

Slain Nun's Memorial Will Be at Shelter

After she'd finished reading the story under the headline in the *Mirror,* she looked at Brady.

"I want to go to Sister Anne's funeral at the shelter."

"Why?"

"She came to our school once with these other nuns."

"I know, and they helped with the big auction for charity."

"Sister Anne had asked me to help her move some boxes and she started talking to me. I didn't even know her, but she was asking me about Dad, and how we were doing. I guess a teacher told her that he had died and stuff. She seemed almost worried, like she knew me or something."

"Nuns can be nice like that."

"She was really nice and I liked her. She said she was going to pray for us."

"That was kind."

"I never told anybody this, but because she was so nice, and taking a picture, smiling, talking like she knew me and stuff, it kinda felt like she was my guardian angel."

"Oh, honey."

"So can we go? It's going to be downtown at the shelter."

Rhonda reviewed the time and location of the memorial service for Sister Anne Braxton.

"You really want to do this?"

Brady nodded.

"All right."

Brady took the newspaper from her and reread it.

"Mom, why would anyone want to kill her?"

"That's a question only God can answer, sweetie."

"And one other person."

"Who?"

"The person who killed her."

She pulled him close and looked out the window. Outside, a gentle wind lifted the branches of the elm trees, carrying a few dead leaves down the street, where they skipped over the sedan parked at the end of the block in the shade of a big-leaf maple tree.

23

Nothing was working.

Jason was on his phone in the newsroom holding for a cop source. The tenth one he'd tried today. And here it was early in the evening, the clock ticking closer to the first-edition deadline and nothing.

Absolutely zip for a fresh angle to advance the story of Sister Anne's murder. Tapping his pen, he noticed that his hands were sweaty.

Wait. He had an idea. A long shot but worth a try. He could—

"You there, Wade?"

"Yeah," he squeezed the phone, "you hearing anything? Anything new?"

"Just what I see in today's *Times* and the *P-I.*"

"Thanks."

He tossed his pen and cursed.

He did not need to be reminded that his competition had killed him with reports about investigators building a suspect pool of violent ex-cons who'd had run-ins with the nun. Both papers played their stories big today on their front pages. And all day they mocked Jason like a victorious middle finger.

What goes around, comes around.

Yeah, well he'd beaten them earlier with his story about the knife from the shelter being used as the murder weapon.

Jason's boss didn't care. Yesterday's news was today's fish wrap and Reep had been in his face to break another exclusive.

"The *Mirror* has to own this story, Wade. Anything less is unacceptable."

Jason had tried everything. Right from the get-go. This morning his old man had gone to his own sources to try to coax the names of any new potential suspects from them. So far, every effort had dead-ended. And Jason's calls to Grace Garner had not been returned.

For a moment, Jason let his thoughts go to his dad's revelation about his past.

What really happened to him?

"Wade!"

Reep stood at his office doorway beckoning him with a crooked finger, then rolled up his sleeves, as if preparing for a fight.

"You're still not on the sked. What have you got for me?"

"An idea."

"And how do I get that into the paper?"

"Listen, it's going to take time—"

"No, you listen. You've got jack. And sitting in here on your ass just doesn't cut it. I want something for tomorrow's paper. Something that will put us back out front. You've only got a couple of hours."

"I've got to try to find a guy who—"

"You're taking Cassie with you."

"Eldon, it'd be better if I go alone, it could be dangerous."

"Stop the horseshit. You're forgetting that I assigned Cassie to this story with you. Do as you're told."

Cassie was wearing a V-neck sweater, jacket, and form-fitting jeans that complemented her figure as they headed across the *Mirror* parking lot to his Falcon.

She never smiled as she sipped from her Styro cup of cafeteria coffee.

Before Jason started the car, she opened her notebook. The sound of her flipping pages filled the awkward silence. Jason stared at her for a moment.

"Let's get one thing straight," he said. "I had no part of your screwup with Brian Pillar."

She looked away from him and out the window.

"That's not how I remember it."

"Then your credibility with me is dead."

"Why don't you let me handle my credibility?"

Jason looked at her.

"I'm searching for a man who may have talked to the nun's killer. This is my story, you're just along for the ride."

"You'd better start the car."

Jason shook his head then slid "Radar Love" into his player and laid six feet of rubber pulling out of the lot. Like most reporters, he functioned with a near-psychic connection to his deadline. He never wasted time. The clock was ticking on him.

It always was.

The sun had set as they came upon the edge of the Pioneer Square District. Jason parked the Falcon in an alley near a loading zone. As sirens wailed, he got out and started for the Compassionate Heart of Mercy Shelter.

Cassie didn't move.

"Coming?"

She hesitated. "It's creepy downtown at night."

"Figures," Jason said.

He headed for the shelter to the sound of Cassie changing her mind: car door opening and closing, shoes clicking as she hurried after him. He refused to slow down. The shelter's serving of the evening meal had already ended and Jason clung to the hope that he could catch some of the men before they vanished into the night.

Taking stock of the lingering stragglers, he approached a group of men huddled in a dim corner, passing a paper bag among themselves.

"Excuse me. I'm sorry to trouble you, but I'm looking for a man who comes here."

Cold hard eyes met his, then went to Cassie.

"Who're you?" a voice asked.

"Jason Wade, a reporter with the *Mirror*."

"And what does she do?"

Mumbling, the swish of liquid and soft, dark laughter went round the circle.

"Whatever it is," one said, "I bet she does it real nice."

The men laughed.

"She's a reporter, too," which was harder for Jason to swallow than the stuff they were drinking. "I don't know the name of the guy I'm looking for, but he's kinda heavyset, maybe in his late forties. Has long hair and a beard, maybe wears a field jacket with desert camouflage and military pants."

"Sounds like Coop. You're talking about Coop," one man said.

"Dark, intense eyes?"

"Angry eyes. That's Coop. Didn't come down tonight. He's taking things real hard. Sister Anne is the only one who could get through to him, and her funeral's going to be right here in the shelter tomorrow. So he's having a hard time."

"You know where he lives, where I can find him?"

"He stays near the International District. But you'd best keep away from him."

Jason took a note. "A mission, hostel? You got an address?"

"Did you hear what I said?"

"I know but it's important that we talk to him tonight. Please, do you have an address?"

"Here." Scarred, ruddy hands reached for Jason's pad and pen. "I'll draw you a map, but I would not be messing with him."

The man's sketching was clear and neat. Jason studied it, realizing that although the location was near, getting to Coop's place would not be easy.

"Be careful, he doesn't take kindly to people. Period."

"What's his full name?"

"Psycho," one of them chuckled.

"Shut up! You don't know him," a voice from the circle said. "John Cooper. But he likes to be called Coop."

"What's his story? I mean why call him that other name?"

A long silence passed.

The glass neck of the bottle flashed and liquid sloshed.

"You find him and you'll find out."

24

The International District wasn't far from Pioneer Square, its southern fringes just north of the stadiums where the Mariners and Seahawks played.

According to the men at the shelter, Jason would find John Cooper there, near the edge of the International District, at the location marked by the "X" on the map they'd drawn for him.

He parked his Falcon next to a Dumpster, near a back alley, took stock of his surroundings, then double-checked the map. Hing Hay Park, the boutiques, markets, restaurants, and the slopes of Kobe Terrace, laced with private gardens, were not far. Neither were First Hill with its million-dollar condo views of Seattle's skyline and Yesler Terrace—the area near Sister Anne's town house.

Look in another direction and it was a whole other world.

Beyond the parking lots, the chain-link fences, and the old site of the homeless encampment, Interstate 5 cut a multilane swath through Seattle, the traffic droning like an ominous chant lifting to the sky. Concrete columns rose to support the freeway, along with vast sloping retaining walls that disappeared from view to meet its underbelly in a darkness deeper than the night.

"He's up in there," Jason nodded to the sloping wall under the overpass. "Let's go, we don't have much time before deadline."

"Climb up there? You've got to be kidding."

"They said he lives up there, under the overpass."

"They also called him Psycho and warned us to leave him alone."

Jason said nothing. He was fishing for something in his pocket.

"Jason, you can't see anything. It's so creepy."

He tested the batteries of his penlight. They were strong.

"Stay in the car if you can't handle it. I don't have a lot of time."

Sirens echoed amid the canyons of Seattle's glittering skyscrapers as he set out to ascend the vast incline. He didn't care if Cassie came. He preferred to go alone. He didn't have time to babysit her.

Newspapers and fast food take-out bags skipped along, propelled by the rush of the traffic that flowed above and the gusts off Elliott Bay that fingered their way through the city. The stench of urine and bird shit assailed him as he progressed. It was like stepping into the great yawning jaw of some nether region. He used his penlight to find his way to the summit where the narrow beam revealed walls encrusted with multiple coatings of cascading guano, the gagging smell mingling with those of engine exhaust, motor oil, and rubber.

Pigeons cooed, then several dark things scurried near his feet ahead of him. Claws scraping. He glimpsed tails, matted fur. Rats. It was gross, but Jason was undaunted. He'd faced worse.

His light caught the fragment of a red blanket beckoning from a crevasselike opening between two large concrete walls. The blanket served as a curtain, suspended from a guano-layered drainage pipe, dripping with foul-smelling water.

This was it.

"Mr. Cooper!" Jason raised his voice over the rumble of the traffic. "Jason Wade from the *Seattle Mirror*! We met at the shelter! Can I have a word with you, sir?"

No answer. Jason waited then repeated his call, louder the second time.

Again, no response.

Cooper was there.

Physically.

Mentally, he was in the busy market near the Syrian border beyond Tal Afar. In one hand he held a bottle. The other was tight around the handle of a knife, ready for the attackers.

Seattle's traffic above him was roaring like the firefight.

It would be different this time—this time Coop would kill them all. Button up.

Save his crew.

Then they would stop screaming.

Out front, Jason drew back the blanket.

It was like the crack at the entrance of a spider's hole. The smell was powerful. His light reached partway down a narrow corridor lined with blankets, plastic sheeting, a shopping cart, wooden crates. He followed one electrical cord from a utility maintenance outlet to a hotplate, utensils. An assortment of mismatched spoons, forks.

Knives.

Jason glimpsed pair after pair of combat boots, shoes, sneakers, jackets, parkas, pants, sweaters, worn woollen socks, tattered shirts. Heaps of toilet paper under plastic sheets, cans of dried goods, beans, soup, stews, boxes of dried cereal. Rations.

It's like the guy's still at war, Jason thought.

More blanket curtains led to other chambers deeper down.

A lull in the traffic and Jason heard a bottle swish.

"Coop! Coop! Can you hear me?"

Something moved in the blackness beyond the curtain. Jason couldn't see anything.

"Get out! Get out!"

The attackers were coming and coming. Cooper gripped his knife. He could hear Yordan, Bricker, Rose, calling him.

Coop!

They were next to him now—getting closer.

"Get the fuck out!"

"Coop!" Jason shouted. "Hold on! It's Jason Wade. We talked, remember? Are you okay? Sir, it's Jason Wade from the *Mirror*. You wanted to help me!"

Help me help me help me.

Jason's words seemed to echo before they died in the sudden thunder of traffic hammering overhead, followed by an anguished groan from the other side of a blanket.

"Reporter?" Coop repeated.

"Yes, you spoke to me about Sister Anne, you wanted to help me. Remember?"

"Leave me alone."

"Coop, please, help me."

Coop help me.

Jason could not know how the phrase he'd spoken cut into Cooper.

"Sir, you wanted me to know about the man."

"What?"

"The man who took the knife from the shelter. The man who argued with Sister Anne before she was murdered."

Coop processed the information, his memory flickering back.

"Did they find that mother?" He shouted. "Because he's the one—I just know—the way he hurt her."

He's the one.

Jason felt something tingling at the back of his neck.

"He's the one?" Jason repeated. "Did you see something, did you talk to police?"

"No goddam cops. I never talk to them."

"But why do you think—?"

"Because I goddam heard him talking to Sister. This goof was so angry. Sister took him to the little office to be alone, but I was watching over her. She's my angel, and he was making her upset."

Jason's penlight was in his mouth, shining on his pad. He wrote fast before withdrawing it to ask another question.

"Tell me what you heard, Coop, can you tell me, please?"

"He wanted something from her."

"What?"

"I don't know. She wanted to forgive him but, no, no, he was angry, he didn't want that from her."

"Forgive him for what?"

"His sins."

"What sins?"

"We all have sins."

"Coop. Who's this man? Tell me about this man."

Traffic pounded overhead, reminding Jason that his deadline was coming fast. Damn it. He had no time to get a photographer up here to get a pic of Cooper in tomorrow's paper. Cooper likely wouldn't even agree to it.

"You want to know who this man was?" Coop asked.

"Yes."

"He could be anybody."

"I don't understand. Did you ever see him before, did you know him?"

"I don't even know myself, man."

An anguished groan and a bottle sloshed.

"I couldn't save them."

"Who?"

"Yordan, Bricker, and Rose. My crew. I was their commander. I tried. It happened so fast. I tried to close the hatch but they were on us so fast."

Jason didn't understand.

"It must've been hard for you, Coop."

"They're always talking to me. I can hear 'em just like we was still there. It's always the same. Why'd you leave us, Coop? Why? Sister Anne understood. She told me to forgive myself."

The bottle swished.

"But I can't."

"Did you try to get help, Coop?"

"Nothing can save me now. Sister said she'd forgiven me. She said she'd pray for me. And she did. And for a while there, my crew left me alone. But then they started coming back. Asking me the same thing: Why, Coop? I told them I tried. I swear, I tried to close the hatch! But those mothers just kept coming, kept climbing on us so fast, man I tried. I tried and tried to save them."

"I know, Coop," Jason said. "Tell me about the man."

"Once I told Sister I couldn't take it anymore. I told

her to stop. To stop forgiving me, stop praying for me. I wasn't worth it. I told her that. But she wouldn't stop."

"Coop, please tell me about the man."

"No, you tell me, asshole! You tell me, now that she's gone, gone like Yordan, Bricker, and Rose, they're all gone and now she's gone, so you tell me who's going to pray for me now? I can never be forgiven for what I've done!"

"What do you mean, Coop? What did you do?"

Traffic hummed but no answer came.

Slowly, Jason pulled back the curtain and the tiny hairs on the back of his neck stood up.

Cooper was squatting against the wall, swinging his knife.

The blade glinting in the weakening light.

25

Please God, tell me what to do.

Sister Denise was alone in her room crying.

She'd told no one about what she'd found hidden under the floorboards in the closet of Sister Anne's room. Of course, her first impulse had been to turn it over to her superior, Sister Vivian, and to tell the others. But for some powerful and inexplicable reason, Denise felt compelled to keep her discovery secret.

To protect it because no one should see it.

Maybe this was God's way of speaking to her. Denise didn't know. A moral war was raging in her heart. Should she tell someone, or forget that she'd ever found it?

Throughout the town house she could hear the sisters making last-minute arrangements for the funeral service at the shelter. It would begin in a few hours and they would leave very soon.

Denise had little time.

Drying her tears, she locked her door, knelt by her bed, made the sign of the cross, and prayed. Then she

reached under her mattress and retrieved the cardboard box she found under the floor in Anne's room.

The box had been used to store candles and was
about the size of a hardcover book. It was ancient with
frayed, deteriorating corners that were held together
with adhesive tape yellowed with age. It smelled of wax
when she lifted the lid.

She reached inside and removed the red notebook.
It was a number 82, plain, four-star line, with a red hard-
board cover. The pages crackled when she opened it to
the secrets of Sister Anne Braxton's life.

> *It was fitting that it was raining when I entered the
> little church in Paris to make my amputation with my
> past life. The warm water against my skin was my bap-
> tism. . . .*

So began the first entry of Anne's journal, dated well
over twenty years ago. It was written with a fountain pen
in Anne's elegant hand, the revelations of a young
woman at the threshold of devoting her life to God.

In reading on, Denise empathized with how Anne
had struggled with the same deep concerns that confront all women who contemplate a religious life. How
they must accept that they will never bear children,
never marry, never have a family or grandchildren, and
are destined to live simply in humility and poverty. Anne
seemed resolute in her readiness to embrace the realities of becoming a nun.

But as Denise read the entries again, she was troubled by the undercurrent that accompanied all of
Anne's thoughts.

Guilt.

Although Anne offered no details of past acts, and

only alluded to remorse for them, an air of atonement accompanied all of her entries.

If we say that we have no sin, we deceive ourselves and the truth is not in us.

Denise knew that one from The First Epistle of John, along with the rest of it, which Anne had written at the outset of her journal and throughout.

If we confess our sins, He is faithful and just to forgive us our sins, and to cleanse us from all unrighteousness.

Flipping through the pages and the years of Anne's life, Denise kept coming back to Anne's personal torment over something that had happened long ago.

Oh heavenly Father, can I ever be forgiven for what I did, for the pain I caused? Although I am not worthy, please forgive me.

It was a consistent theme of Anne's writing, one she kept returning to even in the last months of her life.

I deeply regret the mistakes I have made and will accept your judgment of me.

What was it? What had she done? What could she possibly have done that would account for such mental agony?

It fits now.

Denise suddenly recalled one of her last conversations she'd had with Sister Anne. They'd gone alone for a Sunday walk near the park. Sister Anne seemed to be

tormented by something before she had finally confided to Denise.

"I believe with all my heart that I will be judged by
the sins of my past life and not the religious one I've
strived to live." Anne stopped. "And I believe that my
judgment could come soon. In the end, I believe God
will determine if my struggle to atone was worthy."

"Atone for what? I'm not sure I understand, Anne."

"When I was young, I did the most horrible thing."

"Everyone makes mistakes."

"I destroyed lives."

"Destroyed lives? What do you mean? Did you break
a young man's heart?"

Anne looked off.

"God knows what I did. God, and one other living
person. Please, Denise. I've said more about this than
I've ever told anyone. Please, you must keep my confidence. Promise me."

"Of course, Anne. But I don't understand."

"If we're patient, God will reveal all mysteries. After
all, He does work in mysterious ways." Anne hugged her
and never spoke of the subject again.

It was so cryptic. "I destroyed lives." What did she mean?

A sudden knock on her door, and Denise's heart
leapt.

"Are you almost ready, Denise?"

"See you downstairs in a couple more minutes, Flo."

Denise was coming to a decision. The journal was
not her property. Being aware of it, and given all of the
tragic circumstances, she must give it to Vivian. Perhaps
Denise had hesitated earlier because she'd been upset
with Vivian.

She'd reached a decision.

Closing the journal, putting it in the box, she took it
with her down the hall, where she knocked softly on the

door to Anne's, well, Vivian's room. It was weird how she insisted on staying there. The others had whispered how they thought it was macabre, but no one dared question Vivian.

"Who is it?"

"Denise."

"I'll be downstairs in a minute."

"I'd like to talk to you privately."

"Can it wait?"

"I don't think so."

"Come in then, for a moment."

The room still smelled of ammonia, which Denise would now and forever associate with Anne's murder. Vivian was a portrait of the imposing leader, writing notes for the memorial service.

"What is it? I have to hurry ahead to meet Father Mercer, he'll be celebrating the mass today and is going directly to the shelter."

"I need to show you what I discovered when I was cleaning."

Denise went to the closet, pried out the floorboards, revealed the hole, then passed the box to Vivian, who was perplexed.

"Anne had hidden this under the floor. It's her journal."

"Journal?"

Vivian started flipping through it. Slowly at first, then faster as she absorbed its contents.

"Did you know she'd kept a journal?" Denise asked.

Vivian shook her head without lifting it from the book.

"You knew her longer than the rest of us. Do you know what she's talking about when she says she regrets the mistakes she made in the past?"

"No, what?" Vivian's head remained in the book, reading. "No. But what human being doesn't regret past mistakes?" Finally she lifted her head, her eyes boring into Denise. "Did you tell anyone about this?"

"No."

"Show it to anyone?"

"No, just you. I thought maybe we might use some of her words at the memorial, then maybe pass it to the detectives."

"Perhaps later, but not at this time. And you will tell no one, absolutely no one, about this book. Is that understood?"

"But why?"

"This is a very private journal and I'll need time to study it more carefully before we decide on how to proceed. *Is that understood?*"

Denise said nothing, watching Vivian slide Anne's journal into her valise among the files she was taking with her to the shelter.

"Is that clear, Sister Denise?"

"Yes, Sister."

26

"HE'S THE ONE."
On the Trail of Sister Anne's Killer:
MIRROR *Exclusive*

The headline above Jason Wade's byline stretched six columns across the *Mirror*'s front page above the fold. After reading his article for the third time, Grace Garner jabbed Jason's number on her cell.

"Grace," Perelli cautioned her as he drove their unmarked Malibu toward the shelter for Sister Anne's funeral. "Let it go."

She waved him off as Jason's line was answered.

"Jason Wade, *Seattle Mirror*."

"Nice story."

"Grace?"

"Is it bull, or is Cooper's information solid?"

"Judge for yourself. It's all there in the paper."

"We want to find him so we can chat."

"Why? Have you got something on the guy he's talking about? Why call me?"

"Seems Cooper wanders a bit. Thought you might point me in the right direction. Save me time."

"Will you give me a jump if something breaks?"

"Like you did for me on your story today?"

"Hey, I don't work for you. Everything I know about Cooper's brush with the mystery man is in my story."

"You know what I mean."

"No, I don't."

"I don't believe this." She searched the traffic for the right words. "It would've been nice if you'd told me this was coming out today, Jason."

"And it would've been nice if you'd returned my calls," he said. "But, *as usual, Grace*, you didn't."

"So this is how it's going to be?"

"This is how it is."

She hung up, shaking her head. He was still hurt. That's what this was all about. Maybe she was wrong to have ever started up with him. Well, that's his problem, not hers, she ruminated until Perelli interrupted her.

"I don't know why you called him. He's always in our face for help but it's never quid pro quo with him. It's a one-way street."

She stared at the buildings rolling by.

Maybe she was wrong to end it with him.

"Focus, Grace," Perelli said. "You don't need Wade. We've got people looking for Cooper in the International District. We've got word out on the street. It's just a matter of time before we find him. Focus on what you've got because it's good."

Perelli was right. Piece by piece she was building her case. As he wheeled into Pioneer Square, Grace reviewed the pictures on her camera phone. First, the knife. The murder weapon. It came from the shelter. Then a foot impression that was consistent with the type of sneaker issued only by the Washington Department of Corrections.

The Seattle PD was set up at the memorial service. The undercover surveillance unit was in the white panel van parked near the shelter entrance, secretly videotaping every person filing into the shelter for Sister Anne's funeral. Maybe, just maybe, they would find someone wearing state-issued shoes.

And maybe they would find the killer attached to them.

Inside the shelter, Sister Anne's garlanded pine casket rested at one end of the dining room. An enlarged photograph of her laughing among the day care's children was raised on a tripod next to it. Nearby, one of the plastic-covered bingo tables had been draped with a white sheet to serve as a makeshift altar. It stood before several hundred mourners in hard-back chairs that had been neatly arranged into pewlike rows.

Dignitaries representing the state, the county, the city, the Vatican, and the Archdiocese were not afforded any special seating. Conscious of the news cameras and reporters at the back, they did their best to look at ease among the homeless, the poor, and their children—the people Sister Anne helped and loved. The children were hushed during the service.

Father Jeb Mercer, a retired priest and old friend of Sister Vivian's, had flown in from the east that morning, arriving just in time to celebrate the funeral mass. Between hymns and psalms, a stream of officials delivered eulogies from the podium near her casket.

In a prepared tribute read by a local senator, the governor called Sister Anne, "An angel of mercy who eased pain." Then the mayor said she was, "the Saint of Seattle," and promised that the council would name a park in her honor.

The cardinal compared her compassion and devotion to that of Jesus Christ, then read condolences from the Vatican. "She inspired us because her love was blind to race, blind to social standing, blind to human failings. She restored dignity and worth to their rightful owners. She was Heaven's grace."

Then Krissie, a nine-year-old girl from the shelter's day care, went to the podium alone. She looked at her young, single mom, who nodded tearfully as Krissie unfolded a crisp sheet of paper and read, "You made us feel important, like we counted. My mom said you saved us. We love you and we will miss you. God bless you."

Finally, Sister Vivian spoke on behalf of the other nuns.

"She is the light in the darkness and we will carry on with her mission but with broken hearts, for Anne was our sister, our friend, and we loved her."

But she was not perfect.

Not a mention of her own failings, her shortcomings, and the self-doubt she battled with on the pages of her journal, Sister Denise thought as she listened to Vivian. Why not mention that Anne Braxton was also very human like the people she helped every day?

Denise didn't understand.

She didn't understand why Vivian was so determined to protect Anne's cryptic past. Why not let everyone hear Anne's own words at her funeral? Denise didn't understand anything anymore and pressed a tissue to her eyes.

Some sixteen rows back from Sister Anne's casket, Rhonda Boland squeezed Brady's hand. She prayed for him, and for Sister Anne, a woman she never knew but would have liked to have known. Sister Anne would've been a good person to turn to—a person she could have gone to for comfort, now, in her most desperate time.

She was the "light in the darkness."

Rhonda glanced at Brady, reading his prayer book. She was puzzled by whatever mysterious cosmic forces

gave rise to his desire to be here. She took some comfort in the fact they'd come. She needed help, even if it
was spiritual assurance, because Brady was just a little
boy who'd known death too well. His father and now
Sister Anne. Maybe God was preparing Brady for the
worst.

Maybe God was preparing her?

Between speakers, Rhonda looked around at the
mourners jammed into the room. Nearly all were street
people. She met the eyes of one man who seemed to be
fixated on her and Brady. Rhonda shrugged it off and
looked away.

Several moments later, all heads turned to a commotion. It was coming from the entrance, which was
jammed with a line of mourners that spilled out into
the street.

Grace Garner stood at the back of the crowded room
estimating the number of news people among the cameras along the side. She spotted Jason Wade but didn't
make eye contact. Focus, she told herself, while through
her earpiece she received updates from the surveillance
unit and the plainclothes detectives who were posted
everywhere.

"Absolutely no sign of anyone wearing the DOC
sneakers, Grace."

"Thanks."

For most of the service, John Cooper sat quietly on a
hard-back chair in a far corner of the room with his face
buried in his hands. Leona Kraver, a retired music teacher
and shelter volunteer, who'd read the *Seattle Mirror* that
morning, had recognized Cooper.

Leona indicated where he was sitting to the two detectives who'd asked for her help prior to the service. The two big men locked on to Cooper and began making their way to him.

"Grace, this is Foley. We've got an ID on our subject. At the back near the door."

In a short time, the two detectives and two uniformed officers managed to get John Cooper outside, where they shoved him against the wall, patted him down, handcuffed him, and placed him in the back of an unmarked car.

It roared off with news crews rushing from the shelter to the street straining to get footage, or a frame, comparing success with each other.

Some grinned, some cursed.

"What the hell was that?"

"Did you get that?"

Jason Wade made it outside in time to see Grace Garner and Perelli get into their car. He rushed to Grace's door and tapped her window.

"What's going on?"

Grace shook her head. She gave Jason nothing as their Malibu squealed away, leaving in its wake a stained page of the *Mirror* to swirl at Jason's feet.

Cassie Appleton emerged, walking toward Jason as she scrawled in her notebook.

"I think they just arrested somebody, Jason. Did you see who it was?"

27

Sister Anne's final journey took her an hour north of Seattle, then east into the breathtaking countryside of Snohomish County.

The hearse and two other vehicles of her small funeral procession moved beyond the farmland and fruit orchards to a cemetery at the base of a steep hillside. It was sheltered by forests of fir and cedar, bordered by thick vines and berry bushes.

She would love it here, Sister Denise thought, as the procession slowed and turned from the old highway onto the soft earthen pathway cutting into the graveyard that was first used by missionaries in the late 1800s.

Father Mercer and Sister Vivian rode in the lead car, followed by the hearse and the Order's big van. Sister Ruth drove the van.

None of the sisters in the van talked much. During the drive, most retreated into their thoughts. Sister Florence and Sister Paula whispered hymns while Denise confronted her problem: Sister Anne's secret journal.

Part of her yearned to tell the others about it so they

could remember Anne as a totally human and flawed woman.

Denise also wanted their support to press Vivian to share her discovery with the detectives. The police might find useful information in Anne's poetic self-deprecation. Admittedly, there weren't many details, but maybe the detectives would find value in the dates, or some other aspect that would lead them to her killer. Anything can be the break that solves a case, her father the police officer used to tell her.

Anything.

Should she disobey Vivian and tell Detective Garner? Tell someone?

Lord, what should I do?

The procession eased to a gentle stop near the open grave, next to the mound of rich, dark Washington earth. A lonely lark flitted by and sparrows sang from the trees. The funeral director and his assistants guided and helped the nuns carry and position Anne's casket.

In all, about a dozen people were gathered for the burial. It was private. No news cameras were permitted. Afterward, the nuns would oversee a reception at the shelter.

Sister Vivian took Father Mercer's arm and helped him from the car. He was well over six feet, but bent by age, with wispy white hair and a phlegmatic face creased by time. The nuns did not know him. He was an old friend of Sister Vivian's, a retired Jesuit who'd flown in from New England to take care of the funeral mass.

Vivian walked him to the casket, where he produced a worn leather-bound Bible, containing cards with rituals written in his hand.

He began by inviting the mourners to reconcile their souls by reflecting in silence. Then he spoke of God's love, the sacrifice of His only son, the mystery of death, and the resurrection of Jesus Christ.

For Scripture, he read from Isaiah 61:1–3.

"The spirit of the Lord God is upon me, because the Lord has anointed me to preach good tidings unto the meek; he hath sent me to bind up the brokenhearted, to proclaim liberty to the captives, the opening of the prison to them that are bound; To proclaim the acceptable year of the Lord; and a day of vengeance of our God; to comfort all who mourn."

Denise didn't really understand that choice. She wondered about it after Mercer ended with the Lord's Prayer. Then each of the nuns kissed the casket and placed a rose on it.

Like the others, Denise also faced the fact that Anne had no husband to mourn her, no children or grandchildren to carry on. This was the reality of a religious life. It was a meaningful life. A good life. But at times it could be overwhelming. All of the sisters accepted it. Self-sacrifice was the burden of a life devoted to God and others.

Still, each sister had a relative, some piece of a family to miss them. But beyond the Order, Anne had no one. And none of them really knew her life before she entered the Order.

Would God ever give Denise the strength to accept Anne's death?

Dear Lord, will the journal help us find her killer?

As Anne's casket was lowered into the ground, Denise wept.

28

At the moment Sister Anne Braxton's coffin was being lowered into the earth of Snohomish County, Henry Wade was miles away in Seattle.

Driving toward his demons.

A mournful Johnny Cash ballad kept him company, soothing his unease as his pickup truck headed west on 50th.

He had to do this.

He turned off the street and entered one of the city's largest cemeteries. It was peaceful but the serenity did not allay his fear. Henry dreaded returning to this place. He hadn't set foot in it since the day they buried his partner.

Vernon Pearce

After Vern's death he'd slipped deeper into the abyss. In the time after it happened, the shrinks told Henry he had to confront the issue.

You must look your worst fear square in the eye.

Henry ignored their advice.

And he'd paid a price

The day Sally walked out, he gave up, let go, and

176   *Rick Mofina*

wrapped himself in the lie of being alive. On the worst nights, he knew the truth. He wasn't working at the brewery. He was entombed there. That was the word for it, Henry thought, easing his pickup by a mausoleum and traveling deeper into the cemetery.

Hell, it got so bad and so lonely back then that he nearly pulled Jason into the darkness with him. But Jason was strong enough to pull Henry back into the light. Jason had never given up on him. Jason stood by him. Forced him to get sober. Forced him to reconnect with the living, which led to his PI job with Don Krofton's agency.

Henry owed his life to his son.

But Krofton's new gun policy had ripped open old wounds and Henry knew he had to do something about it, or this time it would be the end.

He was getting close now.

He knew the way. Even after all these years. Even though the taller trees cast larger shadows, Henry never forgot. He wheeled by the plum trees, the mountain white pines, and a pair of buttonwoods that now reached some seventy-five feet, his tires rolling on the earthen path that was cushioned like casket lining.

He came to a stop.

When Johnny Cash's ballad ended, Henry switched off his engine and looked out at the headstones.

Why don't you admit it? Go on, admit it.

He craved a drink right now. Craved it as a whirlwind of emotions and images swirled around him. The gun, Vern, the blood of wasted lives.

No.

No, he shouldn't be here.

Henry was startled by the sudden ringing of his cell phone. It was Michelle from the agency. He didn't answer, letting her call go to his voice mail, like the others.

Relieved by the distraction, he let a minute pass, then decided to check his messages.

The first was from Michelle at the agency. It had come earlier this morning.

"Hello, Henry, are you coming in today? Will Murphy called asking on the status of his workers' comp case. He's got new data. Give me a ring."

The next message was from Don.

"Krofton. Good work on qualifying. Just heard from Webb at the range. Listen, Henry, got an insurance agent who was looking for you. Wants your help with a claim. Employee theft or something. Kid's name is Ethan, or some shit like that. I never heard of him. I gave him your number. Expect a call."

The next one was from Jason.

"Hey, Dad, I need your help on this nun murder. Give me a call."

And finally, Michelle again.

"Henry, Susan Gorman called from over at Seagriff's, wants to chat about that infidelity case. Where are you, by the way?"

That was it. All right. Stop this right now.

He was procrastinating. Ignoring the issue. He switched off his phone, put both hands on the wheel, and squeezed until his knuckles turned as white as the sheet covering a victim in the morgue.

As white as the fear on the face of . . .

Get out and do this. It's time for battle. Henry glanced at the ocean of grave markers, swallowed hard, then stepped from his truck and started walking.

With each step he remembered Vern's face. The sound of the record scratching, the smell of his house, the look in his eyes, the blur of the gun, the explosion.

The blood.

Oh, God, the blood.

Henry kept walking until he came to the headstone of Seattle Police Officer Vernon Pearce. He stood over it for a long time, feeling numb as he searched the graveyard for inspiration.

"Vern, I'm sorry, it's taken me this long. It's been hard, buddy. So damn hard. We both died that day, but my son brought me back to life. You know that I always wanted to make detective. I just never expected that it would be like this. That it would cost so much. And now here I am, licensed to carry a gun. Again."

Henry's attention went from Vern Pearce's headstone to a distant corner of the burial ground. This battle was far from over.

In fact, it was just beginning.

Other ghosts were still out there pulling him back to that day.

The day they got the call.

They'd come upon the suspect fleeing with a weapon in his hand. They had him dead to rights right there on the street. It's happening so fast.

Too damn fast.

Henry's heart is pounding a blood rush in his ears. He can't think. They draw on him, screaming.

Drop your weapon! Drop your goddamn weapon!

Henry blinks and now the guy's got a hostage.

Oh Jesus, Vern, he's got a goddamn hostage.

Eyes wide with fear are locked on his.

Are pleading with him.

Don't let me die!

This is everything in a heartbeat.

This is all you are and all you will be.

This is your life.

Right here. Right now.

Henry's finger is on the trigger.

Shoot. Don't shoot.

Don't let me die!

29

Sister Denise's anguish intensified after they'd returned to Seattle and were immersed in the large reception at the shelter.

It was noisy and chaotic. So many people had donated food, had volunteered to help, and so many offered their condolences. Strangers, like this woman and boy who'd approached her.

"I'm Rhonda Boland," the woman took Denise's hand. "This is my son Brady."

"I met Sister Anne at my school," Brady said.

"Hello, dear. Sister Anne just loved going to the schools." Denise smiled.

"We wanted to come to pay our respects. She was so kind to Brady. He'd lost his dad a while ago."

"Oh, I'm so sorry. We will pray for you."

"Thank you," Rhonda said, "but since then, Brady has—"

Rhonda was uncertain how, or if, she should tell this nun standing before her, this complete stranger, that she was terrified for her son and thought that maybe it was selfish at a time like this to even raise his situation.

While Rhonda grappled with her emotions, Brady just came out and said it.

"I'm real sick and I need a major operation and we're kind of scared about it."

"Oh, no, sweetheart," Sister Denise said. "We'll say many prayers for you and include you in the masses in the Archdiocese."

"Thank you, Sister," Rhonda said.

"Thanks," Brady said.

"Well, it's exactly what Sister Anne would've done. Thank you both for coming."

Those warm condolences from strangers were like balm for Denise.

Still, she remained conflicted until she found a moment and the courage to pull Sister Vivian aside.

"Sister, I think we should tell the police about Anne's journal."

"This is not the time, Denise."

"The other sisters have a right to know who she was. That she also made mistakes in her youth, whatever they were."

"Sister, I remind you to keep this information confidential. It is private and the journal is property of the Order."

"We should share it with the police. They've asked for our help about her past."

"You don't understand. We must do all we can to take care of her memory."

"I understand."

"I don't think you do."

"I had my hands in her blood, Vivian! I understand!"

"Lower your voice." Vivian saw Sister Ruth coming. "This discussion is over. I'll consider your concerns."

After Denise left, Sister Ruth touched Vivian's arm, then pointed to two uniformed cops who were talking to people taking notes.

"The officers want to talk to you."

Vivian nodded. "First, I need to talk to Father Mercer in the office. I'll be out in a few minutes."

On her way back to her post at the serving table, Denise was approached by a small group of kindly parishioners who placed envelopes in her hand containing cash donations.

"Thank you. God bless you."

Denise headed for the office, to put the donations in a safe place. She saw the door was open a crack and overheard Vivian talking to Father Mercer.

"Jeb, any luck on finding out who screened her? She wrote here . . ." Denise couldn't believe her eyes. Vivian was showing Mercer the journal. ". . . she wrote Sister M."

"May I see that and the date?" After consulting it, Mercer said, "That would be Marie when she was in Paris."

"Is she still living?"

"I believe so. In Montana, or Canada, the western part, Calgary, I think. I'll keep going through my personal files and make some calls."

"I want to know more about Anne's past and if it has anything to do with these cryptic writings in her journal, her agonizing over sins she'd committed. Was there something that was missed when she was screened?"

"Oh Viv, when young women want to enter the Order, they often overdramatize their lives, you know that."

"In Anne's case we don't know what she confided to her screener."

"Do you think it's a factor in her death?"

"Only God knows."

"And the person who killed her," Father Mercer said. "Such a cold-blooded, vile act. May I take Anne's journal with me to read tonight? I'll return it to you before I fly back to Maine tomorrow morning."

"Absolutely."

Mercer flipped the pages.

"I vaguely recall Marie telling me that there was something a little disconcerting about Anne Braxton's history prior to her taking her vows."

"Jeb, it's my duty to find out as much information as we can, so I can determine what we should do."

Denise jumped when a hand grabbed her shoulder. She turned to see Paula and caught her breath. Paula passed her a copy of the *Mirror*. The nuns had been so busy, none of them had seen the papers this morning.

"Look at this," Paula said.

"Goodness." Denise devoured the article and said, "My Lord."

"There's a rumor going around that police arrested Cooper just as the service was ending," Paula said.

"To talk to him, probably. He likely saw something."

"No. People who saw him get arrested are saying the police were acting like Coop was a suspect."

Denise began shaking her head.

"No, no way. Cooper adored her, he would never touch a hair on her head."

"Our people say police are calling him a prime suspect."

"No, not Cooper. Oh no!"

30

Jason's stomach churned with the sick feeling every reporter dreads.

He was missing the story.

They'd arrested somebody at Sister Anne's funeral but he didn't know who and he didn't know why. Was it Cooper? Were they questioning him about the stranger he'd seen arguing with Sister Anne, the guy who stole the knife from the shelter?

Jason didn't know.

No one would tell him anything and not knowing was killing him. He glanced at the clock in the *Mirror*'s cafeteria, resisting the aroma of frying bacon, burgers, and fries. Grabbing only a coffee for his dinner, to go with a plate of adrenaline and fear, he apologized to the early night crews inching their trays toward the cash register.

He jumped the queue and left two crumpled bills without waiting for change.

He had no time.

He had to find out what happened at the funeral. He'd called every source he had, except Detective

Grace Garner. He'd burned a bridge there. At this point, his best hope was his old man.

He took a hit of coffee and felt a pang of guilt.

His dad had enough crap on his mind. Having to carry a gun again had resurrected the pain of seeing his partner's suicide. *Blowing his brains out before his eyes.* It explained all the turmoil in their lives and why his mother walked out on them all those years ago.

Man oh man.

Jason made a mental promise to talk about it all with his dad. But later, after he had his story under control. Until then, he needed his father to pump his old friends inside the Seattle PD for information.

Jason stepped aside, reached for his cell phone and made the call.

"Hey Dad. You get anything?"

"Not much, I'm afraid."

"Damn."

"You know that earlier they'd developed a list of ex-cons, parolees who are regulars at the shelter."

"Yeah."

"Creeps with violent pasts."

"Yeah, yeah, like the usual suspects."

"All of them have been eliminated, cleared."

"So what happened at the funeral today?"

"I wish I knew. I asked about that."

"Did you push hard?"

"I've got to be careful, Jay, I can't risk my license."

"I know. Sorry."

"Of course I pushed, but none of my guys would breathe a word."

"Which means that whatever happened is huge. I don't like this."

"I'll do my best, son."

"Dad, it's fine, thanks. How're you doing? With everything, I mean?"

"I'm doing the best I can. Look, I'd like to talk to you just as soon as you can manage it, son."

"Absolutely. We'll talk once I get a handle on this story. I'm really sorry, but I've got to go. Call me if you get something, okay, Dad?"

Jason headed for the stairs. They would get him to the newsroom faster. He still had some time. Glimpsing a copy of today's front page with his exclusive story on Cooper, Jason thought that this was starting to be a replay of last night. Find a story. Pull it out of the fire. Eldon was pleased with his Cooper story, but it was dead news now.

What you got for tomorrow's paper?

Concentrating on what he could try next, Jason made a beeline for his desk, hoping to avoid Eldon Reep. He failed. Reep was at Vic Beale's desk, where they were huddled with Cassie Appleton, when he spotted Jason.

"Wade! Get over here!"

Cassie had her notebook open, flipping pages filled with her notes. Jason didn't like the air here. Beale and Reep looked pissed off. His stomach tightened.

"Enlighten us," Reep said. "What happened at the funeral today?"

"They arrested somebody."

"Who?"

"I'm trying to confirm it."

"Oh you're trying to confirm it? Well, did you think about maybe getting your ass on the street? Maybe visiting your buddy Cooper, see if he's home under I-5?"

"I've been doing a lot of things."

"So has Cassie here. Inform our all-star here what you've learned."

"After you left, I talked to people. Seems all the street people had a sudden memory loss. Nobody knew who was arrested, or saw much. It happened fast. I just got off the phone with Butch Ettersly. He's a camera-man with WKKR. Turns out I know his sister from my hometown. Apparently it all went down right in front of Butch. He says KKR is the only news team to get it all."

"What do you mean?"

Jason saw Beale reach for the remote for the TV near his desk.

"Here we go," Beale said.

The sound carried a few ominous bass notes then the graphic: BREAKING NEWS WKKR EXCLUSIVE: ARREST IN NUN MURDER filled the screen, then shrank to be placed below the news anchor's desk.

"I'm Carol Carter. We're interrupting our program-ming to bring you this live report. Seattle Police have made an arrest in the murder of Sister Anne Braxton and our WKKR camera was there."

Dramatic footage showed the lightning-fast arrest. Jason's stomach knotted. He recognized the unidenti-fied man as Cooper while it played in slo-mo. After a few seconds Carol Carter returned to say, "WKKR's David Troy has the story. David, what do we know so far?" Carol Carter said to the white teeth and tanned, chiseled face of David Troy, WKKR's veteran crime re-porter, standing in front of the shelter.

"Carol, in a bizarre twist to this tragic case, police ar-rested the man during a moving funeral service for the murdered nun, whom the mayor called the Saint of Seattle."

"Any details on the identity of the man arrested, or why?"

"Not much, but my sources indicate the man is John Randolph Cooper, a troubled war veteran who, after seeing action in Iraq, was a regular at the shelter and very close to Sister Anne—"

"Sounds like he's reading your story, Wade," Beale said.

"We should've got Cooper's picture last night," Reep said.

"He would have refused," Jason said, "believe me."

"We've got photo and the library trying to get unit albums and something from his military records," Beale said.

"And his high school yearbook," Cassie added.

Reep studied the WKKR's report. "Is it Cooper there, Wade?"

Jason nodded.

"David," Carol Carter asked, "have your sources told you if Cooper's a suspect?"

"Not on the record. As you know, police are playing their cards close to their vest on this one. But I'll speculate that he possesses information vital to the case, Carol."

"Thank you, David," Carol Carter said. "Just to recap, WKKR's David Troy brought us the breaking news that police arrested a man during today's funeral service for Sister Anne Braxton, whom the mayor called the Saint of Seattle. That man is believed to be John Randolph Cooper. We now return—"

Beale muted the TV.

"That just kills us," Beale said.

"How could you let this happen, Wade?" Reep said.

"Excuse me?"

"You and Cassie break the story that the murder weapon is a knife from the shelter—"

"Cassie had nothing to do with that story."

"Then you find this Cooper living in a hellhole under the Interstate, a troubled war vet who goes to the shelter and knew the nun."

Jason nodded.

"And he tells you about some stranger he saw who argued with her and took the knife."

"Right"

"And you just saw what happened?"

Beale shot Jason a glare. He couldn't hold his tongue.

"TV just used your story to kick us between the legs and break things wide open, pal."

Jason's mouth went dry with the awful realization.

"That's right, Wade," Reep said. "Now the lights are coming on, now he gets it. Cooper was likely talking about himself. You were likely interviewing the nun's murderer, Wade! We've got no pictures, no confirmation. We've got squat. You should have allowed Cassie to go with you to find Cooper."

"I did. She backed off!"

"You refused to wait up for me. You left me behind."

"Bull!"

"Wade," Reep said, "you dropped the ball!"

Jason swallowed hard, ran his hand over his face, glanced at the time.

"Now listen to me, Wade!" Reep's voice stopped conversations throughout the newsroom. "You get your ass to Homicide, because that's likely who's got him, and you get it confirmed that they believe he's the killer, and you do it before deadline, or you don't come back."

31

The Seattle Homicide Unit's interview room reeked of lies.

Its oppressive fluorescent lighting burned on the pale cinder-block walls holding the mirrored window that reflected Cooper, waiting alone in a metal chair at the bare table.

Staff Sergeant John Randolph Taylor Cooper.

Age: 45. Born in Kent, Washington, according to his military records.

They'd just been faxed from St. Louis, and Grace Garner was studying them from the other side of the mirrored window.

Cooper was commander of an M1 Abrams tank when his patrol came under attack during operations in western Iraq. Three members of his crew died. For his brave action under fire, Cooper was recommended for several medals and awards.

But after the tragedy, he'd suffered severe mental trauma and was sent to a psychiatric ward of a military hospital, where he'd experienced several episodes. In one violent outburst, he'd threatened to plunge his toothbrush into a nurse's throat if she didn't tell him where they were keeping, "Yordan, Bricker, and Rose." Other incidents were hallucinatory, or related to medication.

After eleven months, Cooper was discharged but he couldn't find a steady job and had no family to support him. Haunted by his ordeal, Cooper succumbed to addictions and life on the street. He became a regular at the shelter. And while Sister Anne seemed to be the only person able to reach him, he had been seen arguing with her several times, according to statements from the shelter's staff.

"Grace?" Perelli repeated, "are you ready to go at him?"

She closed Cooper's file and nodded, recalling the advice Lynn Mann gave her over the phone from the King County Prosecuting Attorney's office. "Play it by the book, Grace, by the book."

Grace inhaled. Every time they stepped into the interview room to work on a suspect, the lying game started.

It wasn't me. I wasn't there, that's not my gun, knife, club, whatever. I wasn't there, ask my sister brother mother father daughter son friend or the dude who left town yesterday. I saw this guy running away. He was a tall, short, fat, skinny Hispanic Asian, black, white guy—like eighteen to fifty years old, man. Find him.

But if Grace was lucky, physical evidence, solid physical evidence, could help her leverage a confession.

Upon entering the small room, Perelli set the *Seattle Mirror* on the table, spun it round so Cooper could see today's article.

"You're famous for what you know, Coop," Perelli said.

Cooper didn't respond. Clearly police made him uneasy.

"We need your help," Grace indicated the article, "to see that the right thing is done for Sister Anne."

Cooper considered things, then nodded.

"Good, thank you. But before we go further," Grace said, "I have to tell you that you have the right to remain silent and anything you say can—"

"What's this? Are you charging me with something?"

"No, John," Grace leaned closer, "we're not charging you with anything. We need your help and we're required to follow procedure and advise you of your constitutional right to refuse to help us find the truth about Sister Anne's murder."

"You're ex-military, Coop," Perelli said. "You know regs."

Coop knew a lot of things. He weighed his situation for several moments. Then he shrugged, inviting Grace to resume advising him.

"Anything you say can and will be used against you in a court of law. You have the right to talk to a lawyer and have him present while you are being questioned. If you cannot afford a lawyer, one will be appointed to represent you before any questioning, if you wish one. Do you understand each of these rights as I have explained them to you?"

"I understand."

"Having these rights in mind, do you wish to talk to us now?"

"I'm good. I don't need a lawyer. I get it. You brought me here because you need my help to find this guy?" Coop tapped Jason's article in the *Mirror*.

"We need your help," Grace said, "to learn the truth about what happened."

"Want me to look at a sketch or something?"

"This." She opened her folder and slid an eight-by-ten full-size color photo of the knife. The murder weapon. "Ever see one like that before? It's fairly unique with the maple leaf symbol."

"Sure, it's like the one I saw that guy take from the shelter."

Grace slid a second photo, a series of enlargements showing shoe impressions in blood, and the alley behind the town house near the bush where the knife was found.

"These impressions are like fingerprints and they were made by Sister Anne's killer. And see this," Grace slid another photo, a file photo of a standard pair of tennis shoes standard-issue only by the Washington Department of Corrections. "These are the kind of shoes the killer wore. Guess where we found shoes like these?"

Cooper's face whitened. He's eyes moved along every photograph Grace had set before him and suddenly realization rolled over him.

"Now the lights are coming on, aren't they, Coop?" Perelli eyeballed him, then slammed his hand down on the counter. "We got them from your little penthouse under I-5. Shoes just like the ones her killer wore, Sergeant!"

Cooper shook his head.

"Somebody put them in my cart a long time ago. I don't even wear 'em. I've got a lot of gear there."

Perelli's metal chair scraped and tumbled as he stood to lean into Cooper, drawing his face to within an inch of his.

"Don't lie to us," he whispered. "Make it easy on yourself. Be a man and tell us exactly what happened."

Cooper's eyes widened as he stared at the pictures.

Perelli righted his chair and sat in it.

"John," Grace's voice was almost soothing, "was it a sexual thing, or an argument? Did you follow her to the town house to talk to her? Maybe something was troubling you and she said something that triggered all the bad things that happened to you? John, it'll help you to tell us now. So you can get help, John."

"You owe it to your buddies," Perelli said, "to their memory, to do the honorable thing, here."

Cooper shot Perelli a look. Grace sensed something was seething just under Cooper's skin.

"John, look at me," she said. "Just tell us what happened."

Cooper went back to the pictures. It seemed as if a monumental sadness washed over him. Tears welled in his eyes as he shook his head.

"I loved her."

Grace nodded encouragement.

"I would never hurt her."

"We know, John," Grace said. "Was it an accident?"

"I don't know. I mean," he swallowed, "sometimes, I black out."

Grace exchanged a quick glance with Perelli.

"We know. It's in your records," Grace said.

"I didn't hurt her. I couldn't hurt her. *I don't think I hurt her.*"

Cooper thrust his face into his weathered hands and released a deafening cry of anguish.

"I want a lawyer."

32

Cooper's call for a lawyer took it all to the next level.

Grace alerted Lynn Mann at the King County Prosecuting Attorney's office. Lynn called the Office of the Public Defender on the fourth floor of the Walthew Building.

The OPD scrolled through its network of public defense agencies contracted to provide legal services. Most had conflicts, so the staff sped through the list of assigned attorneys. Next up for a felony: Barbara North, a criminal defense lawyer with Acheson, Kwang, and Myer.

The call caught her on her cell, driving from court to her son's soccer game.

"The nun murder?" Barbara repeated into her phone while at a red light. It had started raining and she switched on her wipers. "Sorry, I didn't get that? He's an indigent street person? Lives under I-5. You mean the guy in today's paper?" She scrawled notes, willing the light to stay red. "Sure. I'll take it but I have to make a few calls. Tell Lynn I'll meet her and Detective Garner at Homicide just as soon as I can get there."

The rain would cancel soccer.

Barbara called her older sister, Mary, and asked her to pick up her son. He wouldn't complain about hanging out at his aunt Mary's. She was a better cook.

"Could be a sleepover, Mary."

"Catch a big case?"

"The biggest."

As Barbara drove, she probed her briefcase for today's *Mirror*. It took four red lights to absorb every detail on the Cooper story. She was a quick-thinking Harvard grad whose passion for law had not waned, despite the disillusioning realities of everyday jurisprudence. She'd handled a number of homicide cases, domestics, drug murders, but never one that had played out on the front pages.

Within forty-five minutes, Barbara found herself in a secured room, contending with the smells of fried chicken, potatoes, Italian salad dressing, and Cooper. As he ate behind the bars of a holding cell, she worked at the small table asking him questions, writing notes on a yellow legal pad, consulting copies of files, reports, and statements she'd requested from Lynn and the Seattle PD.

"So, do you think they're going to charge me with something?"

"We'll know soon enough. Just try to take it easy."

Barbara left the room to meet with the detectives, their sergeant, and Lynn Mann, a deputy prosecuting attorney. Lynn was a veteran of DOP, King County's homicide response team. Lynn was beautiful. She also had fifteen years' more experience than Barbara.

"Here it is," Lynn said. "Your client has a troubled history, with a few violent incidents. He has been known to argue with the victim in front of witnesses at the shelter. Your client had access to the murder weapon, a knife from the shelter. Your client is in possession of shoes consistent with impressions found in the victim's blood and at the location where the weapon was recovered."

"But you haven't charged him," Barbara said. "You don't have a time line and anyone putting him at the scene."

"We've got a compelling case going," Perelli said.

"What you have is reaction to public pressure." Barbara tapped her pad with the point of her pen.

"He's had access to the knife and he's grappling with psychological anguish," Grace said.

"Which is the case with about half of the hundreds of regulars who go to that shelter. Your case is so circumstantial as to be nonexistent."

"At his encampment," Boulder said, "we found other knives consistent with knives belonging to sets at the shelter."

"Circumstantial," Barbara said reaching for the *Mirror.* "Look, Mr. Cooper's indicated that he witnessed a stranger at the shelter arguing with the victim and stealing a knife. Did you even pursue this avenue of investigation?"

"Isn't it funny," Perelli said, "how people with such critical information go to the press first, to put it out there, before coming to us? That's what guilty people do."

"Detective, my client pushes a shopping cart through the streets of this city and lives under a freeway."

"That doesn't make him stupid and it doesn't rule him out," Perelli said.

"Dom," Grace said, "Barbara, we have pursued that avenue and have already eliminated a number of potential suspects."

"The shoes are damning," Lynn said.

"The shoes are state-issued only by DOC. As I understand, my client has no criminal record. He's never been arrested. He's never served time. And you are all well aware that all state-issued clothing is marked with an offender's DOC number. I believe with shoes, it's inside the instep of the right shoe."

"That mark has been removed, carved out," Perelli said.

"My point exactly. My client states the shoes were dropped off near where he stays, which means anyone could have had access to them. The fact that you didn't need a warrant to seize establishes that his 'residence' is actually public property." Barbara reached for the file on the shoes. "Did you contact DOC and see if shoes this size have been reported missing? You know all state-issued clothing must be turned in before offenders are released?"

"We have," Perelli said. "They're checking. Still, doesn't mean Cooper didn't pick them up somewhere."

"Exactly. Virtually all of Cooper's possessions have been previously owned by other people. Again, the man lives on the street, on public property. So how can you tie these shoes to him, beyond all reasonable doubt? How can you connect him to this crime in any way?"

Grace took stock of the others.

"There are ways. And we can get started on them if your client will cooperate."

Barbara experienced a twinge of unease.

"What ways?"

33

"Showtime."

Kay Cataldo put down the phone and turned to Chuck DePew.

The two forensic scientists had been waiting and watching local news on a TV in an empty meeting room down the hall from the Homicide Unit. Garner had summoned them and now it was time for them to do their thing.

"They're bringing him to us now," Cataldo said.

She and DePew went to work in the room, making preparations, moving chairs to create a large comfortable space. Within minutes the chime of cuffs, shackles, and a belly chain preceded Cooper's arrival.

"Mr. Cooper," Cataldo said as Barbara North, Garner, Perelli, and the others took places around the room, "I'd like you to sit in this chair and be comfortable."

Clasping his hands together to ease the pressure of the handcuffs, Cooper took stock of the room, the people, and the chair while Cataldo and DePew tugged on latex gloves.

"Please sit down, sir. This won't take long."

Cooper looked at Barbara, who nodded to him before he sat.

Cataldo and DePew began unlacing his boots.

"Sir, are these boots the footwear you wear most often?" Cataldo asked.

Cooper nodded.

"Now, on the table, you see several sets of footwear taken from your location under the overpass." Cooper scanned them, observing the evidence tags. "Can you please tell us what sets among them you have worn most, or still wear?"

Cooper extended his chin to a pair of worn boots and DePew placed his hand on them to confirm the correct ones. Cooper nodded, DePew made notes, put the boots in a paper bag, then did the same with the boots they'd removed from his feet.

Cataldo then removed two pairs of woollen socks. Cooper's bare feet were in good shape. He bathed every other day at the Mission, near Pike Place.

DePew then reached for a box that was the size and shape of a take-out pizza box cut in half. He opened the lid. It was filled with blue impression-casting foam.

"Now," Cataldo said, "I'm going to take your right foot and guide its descent into the foam. I want you to press as much as I tell you, so we can get a clear cast."

Cooper cooperated.

Cataldo repeated the process with Cooper's left foot.

DePew then closed the boxes, recorded information, and helped Cataldo collect the boots they'd taken from Cooper and the second pair he'd indicated he'd worn.

"Sir, which other shoes would you like us to replace on your feet?"

Cooper nodded to another set of worn boots and Cataldo helped him slip them on after replacing his socks. Then she prepared to leave with DePew.

"So what's next? How does this work?" Barbara North asked.

"Like fingerprints, footprints are unique," Cataldo said.

"Okay . . . ," Barbara said.

"It's pretty much accepted that no two people have the same, identical foot shape, or the same weight-pressure patterns. The differences are reflected on the wear of the insole and the tread and wear patterns of the outsole."

"So what are you going to do?"

"We're going back to the lab to analyze these casts. We'll compare them with the boots Mr. Cooper wears, and we'll compare them with our analysis of the DOC tennis shoes that are consistent with the impressions at the crime scene."

"This technique is widely known in forensics," DePew said. "It's called barefoot morphology. The Royal Canadian Mounted Police developed it."

"That's fine. However, my client has said that he'd recently discovered that the tennis shoes had been placed in his shopping cart. They're not his and he's never worn them," Barbara said.

"Then the evidence should support him," Cataldo said.

As Garner thanked Cataldo and DePew, Barbara looked at Cooper for a long, uncertain moment. This was not going to get any easier for him.

34

On Barbara North's advice, Cooper had agreed to take a lie-detector test.

It would be conducted by Seattle Detective Jim Yamashita, who entered the room carrying his polygraph equipment in a hardshell case.

Soft-spoken and bespectacled, Yamashita was a reserved, slightly built man, who could be taken for an accountant rather than one of the country's top polygraphists.

His hobby was cryptography.

His expertise was truth verification.

Over his sixteen years in detecting deception, he had pointed detectives in the right direction on countless major investigations. He also was involved in ongoing research to refine and improve his profession.

In court, Yamashita was a prosecutor's dream.

Before starting, he met privately with Garner and Perelli to be briefed on their case. Then he prepared Cooper, explaining the process of a polygraph examination.

"The results of the examination are not allowed as

evidence in court in most jurisdictions. So, this is really just a tool, Mr. Cooper."

"I've explained that to my client, Detective," Barbara said.

Yamashita smiled, then tried to put Cooper at ease with his machine—a new standard five-pen analog that he swore by. It would use instruments connected near Cooper's heart and fingertips to electronically measure breathing, perspiration, respiratory activity, galvanic skin reflex, and blood and pulse rate, recording the responses on a moving chart as he answered questions.

Yamashita would pose the questions, then he'd analyze the results and give Garner and Perelli one of three possible outcomes: Cooper was truthful, untruthful, or the results were inconclusive.

"Please understand that I am aware and expect you to be nervous. Everybody is and I account for that."

Then Yamashita asked Perelli to bring a more comfortable cushioned chair into the room. He seated Cooper in it and connected him to the machine. Yamashita started the examination with routine establishing questions, requesting that Cooper answer "yes" or "no."

"Is your name John Randolph Taylor Cooper?"

"Yes."

"Were you born in Kent, Washington?"

"Yes."

"Did you serve in the U.S. armed forces in Iraq?"

"Yes."

"Have you ever killed anyone?"

There was a long silence as the five ink needles scratched the graph paper.

"Have you ever killed anyone?"

"Yes, in combat."

"Answer yes or no, please."

"Yes."

"Do you reside under Interstate 5?"

"Yes."

"Do you have a job?"

"No."

"Do you often visit the Compassionate Heart of Mercy Shelter?"

"Yes."

"Have you ever killed anyone?"

"Yes."

The needles swept across the paper.

"Did you know Sister Anne Braxton, who worked at the shelter?"

"Yes."

"Are you involved in any way in her murder?"

"No."

"Do you possess knives?"

"Yes."

"Do any of them come from the shelter?"

"No."

"Do you possess tennis shoes?"

"You mean do I own—"

"Yes or no, please. Next question: Is today Sunday?"

"No."

"Did you know Sister Anne Braxton?"

"Yes."

"Did you harm her in any way?"

"No."

"Do you possess tennis shoes similar to the tennis shoes in the photographs shown to you today?"

"Yes."

"Did you wear them?"

"No."

"Did you kill Sister Anne Braxton?"

"No."

"Did you see a stranger at the shelter whom you saw argue with Sister Anne and cause her to be upset?"

"Yes."

"Did you witness this stranger take a knife?"

"Yes."

"Was it similar to the knife in the photograph shown to you today by the detectives?"

"Yes."

"Did you ever have any romantic feelings toward Sister Anne Braxton?"

"No."

"Did Sister Anne Braxton ever make you angry, upset?"

"No."

"Did you see Sister Anne in the hours before she was murdered?"

"Yes."

"Did she speak with you?"

"Yes."

"Have you ever had reason to be in her town house near Yesler Terrace?"

"Yes."

"Were you present in her building the night she was killed?"

"No."

"Were you present in the alley behind the town house the night she was killed?"

"No."

"Were you present in her neighborhood the night she was killed?"

"No."

"Are you being truthful?"

"Yes."

"Did you ever have sexual fantasies about Sister Anne?"

"No."

"Do you feel remorse about the deaths of your crew during combat?"

"Yes."

"Do you blame yourself?"

"Yes."

Barbara noticed tears rolling down Cooper's face.

"Do you often hallucinate about that time?"

"Yes."

Yamashita adjusted his glasses as he made notes, then returned to many of the same questions, repeating them.

"Have you ever been violent toward anyone?"

"Yes."

"Have you ever wished to harm anyone?"

"Yes, during duty—"

"Yes or no, please," Yamashita made a note. "Did you ever wear the tennis shoes shown to you in the crime-scene photograph?"

"No."

"Are you angry that Sister Anne was murdered?"

"Yes."

"Do you know who killed her?"

Cooper hesitated for a moment.

"Do you know who killed her?"

"I think I know."

"Answer yes or no, please. Did you ever kill a woman in combat?"

"Yes, but I—"

"Do you know the name of the person who killed Sister Anne?"

"No."

"Do you hallucinate?"

"Yes."

"Do you relive your combat action in which you kill those who killed your crew?"

"Yes."

"Are you a danger to people?"

"I don't know, please, I—"

"Did you ever threaten Sister Anne."

"No."

"Do you sometimes black out?"

"Yes."

"Do you always remember your actions during a blackout?"

"No."

"Did you kill Sister Anne?"

Cooper's face was wet with tears.

"No. God, please no."

35

Damn it. Damn this rain. Damn it.

Time was running out and Jason was losing it.

Seattle Police Headquarters took up half a block of downtown real estate at Cherry and Fifth. The twelve-story complex included the city's municipal court building with its monolithic glass facade.

Tonight it was a fortress.

Jason was pacing in the pissing rain, desperate to talk to Grace Garner. He'd been shut down at every turn. No way were they going to let him inside and up to the Homicide Unit.

Not tonight.

He craned his neck to look up at the seventh-floor lights of the building. He knew Grace was up there with Perelli, likely working on Cooper.

But she wouldn't answer her cell phone. Neither would Perelli, or Stan Boulder. He managed to squeeze a drip of information from Lynn Mann's people at the King County Prosecuting Attorney's Office.

"Lynn's definitely in Homicide with Gracie and this

street guy, Cooper. It all flows from your story but you didn't get it from me, pal."

Damn it. That made it worse.

Were they questioning Cooper? Was he going to lead them to the killer?

Was Cooper the killer?

Maybe they were charging him?

Damn it, had he dropped the ball on the biggest story to hit the city in months?

Jason glanced at the time. If he was going to get anything in the first edition, it would have to be now. All right. An idea struck him. He reached for his cell phone to call back his source in Lynn Mann's office.

After Cooper's polygraph test, Barbara North stared at herself in the mirror of a seventh-floor washroom.

Exhaustion rippled through her, making her entire body tremble. Garner and Lynn Mann had hit them hard. Their physical evidence was strong but there were holes in their case. The results from the foot impression and polygraph would play a key role.

The blackouts would hurt.

And he couldn't account for his whereabouts the night of the crime.

Cooper's arrest before WKKR's camera, his physical appearance, his troubled history, his cryptic claim that a stranger killed Sister Anne, all served to make him look like a deranged nun-killer.

How could she counter that?

Seeing Cooper's tears, hearing his responses, reading his file, in her heart she didn't believe he was guilty. But public perception was difficult to overcome.

Barbara splashed water over her face. It felt good. As she descended the elevator at police headquarters, she decided that she was too tired to make herself dinner. She'd grab something on the way home.

Stepping into the lobby, she rummaged through her bag for her umbrella, then headed for the street, nearly bumping into somebody speaking her name.

"Excuse me, Barbara North? Would you be Barbara North?"

"Yes," she tilted her umbrella up. "And you are?"

"Jason Wade, *Seattle Mirror*. Do you have a minute?"

"Not really, I'm late. How did you—?"

"I've been calling around since John Cooper was taken in earlier today. I understand you're his lawyer, from the Public Defender's Office, is that correct?"

Adjusting her grip on her umbrella, Barbara stared at Jason, contemplating his face, deciding whether or not he was worth her time.

"Let's get out of the rain and go over there," she nodded to a coffee shop down on the corner.

They found a booth and ordered coffee.

"Look, I truly am up against my deadline, right up on it, so forgive me in advance if I'm curt, rude, and rushed."

"Sounds like the name of a law firm. What're you after?"

"So, Cooper's your client?"

"Yes."

"Has he been charged with Sister Anne's murder?"

"No."

"Do you mind?" Jason set a small recorder between them.

"That's fine. I won't be telling you much."

"Where's your client now?"

"In a holding cell."

"Why are they holding him?"

"They can hold him for seventy-two hours before

pressing charges. They're attempting to rule him out as a suspect."

"Or rule him in?"

When their coffees came, Barbara decided she might be able to counter the negative image Seattle would have of Cooper.

"If they had a strong case, they would have charged him. I can tell you he's cooperating fully. He just agreed to a polygraph test."

"*Really?* I can use that?"

Jason had just nailed his exclusive.

"Yes," Barbara sipped her coffee. "He also gave samples of evidence that I will not disclose."

"Samples, like what? DNA? Was Sister Anne sexually assaulted?"

Barbara shook her head.

"Not that type of sample."

"Well, what then?"

"I believe you've written something about shoes? Let's say, relating to footwear."

"Really, that's interesting. What's the result of the polygraph?"

"Won't know until tomorrow. Check with me then."

"Did Cooper kill Sister Anne?"

"Come on."

"Well?"

"No, I don't think he did."

"But he has these spells and when I found him under the Interstate, he was hallucinating and stabbing the air with a knife."

"Yes, all in your story. I read that. Very vivid writing."

"You think I made that up?"

"No, I'm not suggesting that. I acknowledge John Cooper's a troubled man, but I don't believe he's Sister Anne's killer. I believe he's a convenient suspect."

Boom. Jason had his lead and the *Mirror* had a head-line.

Jason's cell phone rang.

"Excuse me, I have to take this."

Then Barbara's phone rang and she took her call, from her son. As she talked lovingly, wishing him a good night, Jason talked to Eldon Reep.

"I think you better hold me space on front, Eldon."

36

The morning after Sister Anne's funeral, Sister Denise was the first to rise in the town house.

Seattle's skyline glowed in the predawn light as she padded to the front door for the morning paper, her heart still aching.

Anne had come to her in a dream, standing at the foot of her bed, resplendent in the light of grace and the fragrance of roses.

Oh Anne, why did your blood point me to your journal? What should I do?

Ease your worried heart, for you will know.

Was that a dream? Or an apparition? A message? Or was it grief? Denise wondered, for she'd asked the same questions during her private morning prayers.

But no answers came.

Maybe they would come during morning prayer with the others, she thought, setting the paper on the kitchen table and starting the kettle. Denise made tea, squeezing in a bit of lemon and a few drips of milk. She took solace in the quiet as the *Seattle Mirror*'s front-page headlines blared at her.

**Homeless Man Held in Nun's Murder:
Arrested at Funeral**
*Sister Anne Braxton Remembered
As the Saint of Seattle*

The papers used that lovely picture of Anne laughing among the children, and there were photos of the crowds entering the shelter. There was also a photograph, an old one of John Cooper, looking much younger, clean-cut. Looked like his military service picture.

The story on Cooper said detectives had subjected him to a lie-detector test and collected forensic evidence. His lawyer said police were treating him as a "convenient suspect."

Denise shook her head in disbelief. Not Cooper. No, they were wrong to think that he might have hurt her. Denise studied every word of every article about Sister Anne. Nothing about her past. Police don't know about her journal and they should know.

What should I do?

Denise heard a gentle knock at the door. Through the front window, she saw the Seattle police car parked out front. The officer was talking to the driver of a taxi that had stopped.

Denise recognized Father Mercer at the door, and opened it. He was leaning on his cane and offered her a kind smile.

"Good morning Sister. My apologies for calling at this hour. I'm on my way to catch an early flight. I have to get back to Maine. Our bishop's not doing too well, I'm afraid."

"Yes, Father."

"I don't imagine Sister Vivian is up?"

"No, Father." Denise saw that he had a large envelope in his hand.

"Could you please ensure she receives this confidentially? Advise her it contains some information sent to me last night by fax, care of the Archdiocese."

He passed the plain brown padded envelope to Denise.

"Is this Sister Anne's material?"

His eyebrows rose.

"How did you know? This is a confidential matter for the Order."

"I'm the one who discovered her journal, Father. While cleaning her—" Denise couldn't speak the words. "While cleaning."

He leaned on his cane and raised his chin slowly.

"Ahh. Then I trust it will remain confidential until Sister Vivian decides how best to proceed?"

"Of course."

"You'll give me your word that will hand-deliver this to her personally."

"My word, Father."

Satisfied, Father Mercer closed his eyes momentarily and smiled.

"God be with you, Sister."

"And with you, Father. Have a safe trip."

After watching Father Mercer's cab disappear around the corner, Sister Denise went to the small office of the town house. Locking the door behind her, she put the envelope on the desk, thrust her face into her hands, and stared at it.

She listened for any noises of anyone stirring.

All remained silent.

The envelope was not sealed with a moistened or sticky adhesive. It had a flap with string tie and button closure. Denise knew exactly what she was going to do next, for she believed that morally she was part owner of this material.

God forgive me, but I feel in my heart this is what Anne wants.

Denise opened the envelope to the original journal. Affixed to it was a short note, handwritten with a fountain pen, from Father Mercer.

"Sister Marie Clermont was the nun who oversaw Sister Anne Braxton's screening when she first approached the Order as a candidate in Europe. Although Sister Marie was thought to have passed away in Brazil, we have now confirmed that she is alive. The information is attached."

The second page was a fax from St. Helen of Mercies Catholic Church in Cardston, Alberta, Canada.

Denise read the information, which was in response to Father Mercer's request, which had been channeled through various levels of church bureaucracy.

". . . We can confirm Sister Marie Clermont is living in the foothills of the Canadian Rockies near Pincher Creek in Southern Alberta. Only last month she reached her 92nd birthday. She is very alert and lucid. A parishioner in the oil industry donated a small cabin where she lives alone, passing her days gardening, painting, and communing with God. Directions are provided below."

A hermit nun.

Denise had read of retired sisters who retreated into a spiritual life of solitude. But would Sister Marie recall anything of Sister Anne as a young candidate and postulant? Would she know what moved her to join the Order as a young woman traveling through Europe? Would she know about her past life?

Age 92. Alert and lucid.

Maybe.

Denise looked at the journal and the documents. Then she looked at the photocopier next to the desk. Reflecting on how everything had unfolded, she was convinced that she'd received the guidance she had sought. She pressed a button and the photocopier began humming. Once it was ready she began making a copy of everything.

Next to the machine, she'd noticed several copies of earlier editions of the *Seattle Times* and the *Seattle Mirror.* Her attention went to the reporter's name, the one she saw most frequently. Jason Wade. The same reporter who'd come here, looking for information. He'd left his card.

At that moment, Denise heard the sounds of movement from the room directly above the office. It was Sister Anne's room. Sister Vivian was coming.

Hurry, please hurry, Denise told the photocopier.

37

Jason positioned his Falcon in the early morning line at a twenty-four-hour donut shop drive-thru in Fremont. As he eased up to the order board, his cell phone rang.

It was Eldon Reep.

"This is what we're doing today, we're going big on how the *Mirror* first tracked him after breaking the story on the murder weapon, etcetera. You give me a first-person on 'the killer's lair under the Interstate,' and use every ounce of color that didn't go into your news story."

"Eldon, they've got to charge him first," Jason said. "Two grape jelly donuts and a jumbo coffee, please. Thanks."

"Wade? Where the hell are you?"

"Getting my breakfast."

"Where are you headed? I'll send Cassie to hook up with you."

Jason fished a five-dollar bill from his jeans at the window and exchanged it for his order.

"No need to send her. That's good, keep the

change," Jason said, checking traffic as he exited the
shop. "I'm good by myself. I'll call you."

"We have to stay out front on this story, you got that,
Wade?"

"You bet. Bye."

Jason slid a Norman Greenbaum CD into his sound
system. He put this morning's *Mirror*, with his two page-
one bylines, on his lap to use as a napkin. He tore into
his donuts, dripping jelly on the faces of Cooper and
Sister Anne as "Spirit in the Sky" flowed through his
speakers.

After the song and his breakfast were done, he pulled
over and called Cooper's lawyer, Barbara North, on her
cell phone and at home, leaving messages at both places.
By the time he hit the Aurora Avenue Bridge spanning
Lake Union, she'd got back to him.

"Jason, it's Barbara."

"Sorry for calling so early. Did you see today's paper?"

"Yes."

"And?"

"I don't like the headline."

"I don't write the headline."

"Otherwise, fair coverage."

"Do you know if Cooper's going to be charged?"

"I'm on my way to meet with Detective Garner and
company as we speak."

"That doesn't answer my question."

"I have no indication one way or the other at this
point."

"You'll let me know, once you know?"

"You have my numbers."

"And you have mine."

In the seventh-floor meeting room of the Homicide
Unit, Grace Garner flipped through her files on John

Randolph Cooper. Next to her, Lynn Mann of the King County Prosecuting Attorney's Office checked her Black-Berry as they waited for the others.

Perelli entered and slapped the *Mirror* on the table.

"What's this *convenient suspect* crap? Did you know this was coming, Grace?"

Grace shook her head.

"Barbara's just protecting her client, Dom," Lynn Mann said. "Countering the image of his arrest. Even the Pope would look bad, taken down in public at a funeral."

Stan Boulder joined the meeting accompanied by Kay Cataldo and Detective Yamashita, the polygraphist.

"What time do we expect Barbara North, Grace?" Boulder asked.

"About twenty minutes or so."

"Okay, everybody was up most of the night, especially Kay, and Yami. Kay, you go first."

"Hold up for a moment," Grace said. "Before we proceed, I want everyone to know that records came up with something last night that we missed."

"Must be old stuff."

"It is. Seems Cooper was twenty years old when officers in a district car observed him acting suspiciously in a car parked down the street from an Ocean First Prudential Bank in Ravenna. He had a disguise, a starter's pistol, and the beginnings of a holdup note. Cooper later pleaded guilty, blamed his action on substance abuse owing to his mother's death in a house fire. Judge gave him four months probation for conspiracy. He never did time inside."

"He's had a terrible time losing people in fires," Boulder said. "Go ahead, Kay."

Cataldo opened her file folder.

"Chuck and I put out full-court press analyzing those casts we took of his feet, looking at weight-pressure patterns, comparing them with the wear of the insole with his shoes and the sneakers from the murder scene."

"What did you find?"

Kay started shaking her head.

"Those sneakers, inside and out, are not consistent with his feet."

"What if he wore them the one time to commit the crime?" Perelli said.

"I could not testify that they are consistent. His weight distribution, the tread wear, the wear on the sole. Look, his foot is a nine and a half and the sneakers are a ten and a half. So while he could easily wear them, the patterns and wear are all off."

Boulder inhaled, then exhaled slowly, while Lynn tapped her pen.

"So the shoes we found at Cooper's place under I-5 do not match the impressions from the murder scene?" Lynn asked.

"Correct," Cataldo said.

"Yami," Boulder said. "You're up."

Yamashita flipped through pages of fanfold graph paper that were punctuated with his neat notes.

"Based on my analysis, the subject was truthful in his responses."

Grace concentrated on her notes.

"What about here?" She slid closer to Yamashita and read aloud.

"Did you meet a stranger at the shelter whom you saw argue with Sister Anne and cause her to be upset?"

"Yes."

"Did you witness this stranger take a knife?"

"Yes."

"Was it similar to the knife in the photograph shown to you today by the detectives?"

"Yes."

"Yami, was there any problem there?"

Yamashita flipped through his graph paper and notes, checking and double-checking. Then he shook his head.

"All consistent with truthful responses."

"We'll be kicking Cooper free once his attorney arrives," Lynn said. "Alert Media Relations to put out a release, clarify things."

"But what if he hallucinates that this happened and believes it?" Perelli asked.

"You're reaching, Dom," Boulder said. "We have to face the fact that her killer is still out there."

38

The elevator stopped at the thirty-third floor of the Columbia Center.

The doors chimed, opening to the gleaming lobby of American Eagle Federated Insurance. The wings of a silhouetted eagle stretched over the company's name above the receptionist's massive wooden desk.

Henry Wade waited for Fiona, *according to her name-plate,* to take her sweet time deciding on a lunch spot with her friend at the other end of her headset phone, before getting around to helping him.

"All right, we'll try Italian, but if it sucks, you're paying," Fiona ended her call with a sincere smile followed by a professional greeting. "May I help you?"

"Henry Wade, from Krofton Investigations. I have an appointment with Ethan Quinn."

Fiona studied Henry's card, pressed a button on her console, and in a hushed, honeyed tone repeated Henry's information into her headset, then said, "Someone will be right out."

"Thank you."

Henry turned, passing the time standing near the

sectional couch, taking in the floor planters, the palms, and the enlarged prints on the wall. Van Goghs. Henry was taken by the deep blue purple sky of *Thatched Cottages at Cordeville*, and what was the other one? It was mesmerizing. He stepped closer to read the caption: *Corridor in the Asylum*.

"Mr. Wade?"

Henry turned to meet a man wearing a navy suit with an untucked orange shirt and no tie. His short hair suggested he'd just rolled out of bed. He had thick Elvis sideburns, a diamond stud in his ear, and a patch of hair under his bottom lip that expanded into a caffeine-charged smile as he extended his hand.

"Thanks for coming. Right this way, sir."

Henry couldn't believe the way people dressed these days—like they just didn't care. Hell, even when he had been drinking, he'd tucked his shirt in.

They went down a long, spacious corridor that was lined with dark mahogany doors to executive offices and meeting rooms with floor-to-ceiling glass walls that offered views of Seattle's skyline. Henry read the plates looking for Ethan Quinn's office when they came to an open office area and a sea of low-walled workstations. They took a labyrinthine route through it before stopping at one cramped cubicle.

It was about eight by eight with fabric-covered walls reaching nearly seven feet. They were covered with calendars, schedules, regulations, snapshots of a Hawaiian vacation. A young woman, beaming while holding a baby in her arms. Another shot of a happy, healthy golden retriever. A flag with a peace symbol.

The computer's monitor was laced with small yellow notes, the screen saver showed U2's latest CD cover. Next to it, an assortment of well-used reference books on investigative techniques. The red message light on the phone was blinking. Stacked files teetered on the desk, threatening to bury the phone as the man began sifting through them.

"Excuse me," Henry said, "but where am I meeting Mr. Quinn? In the call he said he had something to show me and wanted to meet here?"

"Oh, man," he extended his hand again. "I'm Ethan Quinn."

"You're Ethan Quinn?"

Quinn nodded and began removing files from the chair at the small table.

"Yes. And this won't work. Let's duck into an empty meeting room. Can I get you a coffee?"

After stopping at the staff kitchen, they went to a spacious boardroom, with a view of Seattle's business district, Elliott Bay, and the mountains in the distance. They set their mugs at one end of the polished table and Quinn plopped down the bundle of files he'd toted.

"Mr. Wade, let me explain a bit," Quinn said. "I'm a subcontractor, a loss-recovery agent, and I specialize in forgotten, written-off cases."

Henry nodded.

"It's not news that with the emergence of DNA and breakthroughs in technology, a lot of old criminal cases are being pulled out of the archives and cleared."

"Cold cases."

"Exactly. Now, I've got one that goes back a bit." Quinn slid a page with the date and a summary to Henry. "An armored car with U.S. Forged Armored Inc. had just completed a sweep, picking up receipts from supermarkets and retail outlets at malls. In all, it had a load of some $3.3 million.

"The crew's last scheduled pickup was at the Pacific Consolidated Savings & Financial Bank at a strip mall in Lake City. At the time, U.S. Forged Armored Inc., was using routine route scheduling which was easy to learn, wouldn't you agree, Mr. Wade?"

Henry nodded.

"Well," Quinn sipped from his mug, "as you know, the truck was hit at the bank. Armed robbers overwhelmed the two-man crew, wounding both guards. The guards survived but couldn't offer any details on the suspects. I know those were different times, but quite frankly it's beyond me how U.S. Forged Armored Inc. secured armored-car cargo coverage with such a serious cash-in-transit risk. Crazy, huh?"

Henry shrugged.

Quinn continued. "A Seattle police car was within four blocks when it got the call and responded to the heist in progress. One of the suspects panicked, took a bystander hostage, and engaged in a shoot-out with two Seattle officers just as others arrived on the scene. Unfortunately, the bystander was killed. The medical examiner's final report seems to have gone astray due to a flood in the records room. However, a draft was inconclusive. I'm checking with King County Court archives.

"In any event, the other suspects fled with the cargo. The hostage-taker, Leon Dean Sperbeck, was arrested, admitted guilt to second-degree murder to avoid the death penalty, yet he had refused to divulge who his accomplices were. There was no jury trial. The judge gave him a twenty-five-year sentence."

Quinn flipped through his notes.

"Virtually no details were obtained on the other suspects. The FBI and Seattle robbery had no substantial leads. Nothing emerged. It's believed two others were involved and they got away with the $3.3 million. Now, American Eagle paid out on the claim. It also reached an out-of-court settlement with the family of the victim for $1.8 million. So all in all the company took a wicked hit of some $5 million."

Quinn took another sip of coffee.

"That's a huge pile of money for back in the day. For

any time, really. We're talking some serious cash. That's where I come in. I comb through files like these in an effort to recoup the loss. I get paid a basic daily rate and a percentage of any funds I recover. And while it could come into play, the reward for information leading to the recovery of any funds still stands." Quinn steepled his fingers and looked hard at Henry. "I think you know where I'm going with this, don't you, sir?"

A bead of cold sweat rolled down Henry's back.

Henry and Vern Pearce were the two responding officers.

This kid—with his Elvis sideburns—was good. He'd done his homework. Henry swallowed. It was all coming at him full bore.

"Sure, that was our call, Vern Pearce and me."

"I know. And from what I understand, sir, it's taken a toll."

"It has." Henry looked at the skyline. "It was a lifetime ago. So what do you think I can do about it now?"

"The fact that Sperbeck never rolled on his partners suggests to me that he took the fall for his cut when he got out, right?"

"I suspect he's due for release soon."

"That's the thing, he's already been released."

"What?"

Quinn passed a folder bearing the Washington Department of Corrections seal to Henry. "Here's his DOC file. Seems Leon behaved himself inside, paid his bill in full. He was released several months ago."

"Really? But he'd still have a Community Corrections Officer. Besides, the FBI would be your best bet to help you with your theory. They're the lead jurisdiction."

"The FBI did help me."

Quinn slid a photocopy of another document. A single page. Handwritten and signed by Leon Sperbeck.

An evidence tag indicated it was from National Park Service Rangers.

"It's a suicide note."

It was short, printed in block letters, conveying Sperbeck's despair, his loneliness, his inability to find work, feeding his isolation and shame over his crime.

... NO FUCKING POINT IN GOING ON I'LL CLEANSE MY SOUL IN THE RIVER AND START OVER IN THE NEXT LIFE ...

After Henry had read it, Quinn said, "Sperbeck left it nailed to a tree near Cougar Rock at Mount Rainier National Park, then disappeared into the Nisqually River. Although his body still hasn't been recovered, the FBI and DOC verified that Sperbeck wrote it."

Quinn slapped a glossy photograph on the table.

All the spit dried in Henry's mouth. His heart pulled him back through time as he stared into the face of his nightmare. The demon his shrink had urged him to confront all those years ago was staring at him.

You must face him, Henry, or you'll be consumed by what happened.

There he was.

Leon Dean Sperbeck of Wichita, Kansas. Staring back from his arrest photo, taken over twenty-five years ago. Coal-black eyes burning with defiance. Another photo slapped on the table. Sperbeck's recent offender-release photo.

Sperbeck had barely aged.

"I get the feeling that you doubt that Sperbeck is dead?" Henry said.

"In this job you do a lot of research on suicide notes. In some studies, experts were unable to distinguish between genuine suicide notes and fabricated ones."

"But the FBI and DOC both say Sperbeck wrote this."

"I'll buy that. But is it genuine? No one's found his corpse." Quinn leaned forward. "Sperbeck spent twenty-five years in prison without uttering a word about a $3.3 million heist. He served all his time without applying for early release, probably because there are fewer strings attached once you're out. So, I think that if he was despondent, he would have been found hanging in his cell, don't you think?"

"Maybe. What do you want from me?"

"Help me."

"Help you how?"

"I started on this file in anticipation of Sperbeck's release, thinking he'd be a strong lead to the money."

"Well, it looks like it's all dead-ended." Henry slid the documents back, checked his watch. "I really can't help you. I've got a lot on the go."

"I appreciate your situation, but please hear me out."

Henry waited.

"Shortly after the heist, the armored-car company went out of business. It was a small company founded by two ex-Seattle cops. They've since passed away, one from cancer, the other from a heart attack. The guards have passed away, too. Your partner is dead and now the only known suspect is maybe dead. So that leaves only you."

Henry took a moment to absorb matters.

"What the hell are you saying, Ethan?"

"I need your help. I believe that the money's out there somewhere."

"I don't know where it is."

"I think Leon wants us to think he's dead and is out there looking for his share of the money. I'd like you to consider helping me on this case."

"That case cost me a piece of my life."

"I understand."

"I don't know, let me think about it," Henry stood. "Before I go, can I get a copy of the files and his picture?"

39

Bruno Stone's eyes took a slow walk over Rhonda Boland.

She was in her best outfit, a form-fitting JCPenney number, nervously sitting beside him on a stool in the Twisted Palms Bar at the Pacific Eden Rose Hotel.

Bruno ran the Twisted Palms.

He had dyed, gel-slicked hair. His tattooed forearm propped his head and he tapped his teeth with his pinky ring as he went back to reading Rhonda's résumé.

"It says here you worked in Vegas a long time ago."

"For several years, yes."

"You know what I think about Vegas?

How would she know?

"Vegas is like LA. It's a magnet for dreamers."

Rhonda nodded slowly.

"Well, this place is where people bury their dreams. You get what I'm saying?"

"I'm not sure."

"Come on, honey. You gotta know that the Twisted Palms is a dive bar. It's respectable. But it's a dive bar.

That's all there is to it. And working here, you're going to get come-ons, get grabbed, sworn at."

"Ever work a supermarket cash register, Bruno?"

A gap-toothed smile escaped from his face to signal that he liked her. He tapped his ring to his teeth to help him think some more.

"Look, my reading of this tells me you don't know much about tending bar. But you could probably waitress. The tips are good and I usually need waitresses."

Rhonda's hopes soared. She needed a second job.

"The thing is, I don't need any waitresses for the time being. So I'm going to keep your number handy and . . ."

Rhonda stopped listening after that.

It was like her two other interviews. Strikeouts. When she got home, she checked her machine for any callbacks. Nothing but a message from her insurance company confirming that she was not covered for the type of "experimental" surgery Brady was going to have. And Dr. Choy's office had called confirming the date for Brady's appointment.

She didn't have the money for this.

As Rhonda stood alone in the living room, her breathing quickened. She had to do something. *Maybe she could sell the house?* She didn't know if she wanted to sell the house. It wouldn't hurt to get an appraisal from a real estate agent. They were always offering free ones.

She headed for Brady's room and switched on his secondhand computer. As it warmed up, she glanced into Brady's wastepaper basket, noticing a crumpled sheet of paper and the fragment of a letter he'd written. She retrieved it and flattened it out. It was addressed to the circulation manager of the *Seattle Mirror*.

Dear Sir or Madam:
I am writing to enquire if you have any jobs for news-

paper delivery boys in my neighborhood. I am twelve
years old and know my neighborhood pretty well and
therefore would make a good person for the job. Also, my
mom and I really need the extra money so I would be
very responsible.

Yours truly,
Brady Boland

Rhonda blinked back her tears.

At that moment the door opened and Brady called down the hall.

"Hi Mom! Going to the park with Justin and Ryan, be home in time for supper, okay?"

Rhonda swallowed hard to find her voice.

"Did you take your medicine today?"

"Yes. And I feel fine!"

"Be home in one hour, kid!"

"Okay. Bye!"

She heard him leave then the phone rang in the living room and hope fluttered in her stomach.

Maybe a job? Or an overtime shift at the supermarket? Or maybe Dr. Hillier to say there's been a huge mistake with the tests and there's absolutely nothing wrong with Brady? Oh please let it be good news.

"Hello?"

Her answer was swallowed by silence at the other end. Her caller ID showed the incoming number as "Blocked."

"Hello? Who's there?"

Nothing. No breathing. No background noise. Just absolute silence.

But Rhonda sensed someone was on the other end.

"Who are you calling, please?"

Nothing.

She hung up.

This was the third time someone had called to give

her the silent treatment. She waved it off as kids playing on the phone, or some crank.

What else could it be?

Rhonda brushed it off and went to her bedroom to change.

As she undressed, a tiny wave of unease rippled through her just below the surface of her consciousness.

Something's not right.

She stopped breathing and studied herself in the dresser mirror.

What was it?

She couldn't put her finger on it. But damn it, something felt wrong. Rhonda went to her closet, searched through her clothes. Nothing. She went to the bathroom, checked behind the shower curtain. Nothing.

What is it?

Her scalp prickled and an ice coil rushed down her spine.

Had someone been in her home?

Rhonda went to the window at the end of the small hall at the back of the house. What was that? She detected the faint hint of a foreign smell. A trace of a fading scent that she just couldn't identify.

Did it even exist?

Maybe she was smelling the Twisted Palms bar on herself?

Maybe it was nothing.

Like the garage. Like the calls. Was she losing her mind? *This is stupid.* She couldn't handle this right now. Rhonda went back to her bedroom and resumed changing.

You must be losing your grip, she told her reflection, because this is just stupid.

In the kitchen Rhonda began taking inventory to get

supper ready. That's when she stopped and put her hands on her hips.

At the far end of the counter, near the refrigerator, all of her files for Brady were ever so slightly askew. As if someone had picked through them.

Did Brady do that? But he wouldn't. He just wouldn't.

Did she do that? Did she forget that she'd done that?

She inspected them. Brady's school file was out of order and she had not touched this one for at least a week.

Had she?

Rhonda bit her bottom lip and took a few deep breaths. It had to be her imagination. Right? What else could it be?

What the hell else could it be?

40

"Heard what happened at recess?" Ryan bounced his basketball to Brady.

"Nope."

Justin clapped his hands, took Brady's pass, and made a successful backboard shot.

"*Yes!* Dex pulled a knife on Billy Hay in the yard behind the addition."

"Whoa, that's serious," Brady said. "What happened?"

Ryan eyed the ball coming back to him.

"Billy steps into Dex's face, does like a quick kung fu move, grabs Dex's arm, nearly breaks it until Dex drops the knife, then Billy leans it against the pavement and building and stomps the knife, breaks the blade!"

"No way!"

Ryan shoots and misses. The ball swishes under the net.

"Way!" Justin said. "It happened. Billy turned into Superman."

The ball rolled across the basketball court, by the swings, then by the mommies and babies at the kiddie seesaws, and then it bounced along the grass toward a park bench, where a man reading a newspaper tossed it back.

"Thanks," Ryan said.

"Dex is such an asshole," Justin said. "Billy's my hero. He should form a gang and be the leader. Call it the Justice Squad, or something cool like that."

"Hey," Brady said, "You think Spider-Man can beat up Superman?"

"Not in a million years," Ryan said. "Superman's not human and Spider-Man is."

"Well, he could," Justin said bouncing the ball, "if he could web him with green kryptonite."

"What if Superman had, like a tumor?" Brady said.

"A what?" Ryan said.

"Like a brain tumor that was going to kill him unless he had this operation?"

Justin stopped bouncing the ball. He exchanged a look with Ryan, then looked hard at Brady. The three boys had been best friends ever since they could talk.

"That's what you've got, isn't it?"

"That's it."

"You're joking, right?" Ryan said.

"Clue in, doofus," Justin looked at Brady. "This is why you've had all those doctors' appointments and went in that MR deep-sleep-chamber thing, right?"

"Right."

"So, are you going to die?" Ryan asked.

"I'm supposed to have this operation soon to take it out. And if everything goes okay, then I should be fine."

"If it doesn't?" Ryan asked.

"Then, I guess I'll die."

"Does the tumor hurt right now?" Ryan asked.

"No. And I take medicine."

Justin resumed bouncing the ball, giving it hard slam bounces.

"You're not going to die, dude," he said.

"How do you know?"

"Because you're not, okay?"

"But how do you know, Justin?"

Justin turned his back, slam-bouncing the ball, pretending to position himself for a crucial shot.

"Justin, tell me, how do you know?"

"Because you're twelve years old and you're our friend and people close to us are not supposed to die. Not until they're old and shit."

"Brady's dad died, right in front of him," Ryan said.

"Shut up," Justin said. "You just shut up."

"Guys, stop. No one knows what's going to happen to me."

"I do," Justin turned. Still bouncing the ball, his sights locked on the basket. "I'm going to take this shot, and if it's good, Brady will have his operation and live."

"And if you miss?" Ryan said.

"I won't miss. I'm going to make this shot and then we're going to start building that tree house we've always talked about. In the forest behind the warehouse."

Justin softened his bounces, preparing to make the shot.

"Hey"—Brady held his hands out for the ball—"give me the ball. This is kinda dumb. Don't do this, Jus, cause if you miss, everything will get weird."

"I'm not going to miss."

"Justin, listen to Brady."

"I'm doing it!"

Justin raised the ball, moved it slowly behind his head, concentrated on the target, and sent the ball spinning from his fingertips in a high arc. During the time it traveled, the boys held their breath, hearing nothing and seeing nothing but the ball, as if collectively willing it to complete its mission.

Which it did.

In a clean swish.

The boys shot their fists into the air and jumped.

"Yes!" Justin said, "I told you I wouldn't miss."

Out of the corner of his eye, Brady noticed the ball rolling away. Their glorious victory ball. Still wearing a smile, he started chasing it as it followed the same course as before. The ball rolled from the court, passed the swings, and then the mommies and babies at the kiddie seesaws. Then it bounced along the grass toward a park bench until a man's shoe stopped it.

Dead.

The man on the bench set aside his take-out coffee and his copy of the *Seattle Mirror*. He'd been reading the articles under the headlines, HOMELESS MAN HELD IN NUN'S MURDER: ARRESTED AT FUNERAL and SISTER ANNE BRAXTON REMEMBERED AS THE SAINT OF SEATTLE.

The man picked up the ball and spun it playfully in his hands until he raised his head to look directly at Brady, who saw himself reflected in the man's dark glasses. The stranger studied Brady's face for an intense moment, as if it held the key to a mystery.

"This belongs to you?" he said.

"Yes, sir."

"And I bet you expect me to give it back?"

Brady's eyes cast around. He just wanted the ball back.

"I guess, yes."

"When someone has something that belongs to you, it's only right for you to expect them to give it back, right?"

"I guess."

"It's a rule to live by." The man bounced the ball back. "Be sure you remember that."

41

Early the next morning, Sister Denise stood before the *Mirror* building and begged God to forgive her for what she was about to do.

Tightening her grip on her bag, she entered the newspaper offices through the gray limestone archway and walked across the marble floor of the lobby to the woman at the reception desk.

"I'd like to speak with Jason Wade, one of your reporters, please."

"Do you have an appointment, ma'am?"

"No, but he was looking for information regarding Sister Anne."

Denise passed Jason Wade's card to her. The receptionist looked at it, then back at Denise, noticing the small silver cross hanging from the black cord around her neck.

"This is about the murdered nun?"

"Yes. Sister Anne."

"Your name?"

"I'm sorry. I'd like to keep this confidential. Please tell him I'm here to see him privately."

The receptionist knew that "walk-ins" could be critical to a huge story. Her polished fingernail ran down the list of reporters' names and she punched an extension on her console.

"Have a seat, Sister, please. I'll get someone right away."

Ah cripes, Jason winced.

Stepping from the elevator with his first cup of horrid cafeteria coffee, he realized he was not even going to make it to his desk. Eldon Reep had spotted him and was waving him into his glass-walled office.

A great start to the day.

Like a dictator plotting strategy, Reep was hunched over the table in his room studying editions of the *Mirror*, the *Seattle Times*, and the *Post-Intelligencer*.

"The story's going to go flat if we don't find an angle to advance it, Wade."

"There's nothing new. Cooper's no longer a suspect, he's a key witness."

"What are your sources telling you? Has he given them a new prime suspect?"

"Just that mystery guy he claims to have met at the shelter."

"The knife came from the shelter, so it's pretty clear the killer came from there."

"Probably."

"We'll go back to setting up the story like this: She was murdered by someone she tried to help, but the question is why? By all accounts, everyone at the shelter loved her."

"Except for the guy who killed her."

"Okay, somebody flipped out."

"I don't know. There's something different here. He did it in her apartment. There's an indication he confronted her at the shelter, that he knew her, had upset her about something. That he followed her or was waiting for her. Maybe she had a history with the guy. We don't know much about her life."

"All right, you and Cassie go back to the shelter, go back to the nuns, keep pushing, because somebody's going to bust this thing wide open and we're not going to let our guard down. Understand?"

"Excuse me, Jason," a news assistant stood at the door. "Reception says there's a woman here to see you."

"Who?"

"The person won't give her name, but reception's pretty sure it's a nun."

Sister Denise twisted her bag's strap as she waited in the reception area.

The more time that passed, the more she doubted herself.

Was this the right thing to do?

Yes, it was. She had to do this. They had to find the truth, she thought, as a reporter approached. He had an earring, a few days' stubble, and a nice smile.

"I'm Jason Wade," he held out his right hand. "I recognize you from the shelter and the town house, but I didn't get your name."

She kept her voice low, "Denise."

Jason sensed her unease.

"Would you like to go somewhere private?"

"That would be preferable, yes."

They went to the seventh-floor news editors' boardroom. It had high-backed leather executive chairs around a massive table. Mounted on the walls were the stories and news photos that had earned the *Mirror* its Pulitzer Prizes over the years. Dramatic photos of forest fires, war zones, a child rescued from a burning building. They were alone and Jason shut the door.

"Would you like a coffee, tea, or anything?"

"No, thank you."

Jason set his notebook down, flipped to a clear page.

"Okay, Sister, what can I do for you?"

"Please, this must be strictly confidential. You protect sources?"

"I do. You're one of the nuns from the Order?"

"My name is Sister Denise Taylor but you must not print it."

"I understand, Sister. Please, try to relax. Let's start by talking about why you're here."

She twisted the strap of her bag, then her cross.

"I'm a friend of Sister Anne's. Sorry. This is difficult."

"It's all right."

"I don't know where to start. The last few days have been so awful for us."

"Well, start at the beginning. What brought you here? It must be something that you felt was important."

She nodded.

"After Anne was killed, I was cleaning her room."

"Hold on." Jason produced a small recorder. "I just want to get things down right, okay?"

"But you can't use my name. Please give me your word. I need to know that I can trust you."

Jason's pulse kicked up when he glimpsed the envelope peeking from her bag. His instincts told him to play this right.

"I'll give you my word. I won't print your name, or indicate that we've talked, unless you agree to be named, or we negotiate something that puts you at ease."

Denise absorbed what he said before nodding and

glancing at the tiny red light on his machine, indicating that he was recording. Jason twisted his pen.

"After Anne was killed I was cleaning her room and found that she'd hidden a private journal. None of us knew of its existence. It was hidden under the floorboards of her closet."

"Really?" Jason noted that.

"I know it's a private thing but I believe it might hold clues to her past that might point to her killer."

Jason sat up and took careful notes.

"Excuse me, have you gone to any other news organizations with this?"

"My Lord, no. I could barely walk into your building this morning."

"Do the police know about this?"

"No. Let me explain. The contents are cryptic and don't have many facts, but they're clearly self-recriminatory for the way she'd lived her life before she became a nun."

"What do you mean?"

"It's a bit tricky to explain. As lay women, we all had previous lives before we're accepted into the order. We all came from somewhere, we all had families, mothers, fathers, brothers, sisters. We all have shared that divine moment when we realized we wanted to dedicate ourselves to God by living a religious life."

"So where's Sister Anne from? Where's her family?"

"That's just it, no one knows. She was traveling through Europe as a young woman when she realized she wanted to dedicate herself to serving God."

"And before that? Was she from Seattle?"

"We don't know, but her journal offers some indications that she was tormented by her previous life almost until her death."

"And you think this is a factor in her murder?"

"I think that it could be, yes."

"So why not go to the police?"

"This is complicated for me. I passed the journal to my superior and I know that the Order is deciding on whether to go to the detectives with it, but there's another aspect."

"What's that?"

"Before being accepted as a candidate for the Order, you must be screened. The objective of the process is to study your personal history, your health, your psychology, moral standing, family background, everything to assess your acceptability."

"So everything should be in some file somewhere?"

"Not quite. What I understand is that the person who oversaw the process for Sister Anne is a retired hermit nun living in the Canadian Rockies."

"A hermit nun?"

"Old school. Pre–Vatican II, adhering to the monastic code that brings one closer to God."

"So what has the Order found out from its hermit nun?"

"Nothing yet, they've only connected her to Anne and located her a day or so ago. They thought she'd passed away."

"How old is she?"

"Ninety, or ninety-two. Something like that."

"Wow, so you're telling me this old hermit nun holds the key to Sister Anne's past, which might shed some light on who killed her, is that right?"

"Yes, that is my belief."

"So why come to the *Mirror*?"

"I think the Order first wants to privately determine what her past might entail and how it might reflect on the organization before informing the police or anyone."

"Really, in light of abuses and scandals, they'd still play it that way?"

"I'm sure you're aware that institutions always protect themselves first, Jason."

"Right. Even news organizations."

"And there's more. It's just a feeling I have. Shortly before she was killed, she confided to me that she'd done a horrible thing in her youth. Something about destroying lives."

"What did she mean?"

"She never elaborated. I brushed it off, thinking that she'd meant she'd broken a young man's heart. When women leave their secular lives for the church, they often break a young man's heart."

"So why is this a factor now, after all these years?"

"After I found her journal, her comment took on a different meaning for me. It's complicated. I'm sorry this is so confusing and I could be wrong—but I got the sense that she felt something from her past was catching up to her."

Jason stared at her, absorbing everything.

"So what are you proposing, Sister?"

"Here," she produced a photocopy of Anne's journal, and the information on Sister Marie in Canada. "I'll give this information to you with the hope that you'll locate Sister Marie, and determine the truth, whatever it may be. I'll give you three or four days, then I'll be passing this to police."

"Why not go to them now?"

"Your stories have been fair and accurate. I want to know that the truth will be known."

He scanned the journal and the material. It was dynamite.

"If we go ahead, I won't publish your name, but I think the Order is going to know where we got our information."

"The Order will ultimately deal with me as it sees fit. I've accepted that, but I know Anne would want this, which brings me to another reason why I'm coming to you. A man came into our home and murdered our Sister. He's still out there and he could harm others. I know we want him arrested and prosecuted."

"That's vengeful talking for a nun. Aren't you supposed to forgive your enemies?"

"We're also human, we get angry, and we seek what is right and just. Believe me, I have agonized over this."

Jason shook her hand.

"I'll do my best."

"I'll pray for you."

After escorting Denise out, Jason returned to the boardroom and spent half an hour reviewing Sister Anne's journal. Then he went to his desk and made a number of quick calls, to check out a few things.

Next he went to Reep, showed him the documents, and pointed out Sister Denise in the background of recent news photos, assuring him that she was a legitimate source. After he'd heard everything Jason had to tell him, and after flipping through the journal and the fax indicating where Sister Marie could be located, Reep steepled his fingers.

"So you want to go up to Canada, find this hermit nun, and see what secrets she holds about our murdered nun's previous life?"

"I think I could deliver a helluva package."

Reep turned to look at the map on his wall.

"You'd have to fly into Calgary, which is not all that far."

"I checked. I can fly Seattle to Vancouver, British Columbia, connect to Calgary, rent a car, drive to the nun's place. Give me two days, tops."

"What if the nun doesn't talk to you?"

"We've got the 'secret diary' that was hidden under

the floor of her room. That's a heck of a scoop. And I'll give you a Canadian place line, loads of color and intrigue. A *Mirror* exclusive, say, secret diary and hermit nun in Canadian Rockies may hold clues to Seattle nun's murder."

The beginnings of a tense smile flickered on Reep's face.

"Go. Get on the next plane. But, I'm telling you, Wade, you damned well better come back with a big one."

42

"An e-ticket will be waiting for you at the Air Canada counter. Take your passport, it'll make things easier," Maggie in travel told Jason over his cell.

He was driving to his apartment, eye on his rearview mirror because he was speeding. Before he'd left the *Mirror*, Maggie had given him four hundred Canadian dollars and a company credit card.

"You've got over two hours to make your flight," she said. "I'll get a cab rolling to your place to take you to the airport."

At his apartment, Jason packed fast.

He grabbed his laptop, extra batteries, files, and enough clothes for two nights. Traffic was choked due to a wreck on I-5. By the time he arrived at Sea-Tac International, got his ticket, got wanded through security, and cleared Canadian Immigration, preboarding was commencing.

As the queue formed, Jason called Grace Garner. He had to smooth things over, he thought, as her line rang. If something broke on the story while he was away, he'd need help. And if he uncovered critical information on this trip, he might need to broker a deal. He got her voice mail. The sound of her voice resurrected memories of them together. He pushed them aside and he left her a message.

"Grace, it's Jason. I know things have been tense lately, but call me."

The jet to Vancouver was three-quarters full.

Jason had a window seat with no one beside him for the forty-minute flight. In the air, his stomach tightened over the story. What if he struck out and something broke back home while he was away? Not much he could do about that. Chewing gum did not ease his tension.

Things looked gray outside.

A gentle rain was falling when he landed in Vancouver, British Columbia. Before connecting to Calgary, he checked his phone to see if Grace had returned his call.

Nothing.

He tried calling his old man. Maybe his dad had something. More important, Jason was concerned about how his father was holding up.

No answer.

His jet to Calgary departed on time. When the plane leveled off over the mountains, he put his files, recorder, and laptop on the tray table and began working. He scoured the photocopied pages of Sister Anne's journal, studied her graceful handwriting. The bulk of her entries were mundane notes or reflection on experiences of delivering hope in Third World countries. But scores of excerpts hinted cryptically at her past. Jason captured them into a story file, highlighting those that leapt from the page, such as:

> *Oh heavenly Father, can I ever be forgiven for what I did, for the pain I caused? Although I am not worthy, please forgive me.*

Regret and remorse were the underlying tones, he thought, as he read an excerpt written near the last days of her life:

I deeply regret the mistakes I have made and will accept your judgment of me.

What the hell happened? What could a nun have done that would compel such tortured soul-searching? It wasn't clear. She doesn't spell it out here. And he considered what Sister Denise told him about Sister Anne's odd revelation about "destroying lives."

What does it all mean?

Jason gazed out his window for the answer. Was it out there among the Rockies, reaching up from the earth below? All he could see was an ocean of snowcapped peaks that stretched to the edge of the world.

The key had to be in her past life.

And his best shot at finding it would be with the hermit nun, he thought, closing his laptop and his tray as the plane made its descent.

As the jet banked, its wing tipped. Suburbs wheeled by, along with a web of expressways and buildings. When the plane lined up for its final approach, Jason's stomach quaked in time with the hydraulic groan of the landing gear coming down.

Man, he could fail on an epic scale.

Or break this story wide open.

43

Jason didn't have a second to waste.

On the ground in Calgary, he rented a compact car and got directions to Deerfoot Trail, a multilane expressway that sliced through the city.

Heading south, he glided by Calgary's skyline with its gleaming skyscrapers jutting before the Rockies to the west. On his left, perched on a hilltop, he saw the glass-and-brick rectangle that was the *Calgary Herald*, the city's dominant paper. Nice-looking building.

Jason checked his precision-folded map and the blue-inked line the rental clerk had made to guide him south along Deerfoot Trail and out of the city to Highway 2, which was the main provincial road. It ran north-south like an incision through much of Alberta to the Montana border.

About an hour from Calgary, as he passed High River he heard the intro to Led Zepplin's "Rock and Roll" and he cranked the radio's volume and marveled at how the prairie plains met the Rocky Mountains.

Glorious.

Some time later, as he continued south, he was intrigued by the signs for Head-Smashed-In-Buffalo Jump, the ancient site where natives would drive the great herds over the cliff to their deaths for food and clothing. Farther south, after he turned west toward the Crowsnest Pass, he saw the massive wind turbines, giant white windmills harnessing energy.

Cool.

Some four thousand people lived in Pincher Creek, a town nestled amid the ranch country and foothills of the Rockies. Jason got a second-floor room at the Big Wagon Inn Motel, a stucco building with a small, clean restaurant with tables covered with red-checkered tablecloths.

He got a clubhouse sandwich and while paying for it at the cash register, he got directions to Painted Horse Road from the cook, a large, kind, woman whose eyes vanished amid her rosy cheeks when she smiled.

"Sister Marie lives in the Jensen cabin on Whisper Creek Ranch. You go for maybe twenty minutes, turn toward the mountains. Look for the two huge white rocks near the road at the crest of a hill. Got WCR on the gate. You can't miss it."

It was late afternoon and black clouds churned in the sky as Jason's rental ripped along the twists, turns, and dips of Painted Horse Road. Pebbles pinged against the undercarriage and dust plumes rose in the car's wake, disrupting the tranquillity.

No other buildings or signs of civilization were evident.

The dash clock told Jason he'd been traveling some twenty minutes when the landmark rocks appeared. He slowed to turn and his car was swallowed by the dust he'd kicked up.

A long stretch of tired, weatherbeaten fencing led to the pine gate bearing WCR. It was open, inviting Jason to take a grassy path into solitude.

His rental car crept along through a stand of spruce until he glimpsed the red tin roof of a log cabin, sitting perfectly amid a clearing, overlooking a rugged creek and the mountains beyond.

He killed the engine. As it ticked down, the gurgle of creek, the chirp of darting birds, and the cheerful flit of monarch butterflies underscored the serenity. The glazed logs of the cabin gave it a sturdy, clean look; its window frames and edging had been painted a fresh buttery yellow. He came to the door.

His knock was received in silence.

"Hello, Sister Marie!"

Nothing.

He called again only louder and in all directions. The echo of his voice was still in his ears when he heard a faint response, stepped around the cabin, and saw a woman in the distance, farther along the small terraced hills. She was in a chair, working at an easel, beside a patch of garden, overlooking the creek.

She waved to Jason and he waved back.

As he neared her he saw that she'd used a cane to stand. She was dressed in jeans, a gingham shirt, and wore a wide-brimmed straw hat. She lifted her head, revealing thick glasses and a kind, ascetic face that met him with a healing smile. Her painting of flowers and trees was nearly completed. It looked good.

"Sister Marie Clermont?"

"Yes."

"I'm Jason Wade, a reporter with the *Seattle Mirror.*"

"Seattle. Oh my, you're a long way from home, dear."

He noticed she had an accent and guessed it was French.

"Yes," Jason fished for his identification, to reassure her.

She nodded at it, then passed it back.

"Sister, I'm researching the biography of a nun who

was with the Order, the Compassionate Heart of Mercy. I understand that before retiring, you were the senior council member who oversaw the screenings of many sisters."

The old nun nodded. Behind her glasses, her eyes were alert.

"Sister, my trip here concerns, Sister Anne Braxton. I'm sorry to tell you that she was murdered in Seattle."

"I know."

"You know?"

"Yes. An old friend in Olympia saw it on the news and sent a fax to the church in Cardston. We held a Mass for her."

"Well, I have something with me that belongs to her."

The nun leaned on her cane, shifting her weight, listening.

"Her journal."

"Her journal?"

"Yes, and if you'd allow me, I'd like to show it to you. Sister, I've come to ask you to help me understand Sister Anne's life before she became a nun. I'd like to write about it for the *Seattle Mirror*. And I'm afraid I don't have much time."

Sister Marie considered Jason's request for a long moment.

Her eyes took stock of the darkening sky.

"We'd better talk inside. Looks like a nasty storm is coming."

44

The air in Sister Marie's cabin was sweet with the light fragrance of potpourri and soap.

A crucifix, adorned with a rosary, and a print of the Blessed Virgin hung on one of the walls. Jason noticed a tiny bathroom and small bedroom. He could see a narrow bed, crisply made, and thought it looked like one in a monk's cell.

He saw no phone, computer, or TV. One wall of the living area had a floor-to-ceiling shelf crammed with books and papers. He saw a large reading chair with frayed fabric. Next to it were a worn Bible and a magnifying glass. The small kitchen area had a woodstove and a wooden table with two chairs with spindle legs that did not match those of the table. The mismatch and the austere style suggested everything was secondhand.

"This is a special place, Sister, I like it." Jason set his files on the table after returning from the car.

Thunder rumbled outside as the old nun lit the stove to boil water for tea and coffee.

"This section of Whispering Creek Ranch was donated to the Order by an oil family whose matriarch died of cancer in a Calgary hospice the sisters administered."

"And how do you handle it, being out here all alone?"

"God takes care of me, dear. Parishioners check on me every day and my neighbor, half a mile down and across the creek, drops by often. I'm never lonely finding God in the quiet."

A cat emerged and nudged her leg as she prepared the tea and coffee.

"And I've got Sassy here, to protect me from mice."

"You're doing just fine."

"I am." She set Jason's coffee down in a chipped mug. "I've thought much about Anne since I learned of her death. How can help you?"

"I'm trying to complete the story of her life. She was loved by Seattle and it's my job to offer the city a full account of what it lost. We know nothing of her life before she joined the Order."

"But does that matter, dear? She gave herself completely, unselfishly to God and to others. And she gave it without vanity, without seeking credit. I think that's all that needs to be said."

"That is virtuous, but there's an overriding factor."

"What could that be?"

"Sister, the person who murdered her remains at large and could easily harm others. There's strong speculation that she knew her killer. Consequently many people feel that perhaps something in her past could help the police in their investigation."

Sister Marie glanced at Sister Anne's journal and the clippings, suggesting to Jason that the old nun knew something about Anne's past.

"Tell me, Jason, how did you obtain a copy of her diary?"

"Sister," he smiled, "you're not trying to get me to reveal my sources?"

"Is that what you think?" she returned his smile.

"It came to me through channels by those concerned that the truth be known; that everything that can be done to help find Anne's killer is done. Even if it means revealing her inner thoughts, even if it means revealing the mysterious parts of her past that seem to have tormented her."

"And what do you ask of me?"

"Would you please read everything here? It's not a lot, really. I've highlighted the important parts. Afterward, would you please allow me to interview you on your reflections on her journal and your memories of screening Sister Anne into the Order, for a feature I'm writing?"

Sister Marie considered the documents.

"And if I refuse, I suspect you will go ahead with your report based upon your acquiring her personal, private diary?"

"Most likely. Sister, my job is to publish news, not suppress it."

She nodded.

"Give me a little time alone to look them over first, then I'll decide."

Jason nodded to the fire crackling in the woodstove.

"I've got plenty of copies of everything, Sister." He smiled.

"I'm sure you do, dear."

Jason left her for an hour, passing the time by walking along the creek bed, mindful that a storm was brewing. He was amazed by the fact that he'd started the day in the metropolis of Seattle wondering where the story would take him, and now here he was, in some hidden corner of Canada, staring at the Rockies, trying to uncover the truth about the murder of a nun who'd buried her deepest secret.

He glanced back to the little cabin.

Sister Marie knew something. He felt it in his gut.

The afternoon sky had darkened with threatening clouds and lightning flashes when he returned. Sister Marie had finished, but was flipping through the journal.

"I will help you," she said and made him a fresh mug of coffee.

"I don't know how much this help will matter." She leaned hard on her cane and went to her bookshelf and searched along a long section containing several identical notebooks, a collection as expansive as a set of encyclopedias.

"May I record the information and take notes, for accuracy?"

"You may."

After checking the battery, Jason set up his recorder and opened his notebook.

"You know, I helped establish the Order in Paris," Sister Marie began. "We came into existence after World War Two. We broke away from a larger, more established group with the aim of being more progressive, more relevant to everyday lives of Christians. We were ahead of Vatican II. After a fire destroyed our early records, our Mother House was moved to Washington, D.C., then Chicago. We have about seven hundred sisters worldwide."

"Yes, I'd read some of the background."

"I am writing a history of the Order, to leave behind when I'm gone." She plucked a notebook from the shelf and returned to the table just as the rain started coming down hard and the afternoon turned as dark as night.

Sister Marie lit several lanterns, which bathed the cabin in dark golden light, then began flipping though the yellowed handwritten pages of a notebook. From what Jason could see it was all in French.

"Your information is correct. I did oversee assessments and screenings of candidates for the period during which Sister Anne came to us as a candidate."

As lightning flashed, Sister Marie paged through her book and Jason took notes.

"As I'd mentioned, many completed files were lost years ago in a fire. I took some notes, a summary if you will, on many of those that came through me. Sister Anne was approximately twenty-three years old when she came to us in Paris. She was born in St. Louis, Missouri, given up for adoption by her fifteen-year-old mother. She was adopted by a Kansas City bank manager and his wife, who were a childless couple. At age seventeen she was sent to private boarding school in Switzerland. Four years later her parents died in a car accident while en route to see her in Geneva. She was kept on at the school where she studied art and helped younger students. That's what we were told."

Sister Marie stopped, then resumed talking as she returned to the bookshelf for more notes.

"Our screening process was similar to that of many orders. The young candidates submit to psychological and medical tests, background checks, letters of reference."

"Where is that file for Sister Anne?"

"Lost, I believe." The old nun pressed a finger to her lips. "No. Maybe not. Now, as I recall, she didn't go through all that. Just a moment." Sister Marie found another notebook; its pages crackled as she leafed through it.

In the lamplight, beautiful French handwriting reflected in her glasses.

"Yes, it's coming back now. The late Sister Beatrice Dumont made the discovery. Yes. It's here."

"What is it?"

"Sister Anne was first encountered in the back of a

small church. A young woman, praying and crying, begging to be allowed to join the Order. At first, there were concerns about her psychological capacity. She was invited to volunteer at one of our missions. Over time, as she became known to Sister Dumont, it was understood that she was grieving the loss of her parents. The young woman was alone in the world and desperate for guidance. It seems that she bore the guilt of her parents' deaths, as she had desired to attend the school. Later she wanted to leave it and had summoned her parents to come and arrange it."

Jason weighed the revelation.

"Do you think this would account for the agonizing guilt she expressed in her diary?"

Sister Marie thought that it would.

"We gave it time and saw that she truly had felt a divine call to devote her life to helping others."

Jason ruminated over the information.

"She was accepted eventually as a postulant for something like a year, as I recall. Then she became a novice and dedicated herself to her studies and went on to take her temporary vows. I think, in her case, it was close to five years before she took her final vows. And then she went off to various missions around the world."

So that was it, Jason thought, a mundane explanation. Nothing at all that would point to her killer. No deep, dark secret. The part about "destroying lives" must've been her anguish and guilt at the loss of her parents.

"Is that everything, Sister?"

The old nun raised her head from her notebooks as the storm's intensity decreased with the whisper of soft rain.

"No." She turned to her bookshelf. "How could I ever forget? Please forgive my brittle mind." She went to another book but failed to find what she was looking for, as Sassy threaded his way through her legs. She checked another, then another. "Oh, I'm sure it's in one of these blessed books. I've got letters and notes scattered all over. I can never find anything." She tapped her cane to the floor in frustration, sending her cat to the corner.

"What is it, Sister?"

"In the process of becoming a nun you take your vows, which include the big ones, like chastity and poverty. In practical terms, candidates divest themselves of all their worldly goods and come to God, poor in material wealth. It's common for candidates to donate whatever they have to the Church or Order."

"And this was the case with Anne Braxton?"

"Oh, yes, indeed. In fact her donation was critical to the Order's initial success. It seems her father had made several wise investments, the proceeds of which she inherited from her trust at the age of twenty-five. It was held for her in a bank in Zurich, and she arranged to turn it over to the Order."

"She turned her inheritance over to the Order?"

"Yes."

"How much was it?"

"As I recall it was over two million Swiss francs."

"Was that a lot, at the time?"

"At the time, that worked out to over one million U.S. dollars."

Jason stared at the old nun.

45

Leon Dean Sperbeck.

Henry Wade's nightmare.

Sperbeck scowled at him from his DOC photographs, which Henry had propped against the salt and pepper shakers on his kitchen table in his house near Boeing Field.

There was Sperbeck glaring at him, just as he did so long ago during the horrific standoff at the heist.

The terrified eyes of the hostage.

Later, Sperbeck eyed Henry in court as he shuffled off in chains to pay with twenty-five years of his life.

Was it enough for what he did?

Sperbeck's image had tormented Henry the day Vern Pearce put his gun in his mouth and pulled the trigger. It had invaded Henry's sleep, enveloping him like a burial cloth for his years of descent into an alcoholic abyss. And it had mocked Henry the day Sally walked out because she couldn't take it anymore.

Henry didn't blame her.

He blamed Leon Sperbeck.

But was he truly dead?

Henry resumed looking over the files that Ethan Quinn had copied for him. DOC records, court records, old police reports.

Is this how it ends? With Sperbeck's suicide robbing Henry of the chance to find the answer to the one question that had locked Henry in a prison of pain and continued to haunt him.

Was he really dead?

Like Quinn, Henry needed to be certain Sperbeck was dead.

It was critical to his own survival.

Sperbeck's suicide note wasn't much evidence, Henry agreed with Quinn. Until the Nisqually River gave up Sperbeck's corpse, and an autopsy confirmed it was him, all bets were off.

Okay, so what's it going to be?

One way or another, Henry had to come to terms with this thing. It was what his counselors had advised him for over twenty-five years. Twenty-five years. Damn. Henry admitted that a drink would feel good right now.

But it wouldn't help.

All right.

The time for battle had come.

He went back to his files and outlined a plan to investigate. He'd treat Quinn like a client who required verification of Sperbeck's death. Henry began by putting in several calls to sources, reminding himself that he was a detective, licensed by the state to conduct private investigations, and, if necessary, authorized to take a life.

He glanced at his new Glock 22.

He'd picked up the .40-cal pistol late yesterday after he got his letter from the state and completed all the paperwork. Having it around made him uneasy.

He hated the thing.

Hope to God I never have to use it.

Get to work.

First, Henry checked with the NPS Rangers at Mount Rainier National Park on whether they'd found Sperbeck's body.

"Naw. Nothing's turned up," Pike Thornton, a law enforcement officer, told him over the phone. "We sent out Search and Rescue, dragged the river near Cougar Rock, and got nothing."

"Any witnesses see him go in the water?"

"None that were absolutely certain. We had a retired county judge say he saw Sperbeck fishing. We found his pole, tackle, and such."

"What about his vehicle?"

"He told the registration desk that he got a ride from Seattle. No one saw him or spoke to him. Seemed to be a man alone with his thoughts."

Awaiting return calls, Henry went back to Sperbeck's DOC file, which was extensive. Sperbeck had entered the system at WCC, where he was processed and sent on to Washington State Penitentiary at Walla Walla. He spent a lot of time making license plates there. Then he was transferred to Coyote Ridge at Connell, where he received treatment for his addictions while working on the farm.

At Coyote Ridge, Sperbeck also took part in spiritual counseling programs run by groups who visited from across the state. Afterward, he went to Clallam Bay, where he picked up a trade, cabinetmaking, before moving on to McNeil Island, but unlike many offenders, he did not work outside on the barges, tugboats, and ferries.

Even though he qualified for work release and to seek parole, he waived it all, choosing to serve his full time and work toward discharge, reducing the number of strings the system would attach to him.

"Sperbeck had very few conditions of supervision," Herb Kent, Sperbeck's CCO, told Henry when he finally reached him. "He stayed out of trouble inside and

paid his debt in full. There was no indication he was a
risk to reoffend."

"Did he talk about the crime?"

"You mean the money?"

"I mean the money."

"Not a word. He expressed remorse over the damage
he'd inflicted."

"Did he have any kind of support mechanism waiting
for him outside—friends, relatives?"

"Not really."

"What about his visitor list?"

"Spiritual counselors, some teachers, vocational advi-
sors. No family or friends from his past to indicate he
was going to reconnect."

"What do you make of his suicide?"

"It happens, Henry. Especially with long-timers. Guys
get out to find that the world has changed. That there's
no place for them in it. They can't go back to prison. So
what's left for them? Sperbeck had a skill but couldn't
get a job. He called me a couple of times, all despondent. He was slipping back into drugs, circling the
drain."

Kent gave Henry two Seattle addresses that he had
for Sperbeck. One was a run-down motel at the edge of
Capitol Hill, the other a rooming house close to the ID,
the address he was using when he vanished into the
Nisqually River.

Henry got in his pickup truck and did some discreet
door-knocking. He showed people Sperbeck's picture,
which yielded mostly head-shaking, except at the Black
Jet Bar, which was near the rooming house.

"I saw that guy a few times. He used to sit in the back.
Very quiet. No trouble," the bartender told Henry. "But
that cracker was not in great shape. Once he complained about how everybody in the world owed him
for what he did."

"That right? And what did he do?"

"He did not elaborate."

Henry was making notes. "He happen to mention who 'everybody' was? Any names?"

The bartender stuck out his bottom lip and shook his head. "People say a lot of things when they're drinking."

Henry was acutely aware of that.

"Anything else you can remember about him?"

"I heard he used to go to the shelter for meals. I told him to get himself a welfare check and a medical card and see a doctor. Clean himself up."

After thanking the bartender, Henry chided himself for nearly forgetting a basic. It was common for ex-cons to apply for welfare while they searched for a job. Stepping out of the Black Jet, he called an old friend who was a welfare fraud investigator at the Department of Social and Health Services.

"Roland King, Division of Fraud Investigations."

"Rollie, it's Henry Wade."

"Hey, pal. Look, you caught me leaving for court. I have to go."

"Just need a second. Can you help me with a quick check on somebody?"

"Ah, Henry you're going to make more work for us. I know it. And we're already way over our heads as it is. Want to work for DFI?"

"Just want to make you look good."

"I've got about two minutes here. What is it?"

Henry gave him Leon Sperbeck's information, his SSN, his date of birth, known addresses.

"Was he ever a client? That's all I'm asking, Rollie."

Henry could hear King typing on a keyboard as he double-checked Henry's info. As a welfare fraud investigator, King had access to nearly all of the department's computerized databases.

"What's the beef, Henry? This guy cheating?" King asked as he waited for the computer to respond to his queries.

"Not sure."

"Here we go. Yes. I can confirm, confidentially, that he's in our system. He's got a medical card. And we have him on General Assistance Unemployable. His status as an ex-convict armed robber presents a challenge in his effort to find a steady job. That it? Because I really have to go."

"Anything else, there? What about the addresses?"

"Henry, I have to go. Wait, what addresses did you have?"

Henry repeated the two he'd checked.

"Nope, I think there's a couple more. Got a pen?"

Henry took them down. Then heard King typing and cursing under his breath.

"That's not right," King said.

"Find something?" Henry asked.

"We just started sending checks for a new client at one of Sperbeck's addresses. The client's got a different name, but the very same address as Sperbeck. Damn it. I knew it, Henry, you brought me more work."

"So you think Sperbeck's received a check using an alias?"

"Happens all the time."

"Tell me something. When was the last check cashed?"

"Looks to me like two days ago."

46

That guy in the park was weird.

But Brady Boland never told his mom about his encounter the other day because he figured it was no big deal.

Right. If it was no big deal why was he still thinking about it?

Because the guy had made him nervous, especially after Justin and Ryan said they'd seen him before.

"I saw him lurking around here a couple days ago," Justin said.

"Maybe he's a perv," Ryan said.

"Maybe he's some creepy weirdo who likes to say stupid things to kids," Brady said. "Who knows? Who cares?"

Brady did.

That's why he was still thinking about it, here alone in his room today, while his mom was in the kitchen doing stuff. Brady would never ever tell anyone that the stranger had scared him a bit. That the incident made him miss having his dad around to protect him and his mom—but to admit it would make him some sort of baby.

But the truth was he missed his dad.

The truth was, that it wasn't always bad with his dad. Most of the time it was great. What Brady liked best was when he went out on landscaping jobs with him. His dad was teaching him how to drive the rider mower, showing him how to cut in patterns. And he was teaching him about planting, about soil. About how to make it all look "professional."

Every job they went on his father was always digging, "digging deep." And always saying how important it was to give plants, flowers, shrubs, trees, whatever, "lots of plant food."

Brady loved helping him bury the nutrients. They came in capsules, pellets, spikes, and bricks wrapped in plastic. He loved digging and spreading the rich, dark soil. And it really worked. In the end, it always looked great. Those were the happiest times with his dad before things started going bad.

In the time before he died, his dad always seemed to be under a lot of pressure. Always worrying about stuff he'd never talk about. He got angry all the time. Lost his temper.

And hit him.

Brady hated how things got so bad.

One time something happened that he never told his mom about. Once, after a bad time, Brady's father took him aside and privately warned him.

"You listen to me. You keep your goddamn mouth shut about anything that goes on in this house! People are looking for me. Bad people. You do not speak one word about anything! Understand?"

Brady didn't understand.

Nothing made sense back then.

And nothing made sense now with the creep in the park saying weird crap.

And nothing made sense about having a stupid

tumor in your head trying to kill you while your mom was always on the phone, crying and going through papers and files and junk.

And nothing made sense when sometimes he woke up in the night wondering what it would be like to be dead and how he would miss his mom, miss Justin and Ryan.

Just quit it.

Brady got up from his bed and told himself to stop worrying like a baby.

He went to his window and looked up and down the street.

Besides, Justin made the shot.

Which meant everything was going to be fine.

Brady continued scanning his street, looking for anything strange.

Anything at all.

47

Something about the shoes gnawed at Kay Cataldo.

It had cost her a night's sleep, had compelled her to get to her crime lab just after dawn and tear through her files.

It's the shoes. Think, Cataldo! Think!

John Cooper possessed used tennis shoes issued to offenders by the Department of Corrections. But they were not the shoes that had made the impressions at Sister Anne's murder scene. That ruled him out.

Okay, but she'd seen that pattern recently in another open file.

Hadn't she?

Yes.

But where? Where, damn it? She struggled to retrieve it from her memory and her computer, gulping coffee while searching her files. Something blurred by.

Stop.

This one.

Sharla May Forrest.

The teen hooker.

This was the one.

Cataldo examined the crime-scene pictures. There was Sharla May, the runaway, naked on the ground in a back alley with a metal hanger garrotted around her neck. She was so young. It broke Cataldo's heart. There was the Dumpster, the trash, and the semidry mud puddle that had captured a partial right shoe impression.

Here we go.

She called up the cast and the image filled her computer monitor. Very familiar. *This is looking very familiar.* She called up the file notes, read through them, then called up the image of the shoe impression.

"Hold on," Cataldo told herself.

She loaded her computer with shoe files from Sister Anne's homicide, including the work Chuck DePew had done over at the Washington State Patrol's Crime Lab. She called up the images of the shoe impressions, then split the screen of her computer monitor.

How in the world did she overlook this?

Biting her bottom lip, she aligned the photograph from the hooker murder with the sharpest image of the right shoe impression from the nun murder, so that they were in identical scale and attitude.

Cataldo transposed one over the other and set out to look for comparisons.

"Oh boy."

The wear, edges, channeling, the waffle pattern, right down to the fifth ridge with the nice little "X" cut, aligned perfectly.

Cataldo reached for her phone to alert Grace Garner.

They had a multiple murder suspect.

Grace was at her desk at the homicide unit, mining her notes on Cooper's account of the stranger at the shelter.

She was panning for details, anything to aid the Washington Department of Corrections in its search for a con who could fit Cooper's scenario. Trouble was, Cooper's description was just too vague.

Once Perelli clocked in, they were going down to the shelter to recanvass the breakfast crowd. Grace turned to her notes and reports on Sister Anne's work as counselor at prisons and women's shelters.

Damn. The DOC was supposed to get back to her on the prisons Sister Anne had visited and the names of offenders she'd counseled. It ticked Grace off that they had not gotten back to her yet. She would get on their case, she told herself as her line rang.

"Garner, Homicide."

"It's Kay at the lab. Are you sitting down?"

"I'm sitting down."

"Our nun killer also did Sharla May Forrest."

"What?"

"Shoe impressions match at both scenes."

"You're sure?"

"Absolutely."

"But we already looked at Roberto Martell."

"Better look again. He's an ex-con."

Within minutes of Cataldo's call to Grace, a Seattle police emergency dispatcher issued a citywide silent alert to mobile display terminals for Roberto Martell. A couple of days ago, Grace had merely wanted to question Roberto about Sharla May Forrest's murder. Now, the twenty-six-year-old drug-dealing pimp was a suspect in two first-degree homicides.

He was Seattle's most wanted man.

The alert with his physical description and details on his Chrysler and tag were also quietly circulated to every law enforcement agency in King County and the state. At the time it came up, Seattle police officers Dimitri Franz and Dale Gannon were inside a 7-Eleven getting fresh coffee and sugar donuts.

They were unaware of the bulletin when their attention was seized by the screech of rubber in the parking lot and the doom-boom of a car stereo playing at an illegal level. It had interrupted Officer Franz's story about his fishing trip to Montana and disturbed Officer Gannon's enjoyment of a quiet morning.

A gum-chewing girl in her late teens, wearing too much makeup and not enough clothing, unless you counted her thigh-high spike boots and micro mini, strode into the store looking for mouthwash.

Dimitri exchanged a look with Franz, nodding to the girl's man, waiting in the lot behind the wheel of a Chrysler. The exhausted driver's head was thrown back to the headrest. His eyes were closed. He was too tired or too stupid to realize he'd rolled up alongside a marked Seattle police car.

Obviously the girl and her man had been working it all night.

While the music assaulted the air, Franz had slipped into the patrol car and typed into the small computer keyboard to query the Chrysler's tag. His eyebrows climbed a titch when it came back and he saw what they had.

"Oh, my." He pivoted the terminal so his partner could see.

The two cops set their coffees down gently.

Murder suspect Roberto Martell felt the barrel of a police pistol against his head and opened his eyes to see a second pistol leveled at him. He was arrested without incident, except for the sound of a bottle of mouthwash hitting the pavement.

Roberto's girlfriend had not expected her night to end like this.

* * *

Less than an hour later, Perelli folded his arms and looked hard at the man sitting across from him and Grace Garner at the table in the homicide squad's interview room.

"Don't lie to us, Roberto," Grace said. "You were the last to see Sharla May alive."

"No." The chains around Roberto's neck chinked as he shook his head. "Your information is incorrect. The last person to see her alive would be the person who killed her. I swear the truth to you on this."

"What size shoes do you wear?" Perelli asked.

"What? What size? Why?"

"Give me your right shoe."

Roberto looked at Perelli, then at Grace, who nodded.

"I do this, then you let me go?"

"Just give it to me."

Roberto put his sneaker on the table.

"Size eight." Perelli and Grace exchanged a look. No way could Roberto be the killer. Perelli passed it back. "Man, you've got very small, stinkin' feet, Roberto."

"People saw you arguing with Sharla May," Grace said.

"Yes, sure, I'm going to tell you what happened." Roberto slipped his foot back into his shoe. "She owed me two large for her habit."

Grace made notes.

"I was getting angry with her. I'm not her banker, I'm her agent."

"Her agent?"

"She had talent and I introduced her to talent scouts."

"You were her pimp and you beat her," Perelli said.

Roberto held up his hands and appeared offended.

"Okay"—Grace shook her head—"you're her agent."

"In a business sense. And she owed me and, yes, I make my point that she has to pay me."

"You make your point?"

"She brought it on herself. But I can understand how people in the community might misinterpret things, give you incorrect information, make you think I killed her."

"You don't seem too choked up about losing her."

"I've come to terms with my pain in my own way."

Perelli had to restrain himself from drilling his fist into Roberto's head.

"So who was her trick, uh, the last talent scout?" Grace asked.

"I set her up with some guy I met around the ID, at a bar. The Black Jet Bar."

"When was that?"

"I don't know, two, three months ago, like before you found her dead."

"You have a name on this guy?"

Roberto shook his head.

"What did this guy look like?"

"White guy, forties."

"Height? Facial hair?"

"About six feet. He was clean-shaven as I recall."

"His build?"

"Good. Average, but muscular, like he worked out. He was an ex-con."

Grace and Perelli maintained poker faces.

"How do you know he did time?"

"You're forgetting that I was unjustly incarcerated due to the lies a slut told the prosecuting attorney."

"Was her broken jaw also a lie?" Perelli said.

"You want to know about the last man to see Sharla, or do you want to call me a lawyer?"

"Go ahead."

"I got that he'd been inside for a stretch from our little conversation. He was having a beer by himself, looked kind of depressed. I said he'd feel better if he met someone like Sharla May, someone with talent, and that I could set him up."

"Where did this guy live?"

"I don't know."

"Where did he work?"

"I don't know."

"What was he in for?"

Roberto shrugged. "We didn't become soul mates. I just pointed to Sharla May, who was picking songs on the jukebox, doing that little sexy dance she always did, and that sealed the deal. I could see him come alive, once he set eyes on her talent."

"You're a fine slab of humanity, Roberto," Perelli said.

Roberto nodded. "I help girls in trouble."

"Sure, you do," Perelli said. "You're just like the nuns at the shelter."

Grace defused the tension with a question.

"Where did this guy do his time?"

"It was not a subject of conversation."

"Did he have any tattoos?"

"Maybe, on his neck."

"What was it, do you remember?"

"I don't recall, just that maybe he had something on his neck."

Grace threw an over-the-shoulder glance to the one-way glass and Stan Boulder, who was on the other side.

This may have brought them one step closer to the killer.

48

The West Pacific Trust Bank on Yesler Way near 23rd Avenue was a small stand-alone branch, built in the 1980s.

It was a one-story structure with concrete columns and tempered-glass walls that captured Henry Wade's reflection after he'd parked in the lot.

Leon Dean Sperbeck, using the alias Sid Foley, had cashed his welfare check here a few days ago.

Quite a trick for a dead man, Henry thought as he entered the bank. He removed his sunglasses and announced himself to the branch manager, Eloise Sherridan, who'd agreed to a meeting. On the phone with her earlier, Henry had guessed Eloise might be near his age, but in person she looked younger, quite striking in her business suit. Her hand was warm when she shook his.

Eloise closed the door to her neat office.

"So, Mr. Wade, how can I help you? You said you were investigating a security matter, concerning..." She began typing on her keyboard and studied her monitor over her half-frame glasses, "Mr. Sperbeck.

The name and information you'd provided concerned a Mr. Leon Dean Sperbeck and a Sid Richard Foley?"

"My client is the insurance firm for a financial institution that suffered a substantial loss several years ago because of Mr. Sperbeck. He was convicted of that crime, which also involved"—Henry paused to clear his throat—"the shooting death of a customer."

"I see."

"It was many years ago, but since his recent release, it's now believed Sperbeck may still profit from that crime. And in the course of my investigation, I've learned that he may have recently committed another crime, welfare fraud, cashing a check under the name of Sid Richard Foley."

"I see. And you say he cashed that check at this branch." Eloise stared at her monitor.

"Here's his picture. I'd like to confirm by visual ID if he in fact was the person who cashed the check here."

Henry showed Eloise the Department of Corrections photograph of Sperbeck, hoping the psychological effect of a prison photo would help him navigate through the bank's privacy policies.

As Eloise looked at it, Henry nudged her by emphasizing the key facts.

"As I'd mentioned, he was recently released from prison, where he served time for his role in the murder of an innocent bank customer during an armed robbery."

"And you'd like to confirm if he cashed the check for $346.23 three days ago?"

Henry nodded.

"And this concerns a security matter with another financial institution?"

Henry nodded.

"One moment." Eloise stepped from the office, leaving Henry with a hint of lilac in the air before she returned a few minutes later. "Madeline was the teller who handled the check, but she's off today. We're going to run our surveillance recording from that time. I've asked Tim Baker, my assistant manager, to get it for us. It'll only take a moment. We'll run it here. It's on a CD." She smiled.

Henry smiled, but his stomach was tensing, dreading what was surely coming. Several moments later a young man in a suit presented a CD to Eloise.

"It's on here, El, go to 3457. That coincides with the transaction time."

"Thanks, Tim." Eloise slid the CD into her computer and it began downloading. "All counter transactions are synchronized with our cameras. We'll get a look at him from several angles." She typed in a few commands. "Please, come around and see."

Henry went around Eloise's desk. Her large monitor displayed several frames of the man at the counter and Henry's gut twisted.

"It's him."

"That was easy, Mr. Wade. Is that it? Do you want color printouts?"

"Yes. Thanks. And, please, this is the address I have for him. Can you confirm it?"

Henry pulled a page from his briefcase and placed it before her. Eloise consulted it, then double-checked her computer files. "That seems outdated," she said. "He must have moved recently; we have a different one for him. I'll print it out for you."

When the printing finished, Eloise gathered the pages into a plain folder for Henry, who slid them into his case.

"Thank you."

"You're welcome. You know, when I was a teller I experienced several armed robberies. That's why I decided to help you. That, and the fact that you strike me as a trustworthy man who'll keep our business here confidential."

"That's the private part of my job," he said.

Henry's pickup was in the far corner of the lot sheltered under the shade of a tall tree. He got into the cab, but did not turn the key. His breathing quickened.

It was real now.

Sperbeck was free.

Sperbeck had faked his death. Christ, what's he up to?

Henry stared at his files. At Sperbeck's face. At the new address. It was all here in this folder. God, he ached for a drink. He licked his lips and in one motion reached under the passenger seat, felt the brown paper bag, and heard the liquid swish as he set it on his lap.

Whiskey.

Purchased last night.

Without unwrapping the bag, he gripped the bottle with both hands. Felt the hard glass. He held it against his chin, swore he could smell the healing quality of alcohol as he imagined that first hot swallow flowing down his throat.

This was not the answer.

He put the bag back under the seat and his arm nudged against his gun, holstered under his jacket.

He was licensed to end a life. Licensed to kill another human being.

He hated it.

Hated it.

Henry inhaled deeply. His hands were shaking and he gripped the wheel.

Twenty-five years and now Sperbeck was this close again.

It was time Henry Wade put it all to rest. He had to face this head-on. He had to face it sober. If he failed, he would die.

He thought of his son. He needed help.

Jay.

He started his engine and eased out of the lot, unaware that down the street, half a block away, someone was watching him.

Awaiting his next move.

49

One million dollars.

Was it a factor in her murder?

As Jason's plane began its descent for Seattle, he took a hit of coffee and scrolled through his story. He'd started working on it last night in his motel room after leaving Sister Marie's cabin. He wrote until midnight before catching an early morning return flight, writing more as the Canadian Rockies glided under him.

At first he didn't think the money could be linked to Sister Anne's murder. It was so long ago. But as he started building his article, he reexamined key aspects.

Maybe it was all right here before his eyes.

First, there were Sister Anne's own words in her journal. He reread what she'd written in the final days of her life. It was as though she were anticipating a conflict, an accounting, something: "Can I ever be forgiven for what I did, for the pain I caused?" then, "I deeply regret the mistakes I have made and will accept your judgment of me."

These anguished entries appear to have been made *after* Sister Anne's encounter with the stranger at the shelter, the one John Cooper had told him about. Jason put it into context, into a simple time line: A stranger at the shelter confronts her, upsets her about something, then she secretly begs God's forgiveness for mistakes made in her life—*then appears to embrace judgment.*

And the murder weapon came from the shelter.

Mistakes from her past.

". . . the pain I caused . . ."

She donates more than a million dollars to the order. *From a Swiss bank.*

To assuage the guilt of her parents' deaths?

Or something else?

Jason heard the hydraulic groan of the landing gear locking and metropolitan Seattle wheeled below. He closed his laptop, raised his tray, then rushed through a mental checklist of what he had to do on the ground.

After landing, Jason took a cab directly to the *Mirror.*

On the way, he called the news desk to alert them to the exclusive story he'd be filing today. Then he called Kelly Swan, the news librarian.

"Kel, I need an all-out shotgun search now on two people."

"You're back in town already? Hang on, cowboy," Kelly was at her computer and began closing files. "Okay, fire away."

"Their names are Sherman Braxton and Etta Braxton of Cleveland, Ohio." He provided the spellings. "Sherman was a banker. They died together some thirty-odd years ago in a car accident in Switzerland, near Geneva. I need everything we can get on them. Obits, old clips."

Kelly was jotting notes.

"What are you looking for?"

"Every word, utterance, record that concerns them, anything. Everything."

"I've got a friend in the library at the *Cleveland Plain Dealer* and I'll call Mavis, our genealogical contractor.

We'll comb the city directories, the public library, municipal records, voter lists, court records, wills, etcetera. A lot of stuff is on CD now, so we should be able to get data flowing pretty fast."

"Good, I also need you to confirm and locate St. Ursula Savary College." He spelled it. "It's a private Swiss boarding school near Montreux, or Lausanne. If you find it, I know there's a time-zone challenge, but get them to check records, albums, alumni clubs, anything to confirm the registration of an American student named Anne Braxton, of Cleveland, Ohio, for the same period, some thirty years back, give or take."

"But we did a big search for Anne Braxton when she was murdered and found nothing about her."

"I know, Kel, just search this new information, please."

"How soon do you need this?"

"I need it now."

50

They were getting closer.

Grace Garner stabbed a cherry tomato with her fork. Eating her salad quickly at her desk, she checked the time, wishing her phone would ring as she reevaluated the facts before her upcoming case status meeting.

Kay Cataldo's discovery had given her a solid break.

The physical evidence told them that Sharla May Forrest and Sister Anne Braxton's killer wore size-11 tennis shoes issued by the Washington Department of Corrections. Everything pointed to an ex-con. Maybe one who was recently released, or had violated custody.

They had ruled out Cooper. And after talking with Roberto Martell, Grace and Perelli canvassed the bar where Martell said the suspect had encountered Sharla May. Martell's story held up, according to a waitress and a bartender.

Grace and Perelli then went back to the shelter to interview John Cooper again. A picture was emerging. The suspect was a white male in his forties with a muscular build and a tattoo on his neck. And considering the knife used to kill Sister Anne came from the shelter, where Cooper had witnessed him upsetting her, the killer had to have had some connection to the nun.

Was he someone she'd counseled in prison? Or a nut job out of control?

The answer was somewhere with the Department of Corrections. How long had it been since she'd requested the DOC's help?

Too long.

Grace checked the time before her meeting. Perelli was in the records room gathering summaries of cold cases to support a theory he was developing. Grace stared at her phone, hoping against the odds that the DOC had some way of helping them zero in on her guy, or develop a suspect list.

Why haven't they called back yet? This was not good.

She jabbed another tomato and grappled with another problem.

Jason Wade.

His messages seemed almost desperate. Where had he been? They hadn't spoken in a long time. She had to take some of the blame. She had to admit that she liked him. A lot. They were both loners. They both felt like outcasts. They were right for each other. But she'd hurt him and in the process got hurt herself. *What goes around, comes around, kiddo,* she told herself. Maybe when all this was over she would talk to him. Really talk to him. Maybe they could give it another shot? For now she focused on her case.

Grace finished her salad and started making notes when her line rang.

"Homicide, Garner."

"Steve Scannell, with the DOC in Olympia."

"Did you get anything?"

"You're asking us to find a needle in a haystack. I've had my people go at your request five ways to Sunday and we can't pinpoint things the way you'd like." Scannell was high up the command chain of the DOC's Prisons Division.

"What can you tell us so far?"

"Sister Anne's order has been very active with our religious and spiritual programs for years."

"That should help."

"It helps complicate things."

"Well, can you give us a list of all the prisoners she's visited?"

Scannell sighed.

"It doesn't work that way. In some cases she had one-on-ones, in others she was with a spiritual group providing services to a prisoner group."

"Well, can I get a list of names?"

"Detective Garner, we have fifteen institutions and fifteen work releases. We're talking a prison population of some seventeen thousand statewide. Over the years the Order has visited every facility. In some cases, several times. In some cases, there are sign-up logs, in some cases, like when they addressed groups, no sign-up was required."

Grace tapped her pen and thought.

"Let's try this, Steve. We know we're looking for someone who's been out for at least three months. He's a male, white, has a tattoo on his neck, and wears a size-11 tennis shoe, approximately six feet tall, muscular build."

"That's too general. Do you have a specific release date?"

"No."

"Type of release?"

"No."

"Do you know his offense, or length of sentence?"

"No."

"Do you by chance have an offender classification, or institution?"

"No."

"Then, I'm afraid that's way too general."

"Couldn't you run a program or search?"

"Grace, listen to what I'm telling you. Every month we average anywhere from fifteen hundred to eighteen hundred releases of all types. Across the state we have nearly forty-three thousand offenders under field supervision, nearly eleven thousand in King County alone."

"I get it. Needle in a haystack."

"Give us something specific and we can lock onto this guy in a heartbeat. Meanwhile, I've got all of my senior custody staff going full bore on this, getting my captains to check with their lieutenants, their CCOs, and Correctional Unit Supervisors."

"I appreciate that."

"If we find something, you'll be the first to know."

51

In the side mirror of his rented Ford Taurus, Ethan Quinn watched Henry Wade's pickup pull out of the West Pacific Trust Bank half a block down Yesler.

Quinn set his video recorder down, started his sedan, and wheeled round into traffic, careful to keep several cars between him and Wade's truck.

As he gathered speed, Quinn's heart rate picked up and he exhaled slowly. This was the biggest psychological gamble he'd ever taken on a case. And, at the outset, he was certain that he'd blown it.

But now, some forty-eight hours since he'd rolled the dice and began his surveillance of Henry Wade, Quinn was convinced that he was on the right track—convinced that his instincts were right.

Henry Wade was a wise old fox.

Contacting him cold was a calculated risk.

But it yielded the result Quinn needed. He'd caught Henry unawares. Quinn saw it in the old guy's face. As expected, Henry played his grief card, telling him that the case had taken a toll. That he couldn't help, that sort of thing.

That was fine.

That was expected.

All that really mattered were Henry's actions after the meeting.

Quinn had done his homework. He'd studied the files of the case exhaustively for months. Months. Because this old case fascinated him.

Things just did not add up.

The armored-car company was owned by ex-cops. There were a lot of cops there the day it went down and $3.3 million in cash vanished. An innocent bystander died in a botched hostage bid. Leon Sperbeck, the one suspect caught, the only suspect caught, was convicted without breathing a word about the other suspects.

Were there other suspects?

There were witness statements with descriptions so general—two other suspects in ski masks—one was thin, the other heavyset—they were useless.

All of it was very unusual.

The case fades.

As Sperbeck does his time, years roll by. People die. The case grows cold.

None of the money surfaced. No word on the street of it being circulated. And contrary to popular belief, Quinn knew from criminology studies of convicted armed robbers that often those who commit big heists are condemned to live in fear, to always look over their shoulder. Man, in many cases, they're so paranoid, they live modestly because they're afraid to spend the money. They fear that spending the cash would draw attention. It was common to find most of the stolen cash in their possession, even years after the crime.

That was exactly what Quinn believed was at play here.

A textbook case.

Sperbeck and Wade were the only two survivors

linked to the heist. No way did Sperbeck do all that hard time only to walk out and commit suicide. Quinn didn't buy that for a second. Sperbeck likely staged his death so that he could start a new life after he collected his share of the heist.

Henry Wade had to be involved.

Quinn was convinced of it. That's why he'd taken a gamble by contacting Henry, tipping his hand while feeding Henry that line about sharing any recovered portion of the cash. It was a strategic move designed to draw him out, to gauge what he knew about the case— hoping that maybe Henry would lead him to the cash.

And now, Quinn's gamble was paying off.

What was he doing at Sperbeck's bank, talking to a bank manager? No private detective was that fast. That good. No way. Henry Wade played the recovering drunk ex-cop thing like a B-movie actor. For him to move this fast, he had to be working with Sperbeck. Had to know something.

Quinn was certain of it.

He glanced at his camera in the passenger seat, thinking that if he cleared this one, it would be his biggest payday ever.

Upward of $1.5 million.

For a moment, Quinn entertained his financial options when suddenly the rear of a Seattle Metro bus was all he saw in front of him. Rubber screeched as he slammed his brakes, stopping dead.

Traffic ahead halted.

Quinn cranked the wheel to the left, craned his neck to see that a construction crew was working ahead.

No sign of Henry Wade's pickup truck.

Quinn slammed his palms against the wheel.

The roar of a Detroit diesel engine in a dump truck unloading steaming asphalt onto the street ahead drowned out Quinn's cursing.

52

Three hours to deadline.

Jason took stock of the newsroom, the tense clicking of keyboards as reporters concentrated on filing. Senior news editors were emerging from the big glass-walled room at the east end where they'd wrapped up their final news meeting on where stories would play in tomorrow's paper.

Only the night news editor could override their decisions.

At his desk, Jason inserted the CD with his story into his computer, downloaded it, flagged the holes he was going to fill, then sent it to the metro desk for editing.

Next, he went online for info, then called the U.S. Embassy in Bern and requested information from the twenty-four-hour duty desk about the school and two American citizens who died in a car crash near Geneva. He also got numbers for Swiss police who had jurisdiction over the areas.

Then he called the Swiss Embassy in Washington, D.C., and made the same request after he'd reached the on-call press attaché.

Next he called Grace Garner. She didn't answer. He left a message, then headed to the cafeteria for a coffee, cheeseburger, fries, and a Coke. Back at his desk, he'd just lined up his burger for the first bite when Eldon Reep called him into his office, where he had been reading a file on his computer monitor.

"You should've alerted me the instant you got back."

"I called in to the desk. I had a lot to do."

Reep swiveled.

"I'm your boss. I authorized your trip. You report to me first."

Jason rolled his eyes.

"Just finished your story from Canada. You struck out. The hard news just ain't there."

"Bull. It's full of exclusive revelations."

"We might be able to salvage it as an exclusive human interest bio: 'A troubled young heiress becomes a nun in Paris and donated her fortune to her order.' Dedicated her life to helping the poor before her murder."

"I wrote it as a murder mystery."

"Yes, that's why I've ordered the desk to rewrite it as a bio feature."

"What? Are you nuts? Did you even read the thing? It's a start at unraveling the mystery surrounding her murder. We quote her secret diary, the donation, Cooper's account of the mystery man at the shelter who'd '*asked her to forgive him and it upset her.*' I'm telling you, there's something here. We're connecting the dots. The pieces are starting to come together."

"I don't see it, I think you're reaching."

"I don't believe this! Did Vic Beale or Mack Pedge read it yet?"

Reep stood, put his hands on his hips, and invaded Wade's space.

"Set this aside for the moment. I want you to check out something more important right now."

"Like what?"

"Nate Hodge was shooting pictures at a house fire when he overheard a cop talking about rumors of a new lead in the case."

"What sort of lead?"

"That's what you're going to find out. He sent the desk an e-mail. I'll bump it to you. You act on it now."

Cursing under his breath, Jason returned to his desk and opened Nate's e-mail. "I was at house fire near Ravanna and was talking to a cop friend. He got a call on his cell phone. He stepped back but I overheard him say, 'We've got a new lead in the nun murder?'"

The cop was probably referring to a new tip, rather than a solid lead. If it's big, it rarely gets down to the uniforms on the street. Jason wasn't sure what to make of it. He put in another call to Garner, shook his head, then tore into his burger, managing three bites and half a dozen fries before Kelly Swan appeared from the library, tapping a slip of paper in her hand.

"Don't know if this is good or bad—can I have one?" Kelly stole a fry. "But so far no records—absolutely zip—for a Sherman and Etta Braxton in Cleveland, or anywhere in Ohio."

Jason halted chewing.

"And," Kelly continued, "there's no record for St. Ursula Savary College in Switzerland, nothing that even comes close."

Jason resumed chewing, but thoughtfully, noticing, at that moment, the arrival of an e-mail from the press attaché at the Swiss Embassy.

Preliminary queries with authorities indicate no citizens of the United States whose names you provided are listed in records as traffic fatalities. The St. Ursula Savary College is not among the country's schools. Included below is a link to all Swiss private and international schools.

"Thanks, Kelly. Can you please keep checking?"

Quieted by the development, Jason resumed eating and thinking. Thinking of the image of Anne Braxton, a distraught young woman, alone in a church in Paris, begging nuns to allow her into their order.

But did she lie to them about her past?

Why would she do such a thing?

And where did that one million dollars come from? How does a twenty-three-year-old American woman come to have one million dollars in a Swiss bank account?

His line rang.

"Wade, *Mirror*."

"It's Garner."

"Grace," he sat up, "Listen, I've been doing some digging and I've got something."

"Will I be reading it in the paper, or are you going to tell me?"

"I think we need to meet."

"Is that what you think? I think you want something."

"Grace."

"So you're talking to me now. All done with your tantrums, is that it?"

"Grace, please."

"You want to meet now?"

"Now would be good."

"All right. That place beside the old warehouse. In twenty minutes."

53

The Rusted Anchor was an all-night sanctuary for cops and the like who worked 24/7 downtown.

Tucked down a side street near an abandoned warehouse and the waterfront, the narrow building was webbed with vines. Its battered metal door, punctured with several bullet holes, gave newcomers pause.

Even during sunny days, the Anchor remained dim inside. The darkness calmed frayed nerves and eased troubled minds, offering tranquillity and beer as cold as an embittered ex-wife. Low-watt lights hung low over the dark high-backed booths that were evocative of church pews. Jason spotted Grace Garner alone in a corner, poking the ice in her Coke with her straw.

The neon clock on the wall gave him a little over two hours until his deadline.

He sat down and ordered a ginger ale from a bored man in a dirty white apron who had three days' worth of white whiskered growth on his face. They waited in awkward silence until Jason's drink arrived.

"Okay, Wade, I made a mistake. Can we move on?"

Jason held up two fingers.

"Two mistakes: You dumped me. And you went out with Special Agent Asshole."

"How did you know?"

"You're not the only paid investigator at this table."

She looked away.

"Grace, what happened? Just tell me what happened?"

"I got scared."

"Of what?"

"It felt so right with you. We were moving fast, but it felt so right I caught myself thinking long-term, even though I realized it ain't going to happen."

"You don't know that. You got to take things one step at a time."

"Okay, I messed up. Can we move on?"

He looked into her eyes until all the hostility between them subsided. After a few moments, Grace drank from her glass and said, "You said you may have something."

"The paper got a tip on Sister Anne that led to Canada. I went there to follow it up and just got back."

"Canada? What sort of tip did you get?"

"We received some information about her life before she entered the Order."

"And?"

"Sister Anne may have lied to the nuns about her past before joining their Order and it involves her family and a lot of money."

"How much money?"

"Enough to put in a Swiss bank."

"How much?"

"About a million dollars. She gave it to the nuns. I interviewed the nun who screened her into the order. Sister Marie. She lives alone in the Canadian Rockies. The old nun told me that the money came to the Order by way of a Swiss bank account. She said that Anne Braxton had told the nuns that it was part of her inheritance after her parents were killed in a car crash when she was a teen."

"And?"

"None of the information checks out, so far. We've been digging into it. The names of her parents don't exist. There's no record of a car accident. The private school she claimed to have attended does not exist, according to Swiss authorities."

"What do you think?"

"She also kept a diary in which she agonizes over sins she's committed and begs for forgiveness."

"What kind of sins?"

"She never says. She supposedly told another nun that she'd 'destroyed lives.' Her journal has no details. It's all vague, with a lot of Scripture."

"Who has this diary?"

"I'll share it with you after our story runs in tomorrow's paper."

"Why do you think she lied? What did she do? What was she hiding?"

"That's what I want to find out. Are you interested in this stuff?"

"I'd like to see your information."

"We'll work that out. Now, I've got a question for you."

"Make it quick."

"Is there a new lead in the case?"

"What are you hearing?"

"I'm hearing there's a new lead, come on."

"Maybe."

"Come on, Grace. I just gave you my exclusive."

"We're looking hard at the possibility that the person who murdered Sister Anne may have murdered another woman."

"What? Before or after Sister Anne?"

"Before."

"Based upon . . . ?"

"New information."

"How are they linked? Have you got a serial killer?"

"Way too soon to speculate on that but I don't think it's going that way."

"Is the earlier case in Seattle?"

"Yes."

"How far back does it go?"

"We're not disclosing that at this time."

"Can you tell me who the victim is? How the two cases are linked?"

"We're not releasing anything."

"I want to use this. Does anyone else have this?"

"It's all yours. Just keep my name out of the paper. I have to go."

"Me, too. Listen, I was wondering—"

She looked at him.

"Yes?" she said.

"That we keep in touch."

"Keep in touch?"

"On the case."

"Sure."

Driving back to the paper, Jason had just under two hours before the first edition deadline; he called Eldon Reep to alert him to the exclusive news of the second homicide.

"I think we can line this on the front page. This is good," Reep said. "We'll use it as a page-one hit to key to your Canadian secret past and diary story."

After he finished the call Jason's cell phone rang.

"Wade."

"Jay, it's me, son."

"Dad. Oh, man, I am so sorry. I've been out of town on this nun murder and—"

"I really need to see you. I need your help."

"Dad, I don't know if I can get away. It's a bad time right now."

"Jay, I've got to take care of something. If you help me with what I have to do, it'll put an end to everything."

"Okay, okay . . . I'll try to steal a couple of hours in the morning."

54

Bitter northwest winds were forking like a serpent's tongue over the Olympic Mountains and reconverging over Puget Sound to deliver a thunderstorm to Seattle.

Rhonda Boland had finished an overtime shift at the supermarket. Her feet were throbbing and her back was aching as she arrived at Alice Valeeni's house. Alice was the Italian grandmother who lived three doors down from the Boland home and watched Brady whenever Rhonda needed help.

The early evening sky had turned black and winds were kicking up when Rhonda and Brady arrived home. They ordered Brady's favorite, a large pizza with the works.

They spent the rest of the evening watching a rerun of *Planet of the Apes*.

Afterward, Brady got into bed with a Superman comic and Rhonda drew a hot bath. She added a ribbon of fragrant bubble bath she'd picked up from the discount bin because the cap had split. It saved her three bucks. The bubbles smelled like roses.

Like the roses on Sister Anne's casket.

Easing herself into the water, Rhonda tried not to

think of her money problems. Tried not to bother God again about Brady. But it was impossible. Not an hour, not a minute, not a second passed that she did not agonize over the prospect of losing her son.

Please don't take him. Please. He's all I have. Please.

She stifled a sob with her hands until the moment passed.

Soaking in the bubbles, the hot water soothing her, Rhonda considered her life so far, her dreams, the choices she'd made, and all that fate had visited upon her. She scolded herself, told herself that no matter how bad she thought she'd had it, someone, somewhere had it worse.

Again, Rhonda asked God to forgive her. She was sorry. She was just so tired. The hot water relaxed her. It felt good. So soothing. The water was so warm, like a Caribbean beach, the warm azure sea caressing her toes, palm fronds hissing in the breeze. Her muscles slackened. She grew drowsy and fell asleep, dreaming of palm trees and a better life when thunder woke her.

She didn't know how long she'd been sleeping.

Rhonda drained the tub, slipped on her robe. She was exhausted, ready for bed as she padded through the still house, switching off lights. She knew every creak and groan of her home. She heard the hiss of the rain, punctuated with the rumble of thunder. The TV was off. The refrigerator clicked and ran with a rattle as she double-checked the locks on the doors.

Everything was fine. Secure.

Before going to her bedroom, Rhonda started for Brady's room to check on him. His reading light was on, his door half open.

A few steps away, Rhonda froze.

Brady's bed squeaked in a way she'd never heard before. Then everything went quiet.

Deathly quiet. Something wasn't right.

"Brady?"

Nothing but the rain. Rhonda moved closer to the door.

"Brady, honey, are you up?"

A shadow flickered like a passing spirit on her son's bedroom wall.

"Okay, sweetie, joke's over, mommy's ti—"

The bed squeak-creaked again, this time with a faint desperate vocal sound as Rhonda inched closer to the door.

She didn't believe what she saw.

It couldn't be real.

Before her jaw opened to shriek, before her brain could issue the cognitive command to react, her knees buckled, and she steadied herself against the door frame.

"Oh, Jesus!"

Brady was sitting up on the edge of his bed, fear pushing his eyes wide open.

A man's right gloved hand was clamped over Brady's mouth. In his left, the man held a serrated hunting knife.

Rhonda stepped toward them and met the man's cold eyes.

"Don't you fucking move!" he said.

"Please, please, let him go."

"Do as I say and he'll live."

"What do you want? Who are you?"

"Sit down and listen."

Rhonda held her arms toward Brady.

"Sit!"

Rhonda sat on Brady's swivel chair near his desk.

"This will be simple. I think your pup here's already grasped the concept of property when we met in the park the other day. Right, sport?"

"Please don't hurt him. Oh, please."

"Your husband was Jack Boland, that's what he called himself."

Rhonda nodded.

"He owes me from an old business transaction and I've come to collect."

"Business? But his landscaping business failed when he died. I'm paying off all of his debts."

"This was *old* business."

"I'm sorry. I don't know you. I don't know what you're talking about. Was it gambling? Because he gambled."

"We were partners on a project. I kept up my end and now I want my money. In full. With interest!"

"How much? I don't understand. The accountants— I mean—we don't—"

"One and a half million dollars."

"My God!"

"I know you have it."

"No. We have nothing. You've made a mistake."

"Don't lie! Don't you fucking lie!"

"Mister, I don't know who you are, or what you think you know! But you're wrong! Look around! Look at how we live! I'm a supermarket cashier! Jack left us in debt! My son's sick and I don't know how I'm going to pay for the operation he needs to save his life! You're wrong about us!"

"Look on the computer keyboard."

"What?"

"Look!"

Rhonda turned in the chair and picked up a snapshot she'd never seen before. Brady with Sister Anne Braxton, the murdered nun. Taken at his school.

"Where did you get this?"

"From Sister Anne. I saw you and your pup here at her funeral. Both of you."

Rhonda's control swirled between fear and anger.

"I swear I don't know what you're talking about!"

"Don't move!"

The man reached into his rear pocket for handcuffs, snapping them on Brady, deftly binding him to his headboard, keeping the knife to his throat and Rhonda at bay.

"Don't!" Brady shouted.

Instantly the man backhanded his fist across Rhonda's face, shocking her as he reached under the bed for a large roll of duct tape, swiftly peeling and spinning it around her until she was restrained in Brady's chair in a silver cocoon.

Then he grabbed the cup of water on the desk. Next to it were four pills. He showed her the brand marking on the pills.

"These are sleeping pills, Rhonda. Harmless."

He shoved them in her mouth and held her nose and clamped his gloved hand over her face as she struggled.

"Swallow them now!"

"Leave my mom alone!"

She continued resisting.

"Swallow the goddam pills or I'll keep you awake to watch him bleed!"

She swallowed them. He let her breathe and checked her mouth, his finger roughly probing under her tongue and along her gums.

"When you wake, find a way to get yourself out of this tape because I'm going to call. When I do, you will have twenty-four hours to clear your husband's debt with me. I'm going to be watching you. If you contact the police, or anyone, you will never see your pup again. I've got a perfect grave ready for him. Do you believe me?"

Rhonda nodded.

He drew his face close until his eyes burned into hers.

"You'll never know the price I've paid, or the things I've done to find you! *You will get me my money!* I'll contact you with more instructions. When I have my money, your pup comes back. Be smart, Rhonda. Your asshole husband held my money. Find it and we're done! Fuck up, and you're going to another funeral."

As the man looped tape around Rhonda's mouth, she would not take her eyes from Brady.

She prayed.

Soon her muscles refused to obey her and she grew semiconscious. She wanted to call the police. She wanted to run screaming into the street but her body was turning to stone.

Her eyes started to flicker.

Her lids became heavy.

She couldn't hold them open.

Her final image was of Brady and the glint of the knife against his throat.

55

So far this morning, Bob Germain was four for four.

Rare on residential routes, he thought as he stopped his Escort wagon in front of number five and reached for his clipboard. Let's see. He ran his finger down the page with the Super Quick & Friendly Delivery letterhead.

Recipient is Rhonda Boland. A letter from an insurance company.

"Help me, Rhonda," Germain chuckled to himself after ringing the doorbell, wondering if he'd be lucky enough to have all twenty-five of his deliveries be home. Could be a record-setting day.

He rang the bell again. As time ticked by in silence, his hope faded.

"Figures."

He reached for his pad to leave the message that he'd return later. His pen was poised when he was stopped by a noise from inside. What the heck was that? Sounded like a cry. He banged on the door.

"Hello!"

He tried the handle, surprised to find it was unlocked.

"Anybody home? You have a delivery! Hello!"

He heard another sound like a woman's muffled groan. He entered, calling as he moved farther into the house, scanning it for a clue, hoping that he wasn't going to come upon a love session, like his buddy did.

Getting down in Tacoma.

Germain stopped in his tracks.

First hair, then a forehead and a woman's face, her mouth covered with tape. She was on the floor, on her back, taped to a chair, moaning, rolling her head.

Germain rushed to her side, pulled the tape from her mouth.

"Please, he's got my son!"

Her face was bruised. He checked for more signs of injury.

"Who?" Germain glanced around. "Ma'am, are you hurt anywhere else?"

He pulled out his keys, extracted the blade of his pocketknife, and sliced at the tape, freeing her and helping her sit more comfortably.

"Ma'am, I don't know what happened but I think I should call an ambulance."

"No!"

"Ma'am, I think you need help."

"My son! He took my son! Don't call the police! He'll kill him! Oh God!"

"Who? Ma'am we have to call some—"

The phone rang, jerking Rhonda to her feet. She trailed tape as she scrambled, grabbing the phone before the second ring could sound.

"Mom!"

"Brady! Oh, honey are you all right? Where are you, just tell me!"

Rhonda heard a scuffle, traffic noise. It had to be a public phone.

"Brady!"

The stranger came on the line.

"This is your wake-up call!"

"Please don't hurt him! Please let him go! I'll sell my house, anything! I'm begging you! Please!"

"You've got twenty-four hours to pay me in full! Say good-bye to your mother, pup!"

"Mommee!"

"Brady! I love you! Brady!"

The line died in her hand and Rhonda collapsed on the floor. She cradled the receiver, then released an agonizing sob.

Germain was dumbfounded.

"Ma'am, I think you'd better call the police right now."

"*Nooooo!* He'll kill him!"

Germain blinked, then swallowed and looked around until his attention went into the bedroom, the posters of the Mariners, Spider-Man, the models of choppers and cars, ships, the skateboard.

A boy's room.

On the floor he saw the photograph of a woman and a boy.

Isn't that the murdered nun whose picture's been all over the news?

Sister Anne.

Who's the boy? What the hell's going on?

Germain looked at the bed. At the sheets. At the small, dark smears.

Blood?

He reached for his cell phone, pressed 911 to get the police and an ambulance to Rhonda Boland's address when Rhonda hurled herself at him, struggling for his phone.

"I told you no police! Now he'll kill Brady!"

Germain held her back until he'd completed the call.

Rhonda dropped to the floor.

Would she ever see Brady again?

56

The 911 operator kept Bob Germain's information off the air.

The kidnapping suspect could be monitoring police calls over a scanner.

Using the computer-aided dispatch system, the operator sent the call immediately to Officers Ron Lloyd and April Vossek, in the district's nearest unmarked unit. Vossek read the call on the car's Mobile Data Computer. The engine roared as they responded without activating their lights or siren, arriving along with paramedics, who examined Rhonda Boland.

They treated her face. She was hysterical. After calming her and taking stock of the bloodied sheets, the tape, the photograph, and other facts, Lloyd and Vossek quickly determined the gravity of what had happened and its link to Sister Anne Braxton's murder.

Urgent calls were made.

* * *

In her downtown high-rise apartment, Grace Garner was stepping from her shower when Sergeant Stan Boulder phoned her.

"We've got a kidnapping of a boy in a case that looks to be linked to the Braxton homicide."

"What? What do we know?"

Grace had wrapped a towel around herself and made a watery trail to her bedroom.

"Not much. The call's hot. Only a few minutes old. Dom's on his way to take you to the scene. Get there fast, Grace. Find out what you can before the FBI bigfoots this one."

Grace dressed at top speed, grabbed her badge and gun, and trotted to the elevator. In the lobby she picked up a copy of the morning's *Mirror*. Outside, she read Jason Wade's stories and devoured a banana just as Perelli whipped the Malibu up her driveway. She got in and he left several feet of burning rubber.

At the Boland home, Lloyd and Vossek briefed Grace and Perelli. Crime-scene people were rolling. The caller's number had come up as a public phone at a gas station at the edge of Renton.

"Renton PD and King County Sheriff's Office are trying to get any surveillance video," Vossek said. "It doesn't look good. The place is pretty beat up."

Kay Cataldo arrived with her crew from the Seattle Police Crime Scene Investigation Unit.

"I brought help," Cataldo nodded to Chuck DePew, who had a team from Washington State Patrol's Crime Lab.

"We'll divide the load so we can move faster," DePew said.

The vice section sent detectives from special and general investigations. They set up a trap on Rhonda's phone, started searching through Brady's computer files and e-mails. They got records to run urgent and extensive background checks on Rhonda Boland and her deceased husband Jack Boland. Then Special Agent Jim Crawson called from the Bureau's Seattle Field Office to say agents were on their way.

Grace and Perelli didn't wait.

They took Rhonda alone into her kitchen and had her go back to the previous night and give them a time line of how Brady's kidnapping unfolded. All the while, Grace used a microrecorder and took careful notes.

"Why would he ask you for over a million dollars?" Grace asked.

Rhonda shook her head as tears rolled down her swollen face.

"We're broke. I'm looking for a second job to pay for Brady's operation."

"What sort of operation?"

"He has a tumor."

"Does he need medication?"

"Yes."

"We'll put that out now and in the alert," Grace said.

"What about this 'project' the kidnapper claims to have been involved in with your husband?" Perelli asked.

"I don't know anything about any project that would involve that much. Talk to the bankruptcy people. My husband's biggest landscaping clients were in the range of five thousand a year, tops. I don't know what he's talking about."

"What about former employees?"

"He was self-employed. He'd take Brady along, but he ran things on his own."

"What about further back in your husband's past? You said he gambled. Did he deal in drugs? Did he have any outstanding gambling debts?" Perelli asked.

"I don't think so. I don't know."

"What about his family?" Grace asked.

"He had no family. His parents died in a house fire when he was young."

Grace looked hard at the photograph of Brady with Sister Anne.

According to Jason Wade's article in today's *Mirror*, Anne Braxton was also orphaned as a teen and donated one million dollars to the order.

Were these factors at play here?

"How could this guy figure into your husband's business?" Grace asked

"I don't know."

"But before your husband started his landscaping business, he gambled." Grace said.

"Yes, I told you, he said he was a professional gambler. When we met in Las Vegas he was playing the tables."

"And before that?"

"I think he held quite a few jobs. He seemed to know a little about a lot of things."

"Rhonda, did he ever do time in jail or prison?"

"If he did, I'm not aware."

"And you never saw this kidnapper before?" Grace asked.

"No. I don't know who the hell he is."

"Not even in the neighborhood?" Perelli said. "Like, maybe he pretended to be lost, looking for directions?"

"No." Rhonda put her face her hands and shook her head. Then she froze. "Wait! *The park!*"

"What about it?"

"He said he met Brady in the park the other day."

"Met? Was that the word he used? It implies they spoke."

"Yes. Two, no, three days ago, Brady went to the park with his friends, Justin and Ryan."

"Which park?"

"The community-pool park. It's three blocks away."

"We need to talk to the boys now, they may remember something."

Rhonda pointed to her fridge and a list of numbers scrawled in Brady's hand.

Perelli snatched the sheet and started dialing, just as Cataldo called Grace to join her outside. Cataldo was working at a rear window and pointed a latex finger to fresh markings made by a hard-edged tool used to pry open its weak wooden frame.

"Looks like he gained entry here." Cataldo showed Grace the busted lock latch. "More important, look what he left."

Under the window, in the soil bed, a full foot impression.

"Looks like a DOC-issued tennis shoe. We're right behind this guy, Grace. We just need one piece of evidence to lock on to him. We're breathing down his neck."

Grace looked through the window and down the hall at Rhonda Boland.

"I pray we're not too late."

57

Across Seattle in Fremont, Jason Wade sat with his old man in a booth at Ivan's, searching for the right words.

"Dad, I'm sorry. I let you down. You've been wanting to talk and it's just been crazy with the nun story."

"It's all right."

"I've only got a couple of hours to spare today. My editor's been on me hard to break stories. I've been on this one for a solid week and I just got back from Canada chasing this stuff."

Jason spun around that morning's *Mirror*.

"I read them," Henry Wade said. "They're good stories. I know this is a busy time and I wish I could do more to help you. No need to apologize."

"But you sounded like it was bad, like you were at risk again."

"I'm not going to lie to you, it's bad."

"And this is all about your old demon, your partner's death. The old call."

His father's Adam's apple rose and fell as he looked to the street.

"That's right."

"Did you drink, Dad?"

His father's face creased and Jason saw more lines pressing into him from the weight of his struggle.

"Almost."

"You said you needed me to help you put an end to everything. What is it?"

Henry Wade rubbed his chin, thinking about that bottle in his pickup as he gazed to the street and back in time. "The call," Henry said, "it's about the old call Vern and I got on the armed robbery."

"I see."

"I told you how it went bad. How there was a hostage."

"The hostage was shot and the suspect pleaded guilty and was sent away."

"More coffee?" the waitress interrupted.

Henry waved her off.

"The whole world changed that day, Jay."

"I know, Dad, and it took a toll."

"It took a toll on Vern and it took a toll on me. Look what it cost me. Your mother, my job as a cop. I'm still paying for it."

Jason patted his father's hand.

"The other day, this kid, Quinn, he comes from out of nowhere and he starts exhuming the dead."

"Who's Quinn?"

"Hotshot insurance investigator, or loss-recovery agent. Something. He calls me up, he's pushing my buttons about the old case, acting like I know something. Then he's telling me that the monster's out of his cage and he's scheming. I know he's planning something."

"Who's out? Hold on, Dad, I don't understand. What's happening?"

"I can't live like this, Jay. It's eating me alive. I've got to put things to rest."

"Dad?"

"I've been carrying this rot inside me long enough. I'm going to see this guy and I need you to come with me. I have to see him now."

"What guy? And why do you need me? Dad, you're not making sense."

Henry Wade reached inside the chest pocket of his sportcoat and Jason saw the grip of his holstered gun before he unfolded a slip of paper.

"I need you to go with me to this address because I don't know what I'm going to do, how I'm going to react, because he's not dead. I'm going to get in his face with one question—just one question."

"Dad, what's this all about? Tell me what's going on."

"Jay, the hostage was a child."

"Jesus."

"A little boy."

"God."

"He died in my arms."

58

Ryan Taylor and Justin Marshall were scared.

Within minutes of Detective Dominic Perelli's call, the boys were standing in Rhonda Boland's kitchen.

"Where's Brady?" Justin said.

"It's all right fellas. We're working on that." Perelli said. "We need your help."

Ryan and Justin had been hurried to the house by their anxious mothers, Gayleen Taylor and Fanny Marshall, who had always pitied "poor Rhonda" behind her back. Such a tragic case. Widowed by a deadbeat who had the nerve to die in debt.

Gayleen and Fanny surveyed the activity, their fears mounting when they glimpsed Rhonda down the hall in the bedroom talking to two men in suits taking notes. Something worse, much worse, than a burglary had happened.

"What's going on?" Fanny asked.

"A police investigation. We need your sons to help us," Grace said.

"Help with what?" Gayleen asked.

"We need to speak to them privately about what they may have seen in the park the other day. We need to do it as quickly as possible."

"Why, what happened in the park? What does this concern?" Fanny said. "Why won't you tell us? You are going to frighten our boys. Where's Brady?"

Grace nodded to Officers Lloyd and Vossek.

"Mrs. Taylor, Mrs. Marshall," Lloyd said. "If you'd please come with us, we'll explain."

Grace and Perelli took the boys to the backyard, where they sat at a picnic table.

"Guys, you're not in trouble, okay? We need your help," Grace said. "This is extremely important. Do you remember going to the park with Brady the other day?"

"We go every day," Ryan said.

"Do you recall a time recently where Brady talked to anyone, like a stranger, or a man at the park?"

"A couple days ago, there was a guy, some stranger," Ryan said.

"Do you know him?"

Head shakes.

"What did he look like? Black guy, white guy? Tall? Fat? Tattoos?"

"White guy."

"Old? Young?"

"Maybe like him"—Justin pointed at Perelli—"only skinnier."

"And we saw him hanging around and stuff before," Ryan said.

"When before?"

"A couple of days ago, I guess."

"Something bad happened, didn't it?" Justin asked.

Grace glanced at Kay Cataldo working at the window.

"Guys, what was the stranger doing in the park?"

"Sitting on a bench, reading a newspaper," Justin said.

"And drinking coffee," Ryan said.

"Drinking coffee? Like in a take-out cup?"

"I think so."

"Want to go for a short ride in a detective car?" Grace said.

A few minutes later, they stood before the park bench where the stranger had sat.

The trash basket beside it was half-filled. Grace squatted, concentrating on the dates she saw on the discarded newspapers. The trash had not been emptied for several days.

"Guys, you said he was drinking coffee from a take-out cup."

"He was drinking from that one," Ryan said.

"Come closer, show me without touching."

Ryan pulled his face to the trash, pointing to the red, white, and blue take-out cup under the plastic take-out bag.

Perelli and Grace exchanged glances.

It was the only red, white, and blue take-out cup in the trash.

"Are you sure, Ryan?"

"Yes, I saw him crumple it before he left."

Grace was making notes.

"Did you see if he got into a car, or where he went?"

Justin and Ryan shook their heads.

"Can you remember, Ryan, was the man wearing gloves?"

"No gloves."

Dial tones sounded. Perelli had turned away to call Kay Cataldo to get to their location fast.

"Uhm," Justin said, "what happened to Brady?"

Grace looked at the boys.

"We're working on that."

Grace turned back to the cup, pulling it out carefully and holding it as if it were the Holy Grail.

"And this cup may give us the answer."

59

This is it, baby.

At her table in the Seattle Police Crime Scene Investigation Unit near the airport, Kay Cataldo examined the take-out coffee cup plucked from the trash in the park near Brady Boland's home.

She worked on it with near reverence because she knew, knew deep in her heart, that they had something. The cup was abundant with wonderfully clear latents.

Grace was bang-on. This was their Holy Grail.

It was the cup used by the Boland boy's kidnapper, who wore the shoes worn by Sister Anne's and Sharla May Forrest's killer. He'd left a nice size-11 impression under the Bolands' back window.

Thank you.

We are so on to you, you mother—

Cataldo had dusted and photographed the prints with an old reliable CU-5, before collecting them with lifting tape. She had a complete and crisp set of impressions from the right hand.

She studied the loops, whorls, and arches.

Very good.

Time was her enemy.

She worked quickly but with expert efficiency, beginning with the thumb, which in a standard ten-card is "number one." Carefully, she coded its characteristics before moving on to the other fingers. Then she scanned the prints and entered the information into her computer.

Now she could submit them to the automated fingerprint-identification systems, AFIS, for a quick search through massive local, state, and nationwide data banks for a match.

After typing commands on her keyboard, Cataldo finished the last of her bagel and orange juice while her computer processed her data for possible matches. In less than two minutes, it came back with two hits from the Seattle PD's local data bank.

Now we're getting somewhere.

It was a start, she thought, waiting for results from the Washington State Patrol Identification and Criminal History Section (WASIS) and a range of other criminal history database systems.

Her submission was searched through the regional information-sharing systems, like the western states network and the FBI's mother of all data banks, the IAFIS, which stored some seven hundred million impressions from law enforcement agencies across the country.

We're coming for you.

When it was done, her search had yielded a total of five possibles that closely matched her submission from the cup.

Immediately, she began making a visual point-by-point comparison between each of the three candidates and her unidentified set from the cup. She zeroed in on the critical minutiae points, like the trail of ridges near the tip of the number-three finger. Too many dissimilarities there.

So long, candidate number one.

For the next set, Cataldo blew up her sample to visually count the number of ridges on the number-two finger and soon saw distinct differences. That took care of number two.

Let's go to number three.

Cataldo's concentration intensified as she compared her submission with the computer's remaining suggested match. The branching of the ridges matched. All the minutiae points matched. Her pulse quickened as she began counting the points of comparison where the two samples matched.

Looking good.

Some courts required about a dozen clear point matches. She had fourteen and was still counting, knowing that one divergent point instantly eliminated a print. By the time she'd compared the left slanting patterns from the last finger, she had seventeen clear points of comparison.

Then she matched the scales of the prints and used her computer program to superimpose one over the other, the way one would trace a picture.

We have a winner.

Cataldo confirmed the identification number of her new subject, and submitted a query to several law enforcement data banks, including the FBI's National Crime Information Center and the Washington State Department of Corrections. By accessing the various criminal history systems she could verify parolee history, offender identification, arrest records, convictions, holds, and commitments for other law enforcement agencies.

In minutes, Cataldo's computer introduced her to the owner of the fingerprints on the take-out cup.

Gotcha.

The cold, hard eyes of a white man glared from her monitor, as if he were angry that she'd found him. She clicked to his central file summary and read quickly through his offences.

Second-degree murder.

Armed robbery.

A lifetime achiever. These were only the big-ticket items.

According to his ERD, his Earned Release Date, he was released months ago.

Cataldo clicked and the guy's story unfolded before her. Her head snapped back at what she'd read.

"Lord, that can't be!"

Cataldo seized her phone, punched a number.

"Homicide, Garner."

"Grace, it's Kay."

"You got him?"

"Leon Dean Sperbeck. Did twenty-five for second-degree during an armed robbery. Was released to community custody a few months ago."

"Got an address?"

"Grace, you won't believe this. His DOC file is closed. It's marked deceased."

60

Ten minutes after Cataldo locked on to Sperbeck, Grace was on the phone with his community corrections officer.

"Dead men don't leave fingerprints," Grace said. "I need an address."

"Sonofa— Hold on. Are you sure those are Sperbeck's prints on that cup?" Herb Kent, ten months from retirement, pulled a page from the file on his desk. "Because I'm looking at the report from the Rangers at Mount Rainier last month. Leon drowned himself in the Nisqually River."

"I know. But did they find his body?"

"I'm not sure. Sorry, I just came back from sick leave, had surgery to remove two toes." Kent paged through the file. "Nothing here says they found him yet. But I talked to Leon, maybe a week before he went there. He was despondent, like he said in his note."

"Do you have his note?"

"I have a copy in here. I'll fax it to you."

"Did Sperbeck ever talk about the Boland family or Sister Anne Braxton? Did they visit him inside?"

"Let me grab his visitor sheet." Kent sifted through the file. "What I know is that Leon was quiet, kept to himself and out of trouble. When he was assigned to me, his case didn't need a lot of monitoring."

Kent flipped through reports, applications, test results for Sperbeck.

"He served his full time and was no risk to reoffend. He had no family, or much of a support network. I helped him with his release plan, you know, contacting social service agencies, lining up job interviews. He had no violations and he got work as a janitor, but it didn't last and he took it hard. Some guys can't cope after being inside a long time. The world changes, they're stigmatized."

Damn it. Grace had had enough.

Sperbeck had fallen through the cracks. Violent felons were supposed to be tracked, even after release. Sperbeck had obviously staged his death. Those were his prints on the cup.

"Herb. Stop. Just give me Sperbeck's last known address now."

"Well, he had a couple. I'm still checking. He told me one place got flooded. The other was noisy."

"Herb."

"Here we go. This one in the northwest was his last. It's off Market."

Grace took it down.

"And, look here, the answer is, yes. Seems Sister Anne Braxton visited him several times at Washington State, then at Clallam Bay and Coyote Ridge."

"You can confirm that he had contact with her?"

"The file here says she was instrumental in helping Sperbeck with his Moral Reconation Therapy and as his spiritual counselor—hello?"

Grace hung up and alerted SWAT to roll on Sperbeck's residence.

* * *

The SWAT equipment truck and other emergency vehicles moved quickly to set up a command post in the parking lot of Wyslowleski's Funeral Home, about four blocks from Sperbeck's address.

The field commander, Lieutenant Jim Harlan, examined detailed maps and blueprints of the small house where Sperbeck rented a room at the rear. Harlan then briefed SWAT and the Hostage Negotiations Team on the objective: Seal the area, choke off all traffic, evacuate all citizens in the line of fire by stealth. Get a visual on the suspect and the hostage, then determine if a blitz entry was viable.

Police set up an outer perimeter well outside the hot zone and began diverting traffic, while cops dressed in work clothes eased a city utility van to a door down from Sperbeck's building to confirm any movement in his apartment.

Other plainclothes officers quickly and quietly evacuated every resident from the line of fire near the building while SWAT members set up an inner perimeter by keeping out of sight near the house. No one was home in the front section. Then Sergeant Mike Brigger led his SWAT team scouts closer to the building. They would determine safety points for other team members to follow and launch a rescue.

As they waited at the command post, Grace and Perelli studied Sperbeck's old crime, trying to piece everything together. A child hostage was killed in a $3.3 million heist. None of the money had ever surfaced. How did it all fit with the Bolands, Sister Anne, and Sharla May Forrest?

And Henry Wade was one of the responding officers. Jason Wade's old man.

While Perelli worked the phone, Grace went over it again and again.

Nothing made sense.

"Hey, Grace." Perelli finished a call and pulled her out of earshot. "Records says that around the time Sperbeck was released, an investigator for the insurance company that paid out on the claim made some enquiries on the old case. Guy by the name of Ethan Quinn wanted to locate the officers on call that day."

"Maybe this Quinn has new information?"

A crackling radio interjected.

"We have movement in the subject's residence."

Tension tightened the air.

The SWAT team scouts had been followed by the utility man, the breacher, the gas team, and sharpshooters, who moved tight up to the building. At the edge of the inner perimeter, SWAT snipers had taken cover to line up on the house.

A window at the rear of Sperbeck's building came into focus within the crosshairs of the rifle scope of the sharpshooter behind the Dumpster of a welder's shop nearby.

"Movement in the house. White male," the sharpshooter repeated.

Uniformed police at the outer perimeter called in on another channel.

"We got press at the east point. WKKR."

Harlan cursed under his breath.

"Cut his utilities and phone. We can't risk him monitoring news reports."

Harlan was in charge. He had seconds to make a decision that could save a life, or cost him one. This is what he knew: The suspect resided here. The suspect had abducted a child, was violent, and wanted in two first-degree homicides. The suspect was an ex-convict who'd served time for killing a child hostage during an armed robbery.

Negotiation was not an option.

Swift attack.

"Mike, you good to go?"

"We're in position."

"Then go throw chemicals, flash-bangs, go full bore, take him down and extract the hostage."

Brigger signaled his team and some thirty seconds later the quiet street echoed with the *ker-plink* of shattering glass as tear gas canisters catapulted into every window. A thirty-pound steel battering ram took down the door accompanied by the *crack-crack* and blinding flashes of stun grenades. The heavily armed squad in gas masks stormed the apartment.

Flashlight beams and red-line laser sights probed thick smoke for Brady Boland and Leon Dean Sperbeck.

61

At that moment, miles across the city near Seattle's southern limit, Jason Wade and his old man rolled through an urban nightmare.

It was at the fringe of Rat City in a zone still infested with rundown scuz bars and porn shops, a stumble and stagger away to the heartbreak of worn Second World War houses that stood like the ghosts of broken promises.

"Dad, who is this guy that you need to see?"

"Leon Dean Sperbeck."

"Sperbeck took the hostage, the boy who died in your arms?"

"He got out of prison a few months ago and about six weeks back he left a suicide note on a tree near the Nisqually River in Mount Rainier National Park."

"Suicide? So, what are we doing here?"

"Unfinished business." His old man pulled Sperbeck's bank security photo from the file on the front seat of his pickup. "Used an alias to cash a welfare check a couple of days ago. He look dead to you? Sperbeck's up to something, and I've been waiting for twenty-five years to put this all to rest."

Jason stared at Sperbeck, growing increasingly uneasy with the situation and his old man's icy resolve.

Henry Wade stopped his truck near a wheel-less eviscerated Pinto mounted on cinder blocks in front of a duplex with a warped frame, blistered paint, fractured windows, and a roof that was missing shingles.

"Let's go. Sperbeck has the dump on the right."

They knocked on the door, unable to ignore the baseball bat–sized splintered gouge rising from the bottom, as if someone in a fit of rage had taken an ax to it.

"He ain't home," came a voice.

They turned to see the speaker climb from under the Pinto. White guy, midthirties. Beer gut straining his filthy jeans and torn Sonics T-shirt. His grease-coated hands held a bouquet of tools and a small part.

"He rents from me and my mom and he owes us."

"When did you see him last?" Henry Wade walked toward him.

"Couple days ago. I think I heard him come in late last night. Mighta had a girl. But he took off this morning. Looked like he was taking a trip."

Henry showed Sperbeck's picture to the mechanic who took a moment to study it.

"That's him."

"Any idea where he was going?"

"I couldn't say. Likely camping, from what I could see, he put sleeping bags and a couple Seven-Eleven sacks of food into that hunk of junk Chrysler Concorde he's been driving."

"You know the plate?"

"No."

"The year or color?

"Dark blue. Ninety-five. Are you guys cops? Got any ID?"

"No, we're not cops. We have business with Mr. Sperbeck."

"Sperbeck? He told us his name was Kirk Stewart. Does he owe you money, too?"

"Something like that."

"Hey, want to buy this starter? Ten bucks," the mechanic's smile exposed brown teeth.

Henry shook his head, reached into his wallet, and held up a fifty-dollar bill.

"This, for some time alone in his place to look around."

Jason shot his father a look of disbelief.

The mechanic eyed the bill, giving it his full consideration. His mom was at the clinic. He knew where she kept the key. They could have take-out chicken and cold imported beer tonight. Hell, he could almost taste it.

"Fifteen minutes and you don't take, break, or tell."

"Of course."

The mechanic went for the key and they waited at Sperbeck's door.

"Dad, I don't have a good feeling about this. Are you sure you know what you're getting into?"

"Do not doubt it for a second, son."

The mechanic came back with the key, slid it into the lock, opened the door a crack, and stopped. "I go in with you, or it's no deal."

"Fine."

His open palm waited until Henry covered it with the fifty.

Inside they were met with air reeking of alcohol, cigarettes, body odor, and dog.

"Is there a dog in here?" Jason asked.

"Naw. Mom's got a no-pet policy on account of the last mental case that lived here let his pit bull piss on the floor. We're going to repaint, redo the place like on those home improvement shows."

The duplex was cramped, with a small living room,

kitchen, a bathroom, and two small bedrooms. The chipped coffee table was covered with porn magazines, newspapers, maps, empty beer cans, and take-out containers.

Henry Wade went to the kitchen counter and shuffled through letters and bills, copying down information, then checked the bedroom. More porn, beer cans, and crap on the nightstand. Nothing that drew his interest, except for one thing.

"You got another seven minutes." The mechanic scratched himself.

At the coffee table, Jason noticed how parts of his stories on Sister Anne's murder had been circled with a red ballpoint pen. *What's up with that?* he wondered.

His father came out of the bedroom with a neatly folded page from the travel section of the *Seattle Post-Intelligencer*. He showed it to Jason.

A feature on Wolf Tooth Creek.

"Looks like he'd been giving this a lot of thought," his dad said, then went to the trash can in the kitchen and examined its contents. Atop the beer cans, junk food wrappers, cigarette packs, he focused on a yellow paper ball. It was a page ripped from a phone book and balled up.

Henry flattened it on the counter. It concerned businesses. Cottage and cabin rentals. One was underlined in ink. Wolf Tooth Creek Cabins's display ad put its location near the Mount Rainier National Park Area.

"You said you saw Sperbeck leave this morning with sleeping bags and groceries, like he was going camping?" Henry asked.

"Yup." The mechanic was holding the door open. "Time's up."

"Thanks."

When they got back into the truck, Henry turned the ignition.

"I think he went to Wolf Tooth Creek. That's where we're going."

"Dad, I have to get to work soon. I can't be away from the city."

"It's only an hour to get there and its early. Call in. Say you'll be late."

"How about we go later, after my shift?"

"I've been thinking about it for twenty-five goddam years, Jay. We're going now."

"Dad, what's going on?"

"Sperbeck does not get to walk out of prison, start a new life, and leave me behind in hell. Today, I'm going to bury all my shit with that fucker!"

"Jesus, Dad!"

Jason grabbed the armrest and the dash as the pickup growled and Henry Wade's tires squealed until they raised smoke from the pavement.

62

At the takedown off Market, the SWAT team rushed from the aftermath with a suspect.

A white male, early twenties, about five-ten, 175 pounds, faded jeans, AC/DC T-shirt. Clean-cut, doubled over vomiting and coughing from the tear gas. His hands were handcuffed in front of him. Somebody spritzed water in his irritated eyes.

"Where's the boy?" A SWAT cop shouted under his Darth Vader gas mask.

"What boy? What's going on!" he coughed, spit, tears streamed down his inflamed face.

Inside, SWAT members searched the living room, the bathroom, the bedrooms, kitchen, halls, closets. They tapped the ceilings, walls, floors for body mass. No immediate sign of another person. After clearing the residence, crime-scene people went in while detectives dealt with the suspect.

"What's your name, sir?" Grace Garner asked.

"Darrell Stanton. What's this?"

Grace examined the contents of his wallet.

"I'm a student at the University of Washington. I'm from Canberra, Australia. My passport's in my desk. Shit! My eyes are burning!"

Perelli dispatched a SWAT member to get the passport.

Stanton was spritzed again, handed a towel to pat his face, then Leon Sperbeck's photo was held in front of him.

"Do you know this man?" Grace said.

"Albert Crawley." Stanton coughed then looked. "He used to live here."

"Where is he?"

"How the hell should I know?" Stanton coughed. "Haven't seen him for weeks ever since I sold him my car. The bastard owes me money. Shit, my eyes!"

A uniformed officer spritzed Stanton.

"He leave a forwarding address?"

"No, he's an asshole."

"Describe the car you sold to him."

"A 1995 blue Chrysler Concorde. I told him it's got problems and let him have it cheap. He owes me six hundred bucks. Is he the guy you want?"

Perelli had his cell phone pressed to his ear when he held up Stanton's passport, nodding to Garner, Harlan, and Boulder.

"Stanton checks out. He's not in the system," Perelli said.

As Boulder stepped away to take a call, Detective Gilbert Bailey took Grace aside. "Just talked to the guys at the Boland home with the mother."

"Any more calls from Sperbeck, any demands?"

"Nothing. She's going through hell," Bailey said. "The FBI and KCSO said the two other addresses DOC had for Sperbeck are washouts."

"Sperbeck's likely aliased up the wazoo, Gib. Can you

help us prepare an alert to blast out ASAP, the vehicle and photos of Sperbeck and Brady."

After Boulder finished his call, he pulled Grace and Perelli from Stanton for a private moment.

"We've got press. The national networks are threatening to go live. And we've got word from the Command Post that Ethan Quinn's arrived. They're bringing him up now." Boulder indicated the marked car roaring toward them.

Ethan Quinn got out carrying a briefcase. Grace, Perelli, and Boulder walked him down the street to talk quietly.

"You're investigating Sperbeck's original crime?" Grace said.

"Yes, the robbery-homicide. My client is the insurance firm that paid out."

"Why are you investigating after all these years?"

"The stolen money never surfaced. We had most of the serial numbers. We suspect the cash is still out there, largely intact."

"Exactly what do you know, or suspect?" Perelli said.

"I don't want to jeopardize my investigation."

"This is *our* investigation, Slick," Perelli said. "If you think you're going to collect some sort of finder's fee on this, think again." Perelli jabbed a finger into Quinn's chest. "If you possess material information relating to this child's kidnapping and two homicides, you'd be wise to cooperate right now. So let me ask you again, what do you know?"

Quinn surveyed their faces.

"There were a lot of cops there the day it went down and the money vanished," he said. "It's unusual that Sperbeck, the only person convicted, never named the others involved. Most of the players are dead, including the ex-cops who owned the armored-car company.

"Several units responded to the heist and it's my belief that, whether it was planned, or a reaction to the child's death, maybe officers took the $3.3 million, and covered up the shooting of the little boy. You may recall that the autopsy and ballistics reports were inconclusive on the shooting victim.

"I think Sperbeck worked a deal, pleaded guilty, avoided the death penalty, and expected to be rewarded with his cut in exchange for his silence and his time. Maybe they tucked it away in some interest-bearing offshore account."

"It's an insulting theory," Perelli said. "And it doesn't fit because there are other pieces at play here."

"What pieces?"

"Nice try. Fuck you."

Grace looked hard at Quinn. "What else do you have to support your theory?"

"Henry Wade was one of the many responding officers."

"With Vern Pearce, his partner," Boulder said.

"Henry Wade is now the only surviving officer."

"Henry quit the job and crawled into a bottle after Vern shot himself," Boulder said. "Not many people talk about it. A few old bulls say it was the case, the boy getting shot, all that crap."

"Wade's a private detective now, working for Don Krofton," Quinn said. "You guys should check to see if Krofton was at the scene that day."

"I think you've watched one too many bad movies, Ethan," Perelli said.

Quinn shrugged and opened his briefcase.

"Not long after Sperbeck's release from prison, he staged his own death. Then Henry Wade just happens to follow the 'dead man' to a bank where Sperbeck had some sort of transaction. It's all here. I was surveilling Wade."

Quinn held up a disk from his video recorder.

"Don't you move." Boulder waved a uniform over to keep Quinn company while he took his detectives for a short walk.

"What do you make of Quinn's shit, Grace?" Boulder said.

"There's a lot at play here. Look at the facts. Sperbeck's our guy for Sister Anne, Sharla May Forrest, and Brady. And Sister Anne visited Sperbeck in prison."

"But some twenty-five years ago," Perelli said, "after the robbery, she enters the convent, with over a million. It has to be a link. And her real identity is not what she claimed, according to the *Mirror*. Maybe she was holding the money for Sperbeck."

"But somehow, Sperbeck thinks Rhonda Boland's husband owes him," Boulder said. "This doesn't make sense."

"The pieces are there. They just don't line up yet," Grace said. "Like why did Sperbeck kill Sharla May?"

"That one seems obvious," Boulder said.

"Right," Perelli said. "It was around the time of his release. Remember, Roberto Martell pimps her date with Sperbeck at the Black Jet Bar. Leon likely couldn't get it up, so he took it out on Sharla May. When I worked vice the ex-cons always had problems with hookers because prison messed them up."

"That seems the most likely scenario for Sperbeck doing Sharla May," Boulder said.

"Okay," Grace said. "That brings us back to Quinn's crazy theory on Sperbeck and corrupt cops being involved in the heist."

"I think we have to ask Henry Wade some questions." Boulder looked at his watch. "First we gotta move fast to get that alert out and hold a news conference. We'll do it right here."

Grace nodded and walked away to be alone as she thought of Brady Boland and her two homicides. This was so damn complicated. Nothing made sense.

Everything was at stake.

Was Jason's father caught up in this?

63

The snow-crowned peak of Mount Rainier rose before them from the Cascade range. They were somewhere between Elbe and Ashford, eastbound on 706.

After leaving Seattle, they didn't speak. Jason's old man listened to those sorrowful Johnny Cash ballads and stared at the lush forests rolling by.

As if the truth were out there and he was in desperate pursuit.

Jason feared his father was driving headlong toward a mental breakdown, like the time he showed up drunk in the *Mirror* newsroom. Man, he had to do something, anything to avoid it.

His old man was carrying a gun now.

"Dad, you've got to talk to me! Tell me what's going on!"

His father adjusted his grip on the wheel. His jaw tensed but he refused to answer.

"Dad, tell me the truth about you and Leon Sperbeck."

"Reach under your seat."

Jason's hand felt around, finding the paper bag and

the glass-hard problem inside as he produced the unopened bottle of whiskey.

"Give it to me."

"Dad, no."

"Give me the damn bottle."

The liquid swished as he handed it to him. His father
opened his window and threw the bottle away. Jason
heard it smash into the ditch behind them.

"I'm doing this sober," he said. "Vern and I get to the
call and we come on Sperbeck. Dead cold. Fleeing with
a gun in his hand. This thing all goes down in seconds.
Seconds. But it feels like slow motion because my
heart's going like a jackhammer.

"Sperbeck's cornered. We've got him. We draw down
on him, order him to drop his weapon, get on the
ground. Out of nowhere, this boy steps from a store
looking for his mom. Sperbeck locks his arm around
the kid's neck, drilling his gun into the kid's head.

"He's eight years old and he's looking at me. Scared
out of his mind. Vern's shouting tactics at me. There's
no time to do anything, we're spreading out, edging
closer, one of us is going to get a shot at Sperbeck.

"We're screaming at him to drop his gun, let the kid
go. But Sperbeck's scared, he knows he's going down
and he's going to take all of us with him. I could see the
boy's eyes. He's staring at me, they're wild, like someone who's fallen from a cliff.

"Vern's closing in on the left, I'm closing in on the
right. Sperbeck's sweeping the boy back and forth but
he knows he's exposed on one side and we're going to
take him.

"That's when we hear sirens. Backup is coming fast.
Time's up.

"Sperbeck makes his move and it happens, he swings
to one side, taking a shot at Vern. Vern finds cover but

Sperbeck pins him, fires again, missing Vern both times, but somehow the kid has broken free.

"The boy's eyes are huge as he runs directly to me. Over the kid's shoulder and down my sight, I've got a bead on Sperbeck and see him take aim toward me and the kid who's between us.

"The boy's large in front of me running at me and I'm screaming for him to get on the ground, waving him down as I see Sperbeck's trigger finger pulling.

"I fire.

"It's loud, there's muzzle flash and smoke, so I don't see until it clears and the boy's on the ground. Bleeding. My gut convulses, Vern jumps Sperbeck, cuffs him, and I go to the boy.

"The kid's eyes were wide and he was searching mine. His jaw started to move and he made these soft breathing sounds as the sirens got louder and I held him. He was warm but so still. I held him until everything drained from him and the paramedics came and I'm on the ground holding him and his warm blood is all over me and Vern is shouting and the paramedics are shouting and the sirens, the damn sirens, are wailing and somebody started screaming.

"The boy's mother, who got separated from him in the department store, is shrieking and punching me. Later they told me that I wouldn't give the kid up, that I wouldn't let him go, and it was true because I knew that if I held on to him then he wouldn't leave this earth, he'd still be alive to grow up and live a good life and I wouldn't have to spend the rest of mine knowing that I'd killed him."

His old man swallowed.

"I still see his face. I've always seen his face because I've never been able to forgive myself."

Jason turned away as his father exhaled slowly.

A few miles later, they saw a sign pointing the way to Wolf Tooth Creek, and they turned off 706 and into the backcountry.

"What happened afterward, Dad?"

"Vern swore I missed and that Sperbeck had actually fired at the same time. That Sperbeck killed the kid while trying to shoot me. The court gave weight to Vern's statement."

"What about the autopsy, ballistics, witnesses?"

"The few witnesses gave conflicting accounts. Ballistics was inconclusive. Sperbeck had just come from around the corner where he was involved in the shoot-out that injured the armored-car guards."

"And the autopsy?"

"It said the boy died from a single gunshot. The bullet tore clear through him but the medical examiner couldn't conclude, beyond doubt, the direction, because the child actually had been turning and spun when he was struck, it had entered his side."

"Did they recover the bullet?"

"No, but the ME said the caliber was similar to what was issued to us at the time and Sperbeck was using the same type of weapon."

"Sperbeck could've walked on the boy."

"No. While the judge said it was inconclusive as to who shot the boy, he said Sperbeck's crime contributed to the child's death. And we had Sperbeck on everything else, although his lawyer implied that police were covering up a botched investigation. There was no jury trial. Sperbeck admitted guilt to everything but killing the child. It was understandable because he could've faced the death penalty. In the end, the judge gave him twenty-five years."

"Dad, I don't know what to say."

"There's nothing to say. I need to find Sperbeck. I've

been tormented by that day for too long. I think I'm owed the truth. We're going to stop up ahead."

Jason's dad stopped his pickup at the pumps of Wolf Tooth Gas and Grocery. The station was a log cabin, built of hand-hewn cedar logs with cedar shingles. It had a snack counter, gift shop, and small two-bay garage.

While his dad started filling the truck, Jason got out and gazed toward the mountain.

After all these years, his father had at last told him about his past.

It was good that he did it, but man . . .

The boy, then his partner.

And now Sperbeck.

Jason thought his old man's pathological pursuit of Sperbeck could end up doing him more harm than good. Maybe he should try to convince him to turn around, go home, and take things one step at a time. Maybe see a shrink again.

"Want anything from the store, Dad?"

"No, I'll meet you there. I want to check the oil."

Walking toward the store, Jason felt his cell phone in his pocket and decided to check for messages. Aside from his dad's bombshell, he was uneasy that he'd been out of touch this morning. Surprisingly, it indicated a strong signal.

What was this?

Six missed calls from this morning. Two from Eldon Reep, one from Cassie Appleton, and three from Grace Garner.

What the hell happened? He must've lost his signal somewhere along the way. Damn it. As he entered the store, Jason called Garner.

"Homicide. Garner."

"Grace, it's Wade. What's up?"

"Where the hell are you?"

64

"We've got a child abduction tied to the nun's murder!" Grace Garner said.

"Jesus!"

Jason drew stares from the counter from an unshaven barrel-chested man in a lumberjack's shirt reading a paper behind the register. Beside the man, a girl, who looked about twelve, turned from watching the TV on the shelf, near the mounted head of a Rocky Mountain Elk with a twelve-point rack.

"Jason, the kidnapping suspect may have a link to your father," Grace said.

"What?" Keeping his voice low, he went deeper into the store, behind shelves with canned beans, soup, chili. "My father? How?"

"From your dad's time as a cop. He responded to an armored-car heist. A child died in a hostage taking. Three point three million was never recov—"

"Oh my God."

"We're looking for Leon Dean Sperbeck, who did twenty-five years"—Jason saw his dad paying the lumberjack guy at the cash—"We believe Sperbeck's responsible for Sister Anne's death. I'm going out on a limb telling you, but we're facing a life-and-death situation. The abduction could all be tied to the money from the old heist, your information, Sister Anne, and your dad."

"What the hell? I don't believe this."

"After Sperbeck was released, he staged his death and now he's looking for the money. An insurance investigator reviewing the case has implicated your father, alleging a cover-up of the facts of the crime to hide the cash. He says he's got evidence your father's recently been in contact with Sperbeck—Jason—?"

As Grace continued, the pieces began aligning.

Except one didn't fit. Christ, it couldn't fit.

"—has implicated your father, alleging a cover-up to hide the cash—"

At the counter, his old man was showing Sperbeck's photo to the lumberjack man and the girl.

Cripes! The man and the girl started nodding.

"—Jason, where's your father? We need to talk to him."

"Grace, we might know where Sperbeck is."

"Where? He's threatening to kill that little boy. Tell me, where you are!"

"Wolf Tooth Creek at a gas station off 706. I think he's driving a 95 Chrysler Concorde. Blue."

"That's right! Do you see him?"

"No. I've got to go."

"Wait! Jason!"

"That's him," the girl pointed to the TV. "The man in your picture was here!"

The show had been interrupted with a burst-tone alert, three shrill beeps, then the message, followed by pictures of Brady Boland, aged twelve, and Leon Dean Sperbeck, wanted for two homicides. More information about Brady's need of medication and Sperbeck's car crawled across the bottom of the screen.

"That's him. I swear!" Lumberjack man said. "They left not two minutes before you. Sat here for the longest time waiting on a fan belt from McKenna. Todd told him it wouldn't hold. That he'd have to creep along because his Chrysler's in sorry shape."

"Did you see a boy with him?"

"No, but he had a lot of junk heaped in the back. Kid could've been in there sleeping."

"Which way did he go?" Jason's dad asked.

"Same way you was headed. To the cabins. Turn left after the bridge and go ten miles down Cougar Ridge, the old dirt logging road." Lumberjack man reached for his phone. "I'm calling Pierce County Sheriff's deputies. There must be a reward."

Trees blurred by Jason and his dad as the needle on the Ford Ranger pickup reached ninety-five on the speedometer. Stones popcorned under the truck as it chewed up Cougar Ridge, leaving dust clouds in its wake.

"What did you find out on your call, son?"

Jason was driving and shot his old man a glance.

"Grace Garner says the insurance investigator suspects that you were actually involved in the robbery; that there was some kind of cover-up linked to the money."

His father stared straight ahead. In the distance he saw a fading dust curtain.

"We're gaining on him. Push it harder. She'll take it."

"Damn it, Dad! What really happened that day?"

"Quinn's a smart-ass punk who doesn't know shit!"

"Did a cop kill that boy? Did Vern? Was there some sort of cover-up? Does Sperbeck know the truth?"

"Christ, look at my fucking life! Look at what happened to me, Jason!"

They both caught the chrome glint of a rear bumper half-concealed like a phantom in the dust ahead. The vehicle was dark blue.

"Hang on!"

Jason accelerated, the Ford roared along the narrow route, bobbing on its sudden hills and valleys, sunlight flashing through the thick woods, branches slapping the body as stones boiled against its undercarriage. Jason's ears pounded with each curve as they gained on the car.

"It's him!" his old man said. "It's a Chrylser Concorde."

They saw Sperbeck behind the wheel, then Jason's skin prickled when a small head surfaced from the backseat. They were suddenly looking into the frightened face of Brady Boland.

Henry Wade sucked in a deep breath before sliding a full magazine into his Glock.

"Jesus!" Jason said.

In the Concorde, Sperbeck shook his head and continued ranting about his twenty-five hard years of regret.

"—Hey pup, your old man was a first-class fool to bring his girlfriend in on the job. She was never right for it. I told him, but he wouldn't listen. She fucked us good. It was not supposed to happen the way it did. Then the bitch wants me to 'see the light' after she tries to buy her way to heaven with my fucking money! Bitch. I sent her to hell where she belongs."

Sperbeck snorted and spit out the window.

"You better hope your mom's smarter than that dead bitch cause I got a special place picked out for you. Your mom ain't ever going to see you again if she doesn't find where your daddy hid my money!"

Sperbeck turned his head to glance at Brady and met a ghost.

Henry Wade glared at him from two car lengths back—pointing at him to pull over.

"What the—! Goddamnit!" Sperbeck slammed his fists against the steering wheel. "God-fucking-damnit!"

Sperbeck smashed his foot on the gas pedal and the Chrylser rocketed ahead. The pickup was in better shape and stayed close, ahead of the dust the car was kicking up. The Concorde grabbed air over the next rise, coming down hard and heavy, scraping the oil pan, sliding and grinding on loose gravel.

"Shit!"

A bang sounded under the hood as the fan belt snapped. The steering wheel shuffled through Sperbeck's hands and he struggled in vain for control before the Concorde slid down an embankment, rolling over small trees in a storm of stones, dust, and crumpling metal.

It came to rest on its side against a stand of cedar and pine.

Brady had a small cut on his head but was okay, cushioned by the sleeping bags and clutter in the back. Crawling out of the wreck, he saw a pair of shoes, then Sperbeck seized his arm, hoisted him to his feet, pulling him as they ran, crashing against branches and trees.

"Come on!"

Brady glanced behind them at the two figures gaining on them, then back at Sperbeck, who yanked on his arm. Brady saw the gun in his hand and struggled. They splashed across a creek, the cold water reaching up to Brady's thighs.

They scrambled up the meadow, up a hill toward a clearing.

Brady's legs ached. His ears roared from the blood rush.

The men were getting closer.

Cresting a hill, they'd come to a cliff and a dead drop of some two hundred feet. Sperbeck turned. The men were thirty yards away.

Sperbeck had nowhere to go.

He pulled Brady closer to him, edging back to within ten feet of the cliff.

The men were twenty yards away and separating. One going left. One going right.

Sperbeck used Brady as a shield and placed his gun to the boy's head.

"You're going to give me your keys and let me walk out of here."

Henry Wade leveled his Glock at Sperbeck.

"It's over, Leon. Put your gun down and release the boy."

"I'm taking this pup to hell with me to meet his old man and his girlfriend!"

They could hear the distant thud of a helicopter.

"It's over."

"It's not over! The bitch nun stole from me! She knew this pup's father was holding the rest of my money. I FUCKING WANT IT! I paid for it with twenty-five years of my life!"

"We all paid!" Henry inched closer, lifted his safety, his gun never wavering from Sperbeck's head. "We all paid for what happened that day!"

Henry met Brady's eyes, wild with fear, his heart thumping in time with the distant chopper. Brady struggled against Sperbeck, only to feel his hold tighten into a crushing death grip, forcing Brady to freeze in order to breathe.

"Leon, let him go! Don't make the same mistake again!"

"I'm not going back to prison! I'm not going back into my coffin!"

Jason rolled two rocks at Sperbeck's gun side, distracting him as Brady suddenly squirmed free, scrambled two, three, five, seven steps. Henry Wade, in the stance, waved him to the ground, Brady dove, hitting the ground hard.

Two shots split the air.

Sperbeck spun, stumbled back, collapsed at the cliff, slid over completely. He screamed as he stopped himself at the final moment with one hand gripping a sharp edge of rock as his gun tumbled two hundred feet to the bottom.

The rock was cutting into him, blood webbed down his arm.

"Help me!"

A shadow blocked the sun above him.

"Who shot the boy that day, Leon?"

"Please."

"Who shot the boy?"

"You—"

"I want the truth."

"You, you missed. It was me."

"I want the truth!"

"It's true! They were going to execute me!"

"Jay, help me get him up!"

Henry Wade got on his knees, gripped Sperbeck's arm, and reached for his shoulder. Suddenly, Sperbeck looked into the sun.

"No, I can't go back! I can't! Let me go!"

With his free hand Sperbeck pulled out his knife and slashed at their hands. They fended him off, while struggling to pull him up, but he drove his feet against the rock. Their grip grew slippery as blood gushed from their wounds.

"Let me go!"

Sperbeck continued stabbing at them until he broke free.

As he fell he extended his arms, plummeting fifty,

seventy, one hundred feet before his body dropped into the yawning mouth of a jagged open crack. As he plunged deeper into its narrowing darkness, sharp rock walls peeled off his clothes and skin, transforming him into a lifeless, bleeding mass entombed in granite.

A perfect grave.

Henry looked into the black hole that had swallowed his demon.

Then he turned to Brady, who was standing in the light. The boy had started to cry. Henry held him as the helicopter approached. Bloodied and exhausted, Henry felt Jason's arm around his shoulder.

"I heard what he said, Dad. It's over. It's all over."

Henry nodded and pulled them both tighter.

65

In the days that followed, Rhonda and Brady Boland were questioned.

They were investigated by Grace Garner, Dominic Perelli, FBI agents, and lawyers from the King County Prosecuting Attorney's Office, the U.S. Attorney's Office, and detectives from several other agencies.

The case had so many emerging complexities no one was quick to sign off.

After interviews and analysis of the new evidence on the histories of Jack Boland, Leon Sperbeck, and Anne Braxton, investigators concluded that Rhonda Boland had zero involvement with the original heist and its outcome.

Rhonda Boland was never aware of the stolen money, nor did she gain from it. In fact, she and her son were victimized because of it.

These were the new facts: Some twenty-five years ago in Seattle, Washington, Russell Scott Schallert, of Newark, New Jersey, alias Jack Boland, his girlfriend, Chantal Louise Segretti, of Montreal, Canada, and Leon Dean

Sperbeck, of Wichita, Kansas, while disguised with ski masks, committed the armed robbery of $3.3 million from an armored car operated by a small subsidiary of U.S. Forged Armored Inc.

After shooting and wounding the armored-car guards, the suspects separated and fled. Schallert and Segretti absconded with the cash. Seattle police officers Vernon Pearce and Henry Wade, among the first to respond, encountered Sperbeck, who took a hostage, Timothy Robert Hope, aged eight, of Seattle, Washington.

Sperbeck fired upon Pearce, then at Wade, who returned fire. Hope was killed in the crossfire by Sperbeck.

After Sperbeck's arrest and trial, he refused to identify his accomplices and avoided the death penalty by admitting that his actions contributed to Hope's death. No evidence emerged to identify the other suspects and none of the stolen cash was located, until now.

During an interview with Brady, Grace Garner twigged on something he'd said about his father always digging deep to add nutrients.

"Did you ever see what was in those plastic-wrapped bricks?"

"No. He had them wrapped pretty good."

Upon further study of the old landscaping records, Brady was able to lead police to a dozen locations of former clients where, after securing warrants, they unearthed scores of plastic-wrapped bricks. The bricks were bundles of cash. Serial numbers confirmed they were from the old heist.

The total: $894,380.

Since the story broke with Sister Anne's murder, it never moved from the front page of Seattle's big dailies.

And the *Seattle Mirror* owned it.

Jason Wade scored exclusive after exclusive and the

paper's circulation climbed. In the wake of Sperbeck's death, it remained Seattle's lead story for weeks. It led to others.

After reading about Rhonda and Brady Boland's hard life, a lawyer, a single mom herself, from a high-powered firm stepped forward to represent her and Brady pro bono. She made convincing closed-door arguments to several parties that Rhonda and Brady had a strong case for civil action.

Without assigning blame, it was agreed that authorities should have been suspicious of Sperbeck's activities upon his release. It was also agreed that information provided by Rhonda and Brady Boland was critical to closing the case. Therefore, they qualified for the standing reward which amounted to a percentage of the recovered funds.

"Rhonda and Brady Boland almost lost their lives helping clear this case," the lawyer said.

American Eagle Federated Insurance, in cooperation with state and federal officials, provided Rhonda Boland with $250,000; in addition, the insurance company agreed to provide the Bolands with full medical coverage for life.

Brady underwent the risky surgery to remove his tumor. The operation was successful, and before long he was back at the park playing basketball with Justin and Ryan.

Ethan Quinn received a per diem and $25,000.

Henry Wade was offered $75,000 and requested it be used to establish a scholarship in the name of Timothy Hope.

For the sisters with the Order of the Compassionate Heart of Mercy, the revelation of Sister Anne's past compounded their anguish over their loss, but ultimately they found meaning in it all.

This is what happened.

After the revelation of Sister Anne's involvement in the old heist became national news, Sister Vivian Lansing flew back to Seattle from the Mother House in Chicago, uncertain of what would transpire.

Sister Denise admitted to giving Sister Anne's diary to the press. Vivian did not reprimand her, for she herself had had a change of heart. In the end the information helped save lives by resolving a violent situation. "I regret that you did not discuss it with me, but I'm sure God was guiding your heart and it ultimately led to a greater good."

Sister Anne's story became news in Europe, with French and Swiss authorities debating the prickly issue of what steps to take on Sister Anne's "donation" of $1.5 million to the Order. Did it not arise from a crime?

The victims, the American armored-car company and its insurer, both indicated to European investigators that they would write off the amount as unrecoverable. And given that all those involved in the crime were deceased, no further action would be taken.

The Vatican weighed in.

Rome not only insisted on offering to repay the $1.5 million, but issued a strong indication that it was considering the posthumous excommunication of Sister Anne Braxton, also known as the criminal Chantal Louise Segretti.

That twist in the story was carried on news wires around the world and gave rise to protests that arose among the very street people that Sister Anne had comforted at the Compassionate Heart of Mercy Shelter, at the fringe of Seattle's Pioneer Square District.

Their opposition found support in cities across the

United States and around the world when an online editorial compared Chantal Louise Segretti's case to the story of The Good Thief, who acknowledged his crimes but asked Christ to remember him for good on Judgment Day.

At this time, Jason Wade received a call from Pincher Creek, Alberta. Sister Marie had located a series of letters Sister Anne had written to be opened in the event of her death. She faxed them to the *Mirror* for Jason to print.

> *I could never confess to another human being the horrible things I did. As a young, confused woman I succumbed to drugs and joined a group of lost souls rushing down a road to damnation that culminated with the death of an innocent child.*
>
> *I wanted to end my own life, but realized that was a sinful, selfish act that would achieve nothing. I wanted to surrender, but I did not believe that it was the answer for me. I begged God to help me and after months of torture, while I was praying alone in a tiny church in Paris, He called me.*
>
> *I decided then that I was a failure, unworthy of forgiveness, but I would use every remaining breath of my sinful life to help others overcome their mistakes and find their way to Him.*
>
> *Later, I tried to convince Russell to search his heart and do the right thing himself. But he shut me out. Russell grew paranoid, fearing that Leon would betray us to police one day. So he lived in torment. I don't believe he touched the money. Eventually, I tried to convince Leon to surrender to God, but prison had made him bitter and he was blind to the path of redemption that God was willing to light for him.*
>
> *As for me, I do not ask for forgiveness, for I am not worthy. I do not ask for understanding, for my actions*

were beyond comprehension. All I ask is that you know that God spoke to me, told me to dedicate myself to helping others overcome their human mistakes and turn to the Light.

Chantal Louise Segretti

The day the *Mirror* published Sister Anne's lost letter, Grace met Jason at the Rusted Anchor.

"How's your old man doing?"

"One day at a time."

"How about you?"

Jason shrugged.

"Might take some time off, drive down the coast to Mexico, do some thinking. I got an offer to write a book."

"It's an unbelievable story," Grace said, "when you look at all the people it touched, the impact, and what they carried with them all these years. People dealing with their mistakes, you know?"

"I know."

"I mean, look at the nun. Look at Boland, afraid to spend the money, Rhonda and Brady, what they were facing, Sperbeck gave up twenty-five years for a payday. Then there's your dad and you."

Jason looked into his ginger ale.

"Yup."

"Helluva toll."

"Yup."

"So, uhm, this drive to Mexico, you thinking it'll be one of those solo soul-quest journeys, or what?"

He looked at her, at her smile and what it offered.

"I don't know, Grace. Guess I'm open to 'or what.'"

"Then we'll talk about that."

"We will."

Later, Jason drove his Falcon to his old man's house,

south, between Highway 509 and the west bank of the Duwamish River, not far from the shipyards and Boeing Field. The house where his mother had read him bedtime stories, where he'd dreamed of being a writer.

Since Sperbeck had ended things, Jason's dad wasn't talking much. But Jason's daily visits were like balm to him. Today, as steaks sizzled on the grill, they reflected on the Seahawks, Mariners, and the Sonics, which was their way of putting the broken pieces of their lives back together.

On this night, Jason noticed that his father had taken out an old family album and was looking at a picture of Jason's mother, who'd walked out on them years ago.

"You ever think of looking for her, Dad?"

Henry Wade gazed out beyond his deck toward the sun setting over the ocean.

"Every day, son. Every day."

AUTHOR'S NOTE AND
ACKNOWLEDGMENTS

In getting this story to you, I benefited from the hard work and kind help of many people. My thanks to my editor, Audrey LaFehr, and everyone at Kensington. I would also like to thank Amy Moore-Benson, Mildred Marmur, Jeff Aghassi, Lorella Belli, John and Jeannine Rosenberg, Shannon Whyte, Donna Riddell, Beth Tindall, Chris Rapking, Ib Lauritzen, Therese Greenwood, Sherri Pilgrim, and Cath Collins. A special thanks to Barbara, Laura, and Michael. My thanks to friends everywhere for their support. Again, I am indebted to sales representatives and booksellers for putting my work in your hands. Which brings me to you, the reader. Thank you for your time, for without you a book remains an untold tale. I hope you enjoyed the ride and that you'll be back for the next one. For updates, visit me at www.rick mofina.com.

ABOUT THE AUTHOR

Rick Mofina is the acclaimed author of *If Angels Fall,
Cold Fear, Blood of Others, No Way Back, Be Mine, The Dying
Hour,* and *Every Fear.* He is a two-time winner of the
Arthur Ellis Award. *The Dying Hour,* his first book in his
Jason Wade series, was chosen as a finalist for a Thriller
Award by the International Thriller Writers. He is a for-
mer crime reporter whose work has appeared in such
publications as the *New York Times* and *Reader's Digest.*
Please visit his Web site: www.rickmofina.com.

More Thrilling Suspense From
Your Favorite Thriller Authors